THE
LAZARUS
MACHINE

THE
LAZARUS
MACHINE

A TWEED & NIGHTINGALE ADVENTURE

PAUL CRILLEY

an imprint of **Prometheus Books**
Amherst, NY

Published 2012 by Pyr®, an imprint of Prometheus Books

Cover illustration © Cliff Nielsen
Cover design by Grace M. Conti-Zilsberger

Inquiries should be addressed to

Pyr
59 John Glenn Drive
Amherst, New York 14228–2119
VOICE: 716–691–0133
FAX: 716–691–0137
WWW.PYRSF.COM

16 15 14 13 12   5 4 3 2 1

Library of Congress Cataloging-in-Publication Data

Crilley, Paul, 1975–
    The Lazarus Machine / by Paul Crilley.
        p. cm. — (A Tweed & Nightingale adventure)
    Summary: In an alternate 1899 London, seventeen-year-old Sebastian Tweed searches for his kidnapped father, uncovering both a horrific technological secret and a political conspiracy that could destroy the British Empire.
    ISBN 978–1–61614–688–7 (cloth)
    ISBN 978–1–61614–689–4 (ebook)
    [1. Conspiracies—Fiction. 2. Immortality—Fiction. 3. London (England)—History—19th century—Fiction. 4. Great Britain—History—Victoria, 1837–1901—Fiction. 5. Science fiction.] I. Title.

PZ7.C869276Laz 2012
[Fic]—dc23

                                                                    2012023476

Printed in the United States of America

For Bella and Caeleb.

May you have the curiosity of Tweed, the spirit of Octavia,
the extravagance of Barnaby, the joie de vivre of Jenny and Carter—
and the intelligence of Stepp to know when each is appropriate.

And for Caroline.

May we always look up at the stars and see the lawnmower.

ACKNOWLEDGMENTS

Many thanks to my last-minute beta readers, Candas Jane Dorsey and John Levitt. And to my amazing agent Ginger Clark. Your work and patience is truly appreciated. Thank you to Lou Anders, who let me tell the story I wanted to tell. And finally, my utmost respect and appreciation goes to Sir Arthur Conan Doyle, for writing such wonderful stories and characters.

CHAPTER ONE

Tonight, seventeen-year-old Sebastian Tweed was going to be the voice of a fifty-year-old woman. More specifically, he was going to be the voice of a Mrs. Henrietta Shaw—missing and presumed dead for over a year now.

He wasn't happy about it.

"I'm tired of doing this, Barnaby," he said.

His father glanced at him in the small mirror as he neatened his bow tie. "Oh? And what would you rather we were doing?"

They sat in the cramped carriage of the steamcoach they used to get around the nightmarish streets of London. Bruised and battered, the piece of junk crawled around in a cloud of dirty steam and left behind a trail of leaking oil like a diseased snail that smoked too much.

"*Anything*," said Tweed. "Anything other than tricking old people out of their money. It's not dignified."

"Dignified? You think it's dignified to be out on the streets? You think it's dignified to beg for food?"

"Of course it's not. But at least it's honest. There are other things we could be doing. It doesn't have to be . . ." Tweed waved at their surroundings in disgust. ". . . *this*. Besides, you're going to get caught."

"My boy, I will never get caught. I'm too clever. Plus, I've got you to look out for me."

Tweed shook his head. "I'm serious, Barnaby. I don't want to do this anymore."

"Why not?" said Barnaby in exasperation. "There's no harm! We're giving them peace of mind."

"But none of it's *true*!"

"Truth is a malleable commodity. And wholly subjective. Our clients believe their lost loved ones have spoken to them from beyond the grave, ergo, their lost loved ones *have* spoken to them from beyond the grave. Simple."

"Justify it any way you like, but we're confidence tricksters. That's all there is to it. And I want it to stop."

Barnaby said nothing for a moment, fiddling with his bow tie some more. Finally, he turned around. There was a strange look in his eyes. Irritation, yes—Tweed had expected that—but something else as well. It took Tweed a moment to place it, and when he did, it pulled him up short.

Pride. It was *pride* he saw.

"Fine," said Barnaby. "I was thinking of giving it a rest for a while anyway. Security's a nightmare ever since that Romanov fellow turned up trying to drum up support for his war against Japan. So you go ahead and find us another way to earn a living. Pick whatever you want and we'll give it a try. My only condition is that it must make us rich beyond our wildest dreams."

"What? Don't be absurd!"

Barnaby smiled. "Only jesting. As I say, find something else for us, and I'll look into it. Deal?"

Tweed nodded suspiciously. "All right, then. Deal." He stared hard at his father. "I'm going to hold you to this, old man," he said.

"Oh, I'm sure you will. But right now, we have work to do, yes? Is the spider ready?"

Tweed stood up and lifted the cushion of his seat. Concealed within was a jumble of brass and silver spiders. He took one of them out. Gaslight gleamed on oiled metal and glinted on the cogs and tiny gears that made up its body. It was about the size of his hand, a small body with long, delicate limbs and a tiny optical lens for an eye.

"Are you ready?" asked Tweed. He didn't want to activate it too early, as there was a possibility the Ministry might pick up on the spider's signals and come to investigate. They were getting serious about cracking down on unauthorized automaton transmissions.

Barnaby spread his arms wide and grinned. "My boy, I am *always* ready. It is the sign of the true professional."

He unhinged the door at the rear of the carriage and stepped into the street. As soon as he pushed the door closed, Tweed inserted a small key into the base of the spider and wound it up. The folded legs twitched then extended all the way out and shivered slightly, as if the spider was stretching after a long sleep. Tweed placed it on a fold-down workbench and pulled up the faded carpet, revealing a small trapdoor in the base of the carriage. He lifted the door to reveal his pride and joy, something that would get him thrown into a Ministry cell if it was ever discovered: a homemade Tesla transceiver.

Tweed had designed and built it with the help of a friend of his, a girl who called herself Stepp Reckoner. It wasn't her real name, obviously, but a handle she used in the hope of staying anonymous and out of the Ministry's clutches. Apparently, the name had something to do with computing history. She explained it to him once, but Tweed had stopped listening when she started going on about fluted drums and decimal number systems. There were few things in life worse than an obsessive going on about the subject with which they were obsessed.

Tweed and Stepp had pooled their resources and scavenged bits and pieces to make the transceiver, finding an unused frequency on the Tesla range so they could send commands to their own constructs. Very dangerous. They had almost been caught three times.

But it was worth it.

Tweed inserted a waxed, perforated card into a slot in the side. There was a small click as the machine drew the card deep into its innards. The spider stiffened, turned around, then scuttled off the workbench and dropped to the floor.

Tweed flicked open the tatty crimson curtain. Barnaby stood by the front door of the house. He glanced back at the carriage and lifted his hand for Tweed to go ahead.

Tweed opened the carriage doors. As he did so, a passing automaton turned to look at him. This was one of the new models, the ones made to look like real people. The white light from the human soul locked in the æther cage in its chest shone upward, casting eerie shadows across the construct's features.

Tweed waited till the automaton had walked past, then allowed the spider to scuttle across the cobbles, where it stopped next to Barnaby's foot. Barnaby glanced down to make sure it was out of sight, then knocked on the door. It was opened by the mark, a tall, sad-looking man called Samuel Shaw, and while Barnaby made his greetings, the spider darted inside.

Tweed closed the carriage doors and turned to the transceiver. He pulled a small lever in its side and two doors on the front slid apart, revealing a tiny, rounded piece of glass. Tweed waited expectantly, but nothing happened. He tapped the glass a few times until it flickered to reluctant life, revealing a grainy, sepia image.

Tweed got an impression of blurred movement—the spider moving to its hiding place. A few seconds later the image paused and Tweed found himself looking at a skirting board. The spider turned in a slow circle, calculating how best to fulfill its program.

It picked a bookcase, scrabbling up onto one of the higher shelves. Then it turned and crept forward until its eye looked down at a large round table.

Barnaby and Shaw entered the room.

"This will do perfectly, Mr. Shaw," came Barnaby's tinny, crackly voice, fed to Tweed through a small speaker in the transceiver.

"Good, good," said Shaw. He cast a vague glance around the room. "Um, can I get you a drink?" he asked.

"A sherry would go down well, thank you."

While Samuel poured the drink, Barnaby moved quickly to a sideboard and placed a tiny speechifier behind a framed photograph. He stepped away just as a third man strode into the room. The man stopped short and glared at Barnaby.

"Ah . . . Mr. Tweed, this is my brother, Victor," said Samuel.

Barnaby held out his hand. "A pleasure, sir."

"The pleasure is all yours," Victor said curtly. He turned to his brother. "I warned you not to go through with this, you fool. You're pathetic, you know that?"

Samuel opened his mouth to protest, but his brother turned abruptly and swept out of the room.

"I'm so sorry," said Samuel, wringing his hands. "My brother . . . he is not a believer."

"No need to apologize," said Barnaby. "That's family for you. Always embarrassing you in public. I have a son who can barely string two sentences together. Drools a lot. Has eyes that look in two different directions. But what can you do?"

Tweed needed to test the transmitter anyway, so he picked it up and depressed the metal trigger. "Most amusing," he said.

A brief smile flickered across Barnaby's face as Tweed's voice traveled to the receiver hidden within Barnaby's ear.

Tweed put the transmitter down and sat back with an uneasy frown. Barnaby's original file hadn't even mentioned Samuel Shaw's brother, but Tweed had come across some information while doing his own background check. He had been doing this more and more lately, complementing Barnaby's meager research with his own.

It was laughably easy to get his hands on such things. Tweed simply pretended to be a records clerk at New Scotland Yard and was allowed to come and go as he pleased. His face had become familiar enough to the police that they no longer questioned his presence when he turned up.

It had come to the point where the preparations for each séance were beginning to take up all of Tweed's spare time. He spent days trawling through police archives and newsprint reports in an attempt to assuage his growing guilt, hoping to give the marks something they could take away with them, something that would put them at peace.

Family histories were always the first thing Tweed looked into, just in case someone at the séance asked any awkward questions about dear cousin Roger who had died thirty-odd years ago. But Tweed hadn't expected Victor Shaw to be in attendance tonight. As Samuel said, the man was vehemently against spiritualism of any kind.

There was a knock at the front door of the house. Tweed peered through the steamcoach window and saw three other guests standing on the sidewalk, waiting to be let in. That would be Samuel's sister, Mary, and her daughter and husband.

While Samuel led them through to the sitting room and took care of the introductions, Tweed paged through his files to refresh his memory on the brother.

There wasn't much information. Victor Shaw. Single. Never been married. Owned a manufacturing plant that supplied glass valves to Babbage & Company for their Analytical Machines. Heavy gambler. Not well liked by those who knew him. Attended church every Sunday.

Tweed closed the file and glanced at the screen. The guests were taking their seats around the table. As Barnaby lowered the lights, Victor returned to the room.

"What's going on?" he demanded. "I thought you weren't going to start this charade until eight o' clock?"

"What difference does it make? We're all here. There's no reason for us to waste Mr. Tweed's valuable time any more than we have to."

Victor took his pocket watch out and glared at the clock face as if it had offended him. When Barnaby retook his seat, Victor hesitated for a second, then sat opposite him. That was surprising. Tweed hadn't thought he would be taking part.

A single lantern in the center of the table was the only light in the room. It cast its glow over the six faces watching Barnaby. Tweed had frequently argued with Barnaby about this, as it made it difficult for him to see, but his father always said he needed the atmosphere, that it did fifty percent of the work for him.

Tweed turned a dial on the transceiver, opening the iris of the spider's eye. The picture brightened until Tweed could see everyone's faces.

But his eyes were fixed on Victor Shaw. There was something about the way he looked at Barnaby that made Tweed incredibly uneasy.

Tweed picked up a transmitter and pushed the button. "Watch out for Victor. He's up to something."

Barnaby's eyes flickered briefly toward the spider on the bookcase, then he spread out his hands. "We must join in a circle," he said in a quiet voice.

Everyone around the table linked hands. Even Victor, though he did so reluctantly.

Barnaby sat in silence for a while. Then he moaned, "Oh ye that dwell beyond the veil, hear us humble petitioners as we call to you."

Barnaby fell silent for another minute before continuing, "Henrietta Shaw. Are you there? If you are present, will you join us? Your husband has questions he would ask."

Tweed picked up the transmitter, ready to be the voice of Henrietta Shaw. The voice would seem to come from all around the room, though it would really come from the spider and the speechifier that Barnaby had hidden on the sideboard.

"We call through the veil, asking that Henrietta Shaw joins us. Can you hear me, Henrietta?"

Barnaby paused to let the tension build. "I'm getting something. It's . . . it's Henrietta. She's here, Samuel. She's come to see you."

Samuel drew in a sobbing breath. "Henrietta?"

Tweed depressed the transmitter trigger, hating himself all the while. "I am here, my love," he whispered in what he called his "middle-aged woman number two" voice.

The husband of Samuel's niece screamed rather shrilly and broke the circle. Victor lunged to his feet, knocking over his chair.

"Enough of this!" he shouted. Victor turned the gas lamps to full strength, flooding the room with light. Tweed winced as his screen flared white, then he partially closed the eye of the spider. Victor stood by the wall, pointing a shaking finger at Barnaby.

"The man is a fraud, Sam. Any fool can see that."

Samuel lifted his tear-stained face. "How can you say that, Victor? We all heard her. My dear Henrietta."

"It's a trick, you fool! Face facts! She didn't love you anymore. She packed her bags and left. What did you expect? All those business trips you took. You were never here!"

"But . . . but I did it all for her!" wailed Samuel, his voice filled with anguish. "So we could afford a better life. Please, Victor. For me. I want to hear what Mr. Tweed has to say."

Victor checked his pocket watch. "I don't think so. I took the liberty of contacting the police before I arrived, Samuel. They will be here soon to arrest this charlatan."

Barnaby's eyes widened. He pushed himself to his feet. "I, ah, see you have some family issues to sort through, Mr. Shaw. I'll come back when it's more convenient, if you don't mind."

Before Barnaby could leave the table, Victor Shaw reached into his jacket and pulled out a small, pearl-handled revolver. He pointed it at Barnaby.

"Why the rush, Mr. Tweed?"

Barnaby nervously licked his lips and sank back into his chair. Tweed flicked the switch that ensured his next transmission went only to Barnaby's ear, then he slowly lifted the transmitter to his lips. "Uh . . . remind me again . . . what was that you were saying about never getting caught?"

Barnaby looked up at the spider and locked eyes with Tweed.

CHAPTER TWO

*T*hink, Tweed. *Think.*

Tweed glanced at the viewing screen, but the picture was the same as it had been for the past ten minutes. Victor Shaw standing with his gun trained on Barnaby.

Tweed had gone through every plan he could think of, all the way from pretending to be the police to setting fire to the house. Brilliant plans, all of them, but to every one he told Barnaby through the transmitter, his father would give a slight shake of his head.

Then what?

Tweed leaned back in the chair. At the very least he could cause some kind of distraction when the police arrived. Maybe he could attack them? That would certainly shift their attention. He seemed to recall seeing a small hand catapult amongst all the junk in the carriage.

No, that was a stupid idea. He felt slightly embarrassed at having even acknowledged the thought as it drifted through his head.

Tweed closed his eyes, taking a deep breath to clear his mind like Barnaby had taught him. *Focus*, he told himself. *Focus on the problem.*

A moment later a thought popped into his head. Tweed's eyes snapped open.

Why had Victor Shaw been so against Barnaby speaking? He was angry they had started early, obviously hoping the police would arrive before anything could be done. But once Samuel insisted they go ahead he had played his hand in order to stop Barnaby from saying *anything*. Even though it meant waiting for the police to arrive.

Almost . . .

Tweed leaned forward in the chair, staring hard at the screen.
Almost as if he were scared Barnaby might be the real thing.
But why would that scare him? Unless . . .

A slow smile spread across Tweed's face. He picked up the transmitter and depressed the trigger.

"Repeat everything I am about to say to you. Do not edit, do not hesitate. I think I've found a way out of this. Understand?"

Barnaby gave the tiniest of nods.

"It must have bruised your ego when Henrietta spurned your advances. Isn't that right, Victor?"

Barnaby hesitated.

"Say it!"

Barnaby sighed. "It must have bruised your ego when Henrietta spurned your advances. Isn't that right, Victor?"

There was an inrush of breath from those around the table. Victor's eyes almost popped out of his head. His face darkened in anger, and in that moment Tweed knew he had guessed the truth.

"You, a highly successful businessman, and your brother nothing more than a traveling salesman. And yet that didn't matter to Henrietta, did it? She cared nothing for power and money."

Barnaby repeated his words and Victor nervously licked his lips.

Tweed carried on. "And the last time Samuel went on his travels, you decided to play your hand. You visited Henrietta, you declared your love. You begged, you pleaded, and when that didn't work, you threatened. Still she rejected you. And that was too much, wasn't it, Victor? Nobody makes a fool of Victor Shaw."

Tweed watched Victor as Barnaby repeated his words. It was a gamble. Victor might simply shoot Barnaby on the spot, but Tweed was hoping that Victor really was the odious coward he appeared to be, and would simply flee from the house.

Unfortunately, Tweed hadn't factored in Samuel Shaw.

The tall, thin man rose to his feet, straightening to his full height. "Victor?" he said. "What is this?"

Victor's eyes shifted between Barnaby and Samuel. Finally, he exploded. "All she had to do was say yes!" he shouted. "But no! She had to be *loyal.*" He said the last word as though it were an obscenity. "Stupid woman. She deserved to die. After all, if I couldn't have her, why should you? *I* deserved her. I'm the one with all the money. What could you have offered her?"

Samuel took a step toward Victor. Even through the grainy screen, Tweed could see tears coursing down his face. "What could I offer her?" he said softly. "I offered Henrietta my love, Victor. And that was enough for her."

Victor snorted. "How poetic. Love fades, dear brother."

"Not ours."

"Oh, because you're somehow special? Is that it? You think you're better than everyone else?"

"No. Not special. We were the most mundane people in the world." Samuel's hands curled into fists. "But we had each other!" he shouted. He launched himself at his brother, grabbing hold of the hand that held the pistol. The gun went off with an explosive *bang!* the bullet shattering a vase on a corner shelf. The three other guests dived under the table as Barnaby hurried forward to help Samuel restrain Victor.

Tweed threw down the transmitter and shot to his feet, banging his head against the roof. He cursed and threw open the doors, setting his feet on the metal steps.

He froze.

Tweed felt it first, a low thrumming that vibrated up through the soles of his shoes. Then he heard it. The *dug-dug-dug* of an approaching airship. The sound grew louder by the second, the vibrations stronger.

Tweed jumped out into the street and looked up. There it was:

21

a small dirigible that slowed to a floating standstill about fifty feet above the ground. But it was unlike any dirigible he'd ever seen. The airship was much smaller than normal, and it was matte black, without any warning lights, making it almost impossible to see from a distance.

As Tweed watched, a huge metal box dropped from the belly of the airship. It sank slowly to the ground, lowered by a thick metal chain that unspooled from within the ship. Tweed moved behind the carriage as the box bumped against the cobbles. The front of the container fell forward and dropped onto the road with an almighty *clang*.

The pulse and flare of blue-white light came from inside. For a moment, nothing happened, but then a strange group of people stepped casually into the street.

There were five of them. All dressed in black. But it was what they wore on their heads that made them look so odd.

The first figure had some kind of metal framework completely encircling his skull. Two rods stuck up from the frame and white electricity jumped from one rod to the other, singeing the air and giving off the smell of burning ozone. Connected to these rods were two solid metal discs, and they shone a bright, flickering light directly into his hidden eyes. But the way he looked around convinced Tweed that the discs in no way hampered his vision.

One of the others wore a protective leather helmet that came down to his chest, like some kind of elaborate gas mask designed to cause fear and terror. The eye holes were covered with black glass and wire, and a long tube hung from the mouthpiece down to his waist. Another figure wore a similar mask but made from metal, like a demonic diving helmet.

But it was the figure standing slightly ahead of the others that made Tweed move even deeper into the shadows, his eyes widening with shock.

He had heard the talk over the past year. Whispers amongst Barnaby's criminal contacts and associates.

He's back, they whispered fearfully. *Come to reclaim his throne.*

Tweed hadn't believed the rumors. Superstitious nonsense, he'd thought. Typical of the kind of thing the uneducated idiots who turned to crime believed in. Except the rumors wouldn't go away. Instead, they got more and more specific. He wore a mask to hide an injury, they said. He surrounded himself with a gang of insane killers. He stalked the streets of London leaving a trail of murder in his wake.

Tweed had thought he was witnessing the birth of genuine folklore, like the legend of Spring-heeled Jack. He'd even thought of writing a paper on it, submitting it to one of the more up market newspapers.

Except here he was, standing no more than thirty feet from Tweed. Exactly as everyone had described him.

The Napoleon of Crime himself.

Professor James Moriarty.

Before he and Sherlock Holmes had tumbled over Reichenbach Falls, no one had known who Moriarty was. He was a manipulator, always hiding in the shadows. But after the Reichenbach tragedy, investigations uncovered a criminal syndicate stretching from London to Eastern Europe, with Moriarty in charge of it all. The man was a genius, a mastermind who would stop at nothing to achieve his aims.

Tweed leaned forward slightly to get a better look. Moriarty wore a much more elaborate mask than the others, tight-fitting and enclosing only his head. It was made from dark brown leather with elegant patterns etched into the surface. Black glass filled the insectoid eye frames. Slim hoses were attached to gold nozzles on the cheeks and lower jaw, the hoses curving over his shoulders to a small canister attached to his back. Did he need the mask to breathe? Had he injured himself when he plummeted over the falls?

Moriarty's clothing matched the style of the helmet. A tight-fitting greatcoat that hugged his body so snugly it was like a second skin. The whole effect put Tweed in mind of a human-shaped scorpion.

As Tweed watched, a last figure stepped out of the metal box and scurried forward to stand behind Moriarty, twitching and giggling as he moved. The man was short, and wore a top hat made from metal wire. Fat worms of electricity arced around the hat, and every time they came around to the front, they hit a copper wire and sparks exploded into the air with the snap of freed electricity. The hat was connected to a metal pipe that the figure clutched protectively to his chest.

Some kind of weapon?

The figures all surveyed the street for a moment. Tweed quickly ducked out of sight. He waited a second, then peered around the side of the steamcoach. They were already moving purposefully across the road.

Straight for Samuel Shaw's house.

Tweed darted into the carriage to check the display unit. Barnaby and Samuel had disarmed Victor and were busy tying him to a chair with what looked like the cords from the curtains. The other three guests had emerged from under the table and were pouring themselves drinks with shaking hands.

Tweed had to warn Barnaby. He picked up the transmitter and depressed the trigger.

"Barnaby!" he said quickly. "You know how I said all your friends were uneducated peasants because they believed that Moriarty was back from the dead? Well, I still think that. But he *is* back. And coming your way. You need to get out of there."

But Barnaby didn't react.

"Barnaby?"

Nothing. *Damn.* Barnaby's earpiece must have fallen out in the scuffle.

Tweed hesitated, then pulled the punchcard out of the transceiver. The image on the screen blurred, then froze at an odd angle. The spider had fallen from its hiding place and was now staring up at the ceiling.

"What the devil . . . ?" said a tinny voice.

Shaw's huge face loomed into view, a mass of deep wrinkles and bushy eyebrows. He picked up the spider and stared at it, then showed it to Barnaby. Barnaby's eyes widened in alarm. He muttered something to Shaw, but before anything could be done, there was a splintering crash. Barnaby whirled around in alarm. Someone cried out. The spider was dropped to the ground and Tweed saw blurred feet rushing around.

He swore and ran outside. The street was empty.

Then the screaming started.

It must have taken Tweed only ten seconds to cross the street, but by the time he reached the front door the screams had already stopped. He peered carefully into the front hall. No one around. He crossed the threshold and entered the sitting room.

When he saw the body of Samuel Shaw lying at his feet, one arm stretched out as if reaching toward him, Tweed staggered to a halt. His eyes flickered around the room. Victor was still tied to the chair, but his head was burnt beyond recognition, his mouth wide open in a soundless scream. Smoke drifted up from inside his mouth, as if his breath were misting on a cold winter's day. There was no sign of Moriarty or his gang, but a second door leading out of the sitting room stood open. The other guests sprawled amidst shattered glasses and spilled brandy on the far side of the room, wisps of smoke curling up from the horrendous wounds burned into their bodies.

Tweed rushed forward to check the corpses. But a moment later he straightened up and frowned.

Barnaby wasn't among them.

He looked around in confusion. Where was he?

Tweed heard someone swearing outside. He hurried over to the window and flicked aside the net curtain. Moriarty and his gang were reentering the metal container, and two of them dragged a kicking and swearing Barnaby between them. Moriarty pulled the metal door back into place and the box started to winch back into the sky.

Tweed didn't hesitate. He sprinted outside and headed straight for the container. It swayed back and forth on the chain, and Tweed could hear muffled shouting from inside as Barnaby struggled with his kidnappers. He leaped into the air and grabbed hold of the thin ledge around the base of the container. The cage dipped, but hopefully they would attribute it to Barnaby's struggles.

Tweed waited, but no one sounded the alarm.

He had gotten away with it. Although, what *it* was, he had no idea. What, *exactly*, did he plan on doing? Barnaby would disapprove. *Acting without thinking*, he would say. *Bad form, lad. Bad form.*

London receded below him as the cage rose slowly upward. The airship started moving as well, heading up toward the lanes of airship traffic that ferried people across the city.

It was actually quite beautiful, thought Tweed distantly. He could see the soft glow of automata as they stalked their heavy way through the streets, the white light of their æther cages combating the orange glow of streetlights. It would actually be quite peaceful if it weren't for the loud thrum of the airship engines and the screech and rattle of the chain winching the container upward.

Tweed's hands started to ache. He was grasping the metal lip with nothing more than his fingertips, and he wasn't sure how long he'd be able to hold on.

As they rose higher the wind started to buffet him, swinging his legs back and forth. He could feel his fingers slipping. He looked down. The houses were tiny. If he fell now a red smear on the cobbles would be all that remained of Sebastian Tweed.

He needed to come up with a plan very quickly. Very quickly indeed.

His attention was distracted from the vast measure of distance between his feet and the ground by the sound of the chain slowing down. He arched back, peering upward. The container was sliding into the base of the airship. Tweed watched as the top of the cage fitted snugly inside the gap.

In fact . . .

He looked at his fingers gripping the edge of the container floor, then up at the airship. There was only the tiniest of gaps between the container and the hole.

So, next question: Fall to his death with his fingers attached, enjoying a very brief period of non-pain, or fall to his death with no fingers, screaming all the way?

Tweed frantically searched the underside of the airship for something he could use. A few feet away was the nearest of the connecting struts that circled the gas-filled balloon. Tweed curled upward and braced his legs against the bottom of the box. Just before it slid all the way into the dirigible he pushed off with his feet and sailed backward through the air. His arms flailed upward, connecting with the strut. But the weight of his body ripped one side of it free. He dropped, then jerked to a stop as the other end held firm. Tweed swung back and forth on the broken arm, buffeted by the wind.

The dirigible rose above the airship lanes. It entered a cloud bank, and heavy moisture clung to Tweed's hair. He reached up, slowly stretching his hand to see if he could grab one of the other struts. He was tall, but not quite tall enough. Typical. The one time when his height would have benefited him, and it did nothing but mock his efforts.

Then the strut he was holding snapped.

He plummeted through the clouds. Water and mist whipped

past his face, tickling his skin. The wind roared in his ears. He forced his eyes to stay open but all he could see was white and grey.

He burst out of the bottom of the clouds. Clear air was all around him. He could see London, the horizon. And—

Tweed had only a second of stunned surprise to see the huge transport dirigible rising rapidly toward him before he slammed into the balloon with enough force to burst the air from his lungs.

He bounced, then started to slide down the curve of the gas bag. He scrabbled frantically with his hands, grabbing hold of the thick wire that held the bag in shape, feeling it cut into his skin.

He slowed, then stopped moving. He waited to make sure nothing else was about to snap or break, then pulled himself back up to the very top of the cigar-shaped dirigible and flopped onto his back. He stared up at the moon as he struggled to regain his shaky breath.

Well.

That just happened.

Tweed sat up. The balloon was huge, one of the massive transport dirigibles that Brunel & Company had recently started building. Huge steam engines at the rear acted as a backup for the Tesla power, pushing it ponderously through the sky, the turbines giving off a deep throbbing that vibrated through the whole airship.

Tweed cast his eyes upward, but Moriarty's zeppelin had vanished somewhere into the bank of clouds. Tweed had lost them.

But on the plus side, at least Barnaby was still alive.

Which meant Tweed still had time to find him.

As he absently drummed his fingers on the thick canvas, wondering exactly what his father had gotten himself mixed up in, a second dirigible rose into view alongside him, drifting into a higher lane of traffic. A small boy stared out of one of the portholes, clearly bored out of his mind.

When he saw Tweed lounging on the top of the airship, his mouth dropped open in shock.

Tweed raised a hand and waved at him. The boy hesitantly waved back, and a moment later his dirigible was swallowed up by the clouds.

CHAPTER THREE

Octavia Nightingale sat next to the fire in a large, wingback chair and attempted to focus on her stitching. Her father would approve. It was a lady-like pursuit, something he was always encouraging her to take more of an interest in.

It was also fiendishly difficult and *incredibly* boring. She squinted at the stitches, tilting the black cloth toward the fire so she could get a better look at her handiwork. She still couldn't see much. She clicked her tongue in irritation and glanced across at Manners, standing at attention next to the door.

"Manners, come here, please."

The automaton moved smoothly toward her. It was the newest model, released only last month. Only the best for her father. She stared at it in distaste. The constructs seemed to be getting more human with every iteration. Octavia wasn't sure she approved. She liked her tools to look like tools. Manners even had articulating facial expressions. It could smile slightly and blink. Unfortunately, it didn't quite know when it was appropriate to use these newfound abilities. Having an automaton tell you it was time for bed with a frozen, creepy smile on its face was quite an alarming experience that had Octavia's fingers itching for her Tesla gun.

"Manners, stand there." Octavia pointed to the carpet directly in front of her. When the automaton had done as instructed, Octavia lifted the protective cover that some of the newer models had over their æther cages. The white light of the soul that powered the construct shone through the thick glass, casting a clear, bright glow across her handiwork.

Octavia had always found it incredibly disturbing to think that most of the automata in the city were powered by human souls. Many decades ago, some government department discovered that it was easier to use human souls extracted from the deceased and trapped inside special "æther cages" to power automata. The discovery was quickly embraced. Finally, an answer to the insolvable problem of delivering instructions to automata out in the street without them having to trail miles upon miles of wires behind them to receive their commands. And the supply of souls? No problem. The Crown offered to "rent" the souls of the deceased from their families, an offer that was enthusiastically embraced by the lower classes.

Of course, nowadays the Tesla Towers helped with all that, but the old-fashioned æther constructs were still the more popular (and affordable) models. Especially as the Crown liked to keep a tight grip on the secrets of Tesla power.

Unfortunately for Octavia, the light from Manners's æther cage only served to illuminate her own failings. Her stitches were large and unevenly spread. Not very nice. Not very nice at all.

Oh, well. At least the thread matched the material, so nobody was likely to notice.

Her father opened the door and peered into the room.

"Oh, hello, Octavia. Not at the paper today?"

Octavia repressed a sigh. It was already past eight in the evening. She had been home from her job at *The Times* for two hours already. Well, she *called* it a job, but she wasn't paid anything. It was more of a volunteer research position that she was allowed to keep because her mother used to work there as a journalist, something Octavia hoped to one day emulate. She forced a smile onto her face. "Finished up for the day, Father. I just wanted to practice my stitching."

"Why don't you just use the Babbage?"

Octavia looked at the wall opposite where a huge, intricately decorated machine made from mahogany and brass stood. It looked more like a church organ than what it was meant to be—a machine that would do your sewing for you. Octavia had tried to use it once, but it had taken her longer to program the stupid thing with the punch-cards than it would to actually sew the material by hand.

But she didn't say that to her father. Ever since her mother's disappearance, her father had been getting more and more absent-minded. More and more distant. She didn't want to do anything that would push him farther away.

Instead she smiled and said, "I wanted to do it myself. I'm afraid I need the practice."

Her father smiled. "Good girl. Your mother would have approved."

No she wouldn't, thought Octavia bitterly, glaring at the door as her father retreated from the room. Her mother would have thought Octavia was wasting her time.

It had been a year since her mother's disappearance. A year of watching her father grow more and more withdrawn, retreating into his work until it was all that kept him going.

He thought her mother was dead, but Octavia didn't believe it. Her mother had been researching a story, looking into rumors that Professor Moriarty had returned from the dead to claim his rightful place as the king of London's underworld. Octavia used to go into work with her mother, something she actively encouraged. Octavia would help with the filing, help with the research, make tea—anything, really, as long as she got to watch how the newspaper worked.

Then one day Octavia's mother was taken. Octavia had witnessed it, seen the strangely dressed gang who swept out of the sky in an unmarked zeppelin, whisking her kicking and screaming mother away into the night.

Ever since, she had done everything she could to try to track her mother down, following rumors, leads, anything to do with Moriarty.

Trying to find out what he was after, why he had returned after he and Sherlock Holmes supposedly perished at Reichenbach Falls.

But the answers had remained elusively out of reach. She was no closer to tracking down Moriarty *or* her mother.

Octavia broke the end of the thread with a vicious tug. She looked around for her needle but couldn't find it anywhere. She was always doing that. She would find it later. Probably when she sat on it.

Octavia climbed the thickly-carpeted stairs to her bedroom. As she opened the door, a small metallic dog bounded across the carpet and banged painfully into her ankle. Octavia winced, leaning down to rub the sore spot.

What had her father been thinking? Her pet dog Phileas had died and he'd actually gone out and paid someone to put the poor thing's spirit into this . . . this . . . *shell*. Octavia honestly didn't know what to do about it. The construct seemed to recognize her and act similarly to Phileas, but she didn't know if that was just the programming of the automaton or the essence of the dog coming through.

Octavia hesitated, then reached down and tentatively patted the thing's brass head. "Good . . . dog," she said. This seemed to please the construct. It trotted over to its basket and lay down as if going to sleep.

Octavia's room was a fairly typical example of its kind: a large bed; a roll-top desk that she kept locked, with a few modifications of her own to make sure no one came snooping; and a dressing table.

However, she did have something that was *not* typical for a girl her age: shelves of books by the likes of Verne, Wells, Flammarion, and Lord Dunsany. Her father had once disapproved of her collection, but she had refused to back down on it, and her mother screamed at him when she found out he wanted to stop Octavia reading them. Octavia remembered feeling sorry for him at the time. You didn't want mother angry at you. She could make your life a living hell.

Octavia was about to ready herself for bed and a re-reading of *The King of Efland's Daughter* when she heard a tapping at the window.

Octavia's heart skipped a beat. She hurried over to the window and slid it open. It made no noise. Octavia made sure the wood was kept well-greased.

A tiny construct barely larger than her hand hopped onto the sill. It looked more like a skeleton than anything else, a brass framework topped with a featureless oval head.

It was one of four messengers Octavia used. The first one hid inside an abandoned building in Holywell Street. It was known to a select few that to contact her a message was to be dropped through the letterbox of that building. This first construct would take the message to the second, the second would take it to the third, and the third would scurry across the rooftops to hand the message to the fourth. Only the fourth knew how to get to the home of "Songbird," the name Octavia had chosen for herself.

Octavia took the small piece of paper from inside the tiny automaton's rib cage and unfolded it. Her heart beat even more rapidly in her chest. It was from Jennings: a request for a meeting. He had information on Moriarty.

Octavia unlocked her desk. She rolled the lid up and quickly scribbled an address on the back of the paper, slipping it back into the construct's rib cage. Once she was finished, the messenger scrambled up the wall and onto the roof, disappearing into the night.

Octavia went to her bed and unfolded the black material she had been sewing. It looked like she would get to put it to use sooner than she'd thought.

It wasn't easy for an unaccompanied young lady to move about London in the middle of the night. Questions would be asked, even nowadays with all the progress being made for equal rights by the followers of the Lovelace Movement.

But an unidentifiable person dressed in old, dirty street clothes, on the other hand, could find it *very* easy to move about. As long as they didn't want to use any of the up market modes of transport. But that didn't matter. An omnibus was an omnibus, whether it had leather chairs, served drinks, and supplied copies of today's newspaper, or whether it was standing room only and stank of the tannery workers who used it last.

Octavia arrived at London Bridge about three hours after the tiny construct had crawled through her window. She leaned on the concrete balustrade, watching the black waters of the Thames rushing between the arches of the bridge. There weren't many people around at this time of night. Certainly nobody of good repute. Ever since they'd built the new, upper level of the bridge, and above that, the wire tracks that moved carriages back and forth across the river, the original level had become the haunt of vagabonds and villains. Up above were lights and patrols, even shops and pubs, mimicking the old bridge of the seventeenth century. But down here there was just darkness, litter, and the homeless trying to shelter from the cold and rain.

Jennings was late. This troubled Octavia. The note said eleven o'clock, and it was already twenty after. He'd never been late before.

Her mother always told Octavia to rely on her gut feelings. She said it was the one thing that would never let you down. And right now, Octavia's gut was telling her to go home.

She drummed her fingers on the balustrade in irritation. She'd been hoping for some new information. Something she could use to track down her mother. Jennings usually had good intelligence.

Octavia thrust her hands into her pockets and turned around.

"Evenin'," said the figure standing before her.

Octavia froze. She narrowed her eyes and studied the man. It certainly wasn't Jennings. Jennings was five foot five with one leg shorter than the other, while the person standing before her now was well over six and a half feet tall.

Octavia carefully moved her hand inside her pocket, curling her fingers around the grip of the Tesla gun hidden deep inside. She usually carried two of the small devices, but the other was still attached to the wall socket in her room, drawing its charge from the Tesla Towers.

"Evening," she said, disguising her already deep voice.

"My name's Colin," said the figure.

"Jolly good for you," said Octavia brightly. "Not that I asked."

"What's your name?"

"Robert," said Octavia promptly. "Robert Blackwood."

"Robert Blackwood?" said Colin. "That's puzzlin'."

"Why, pray tell, is it puzzling?"

"Because I was under the impression that your name was Songbird. At least that's what Jennings told me before I threw his body into the Thames."

Octavia moved her thumb and flicked a small catch on the gun. She could just hear the tell-tale whine building up.

"Songbird? No I'm afraid you're mistaken. As I said, I'm Robert. Now if you'll excuse me—" Octavia took a step to the right, but it was mirrored by Colin the unfriendly giant.

"No need to rush off," he said. "I just want a word, that's all. Just a little word in your ear—" he smiled— "before I rip it off."

"What do you want?"

"You. See, word's got around that someone's been askin' questions about a certain person, and this certain person don't like it. He's put the word out to his chums on the street—" here Colin smiled and spread his arms wide— "and I'm one of them—to find out who it is that's so curious about him."

"And then what?"

"Well, as I understand it, they want to have a little chat with him."

"Ah."

"Yes. 'Ah.'"

"And you are speaking to me . . . why, exactly?"

"I'm speaking to you because Jennings was kind enough to tell me he was supplying information to a certain person called Songbird, and that he was supposed to meet Songbird here. I say 'kind enough to tell me,' but it was all I could do to make out his words. You know, in between all the screaming and crying."

"I see. You know, it's funny you should mention screaming and crying," said Octavia.

"Oh? And why's that?"

Octavia whipped out the Tesla gun and Colin lunged toward her. Octavia pulled the trigger, sending a blue-white bolt of lightning straight into his chest. He screamed, then dropped straight to the ground as his muscles stopped working. Octavia waited while the high-pitched whine built up again, then she fired another bolt into Colin's twitching body.

Octavia walked over and prodded him with her shoe. He didn't move. She bent over and felt for a pulse. Still alive.

"That's why, Colin," she said in her normal voice. "That's why."

CHAPTER FOUR

Tweed stumbled along Whitechapel Street, his mind racing over the events of the past few hours.

His father was gone. It hadn't really sunk in yet. It was too vast for his thoughts to encompass. He kept expecting to see Barnaby striding along beside him, greeting an oyster seller, or laughing about some aspect of the job.

Except he wasn't.

Because Professor Moriarty had taken him.

Why? That was the question. What did he want with Barnaby?

Or maybe that wasn't the question at all. Maybe it was rather, "What had Barnaby done?" It was entirely possible Barnaby had gotten himself involved in something he shouldn't have. It certainly wouldn't be the first time.

Tweed arrived at the rundown building in which they lived and shoved open the door. He stepped into the dark hallway and let the door close behind him.

The house was silent. He looked down at the pile of coats lying on the warped floorboards. Barnaby had left them there after trying them all on as he searched for the perfect accompaniment to his outfit. Tweed had told him to pick them up, but Barnaby had waved his hand negligently and said he'd pick them up when they got back.

Tweed prodded the pile with his foot. He stared blindly at them for a while then trudged through to the living area, a vast space that took up the whole ground floor of their dilapidated house. The walls that once sectioned off the various rooms had been removed by Barnaby on one of his decorating stints. A single set of stairs was all that remained of the original floor plan, climbing up to the bedrooms and bathrooms on the second floor.

Tweed turned up the gas lamps to fend off the gathering dusk, illuminating the chaos and disorder all around him. Scratched and battered desks had been shoved up against every available wall, all of them covered with a bizarre collection of oddities: automaton parts; gears; cogs; glass valves; old, mildewed books; and costume jewelry. Glass jars contained strange animals in formaldehyde: a two-headed snake; ten rats whose tails had wrapped around each other, tying them together into a massive knot; and a tiny brass skeleton that Barnaby had thought amusing to build.

One desk was the home of four ventriloquist's dummies. Tweed had been absolutely terrified of them as a child, convinced that their glass eyes followed him around as he walked. It got to the point where he'd refused to enter the room unless they were covered up. He found out a few years later that his fears had in fact been entirely justified, thanks to a simple mechanism operated by his father, who thought the whole thing was a hilarious joke.

In the far corner was the empty brass shell of an automaton. Barnaby had built it a year ago, spending months on the project, getting every detail exactly right. Tweed thought it was going to be a prop in some sort of elaborate con, but was disappointed to find out Barnaby simply wanted it for a costume party.

Tweed dropped onto the threadbare couch. His gaze drifted around the empty room. It really *was* empty. The house was draped with a deep silence, as if it knew something was missing, the absence of Barnaby leaving behind a faint echo of wrongness.

If everything had gone according to plan, he and Barnaby would be enjoying a nice supper right about now. They always bought good food after a job. They'd been talking about going to a restaurant.

And now?

Now his father had been kidnapped.

Tweed felt the beginning of anger stir in the pit of his stomach, fighting sluggishly against the shock of what had happened. Just who did Moriarty think he was? What gave him the right to just go around kidnapping people?

Fine, yes. Maybe Barnaby wasn't the best father in world, but nobody was perfect. And he *was* Tweed's father. That was the point. And Tweed would be damned if he was going to let some masked freaks whisk him away in the middle of the night without some kind of reckoning.

Tweed knew he and Barnaby had an odd relationship. More . . . *friends* than father and son. Teacher and student instead of close family. And that suited Tweed. He was happy with that. He'd read books where fathers showered their children with praise and love, and all the time he'd read he thought, *Really? People actually say that kind of thing?* He couldn't imagine Barnaby saying he loved him, or even giving him a hug. A clap on the back, yes, if he'd retained some important piece of knowledge, but that was about it.

Barnaby had always said it was his duty to raise Tweed to be the best man he could be, to make sure he could stand on his own two feet and rely on nobody but himself.

Now it seemed Tweed had a chance to put that to the test.

Another thing Barnaby said was that one of the most important things in any situation was to step back and take emotion out of the equation. Emotion clouded judgment, he said. Calculate. Analyze. Theorize. Never act without thinking.

Barnaby had taught him that lesson in this very room. It was one of Tweed's earliest memories. Barnaby, teaching him to use logic in all things. To analyze any emotions he felt and ignore them. To discard sentimentality and embrace rationality.

Tweed had been five years old at the time.

Tweed stood up and started to pace. First things first. List objectives.

One . . . get Barnaby back.

Oh, well done, Tweed, he thought contemptuously. *A truly brilliant analysis of the situation.*

How? That was the question.

Two . . . find out why Moriarty wanted Barnaby.

Better. If he could find that out it would go a long way to answering a lot of questions. In fact—

Three . . . was it really Moriarty? Maybe someone was making themselves up to look like the enigmatic professor.

Hmm. Annoying. That complicated things. Tweed pondered the possibility, but could go nowhere with the thought. He didn't have enough information. Point two would answer number three. So . . . discard that one for the moment.

Another possibility occurred to Tweed, freezing him in mid-stride.

What if they had already killed Barnaby?

He held his breath for a second, then let it out. No. Not possible. They took him alive. They killed everyone else, but took Barnaby. That meant they wanted him for something.

That wasn't to say they wouldn't kill him once they were done, but chances were he was still alive.

Barnaby had contingency plans. Just in case, as he'd often said, some elderly widow came after him with a pistol disguised as a walking stick. He'd told Tweed that should anything ever happen to him, Tweed was to take the emergency funds and go to Carter Flair and Jenny Turner, two old friends of his. Carter and Jenny were married thieves, their specialty up market hotels. Tweed liked Carter and Jenny. He'd known them all his life, and they were good people. *Trustworthy* people. That was what he needed right now.

Tweed gathered up the money Barnaby had hidden away beneath the floorboards. He wished Barnaby hadn't been so against weapons. Tweed would feel a lot safer if he had something to protect himself. But Barnaby had always said it was just as likely that you'd be injured by your own weapon as it was you'd injure your opponent. Tweed wasn't sure he agreed, but nothing he ever said could change his father's mind about it.

Tweed took a last look around the room, then turned off all the lights and stepped out into the street once again. It was about an hour before midnight. A faint haze of rain draped the roads and buildings with a dark, reflective sheen, causing oily, soot-scummed puddles to gather on the uneven pavements. Tweed paused on the step and took a deep breath of the damp air, taking in the comforting aroma of oyster barrows, hops, and tobacco: the familiar perfume of their home.

Tweed loved it here. Their house was in East End, on the corner of Goulsten and Whitechapel High Street. There was a saying among the upper classes of London. *If you're tired of life, move to Whitechapel*, they said. But Tweed saw it differently: *If you're tired of Whitechapel you're tired of life*. Because no matter what time of day or night, there was always something going on in the East End.

All right, so the things going on were usually brawling, screaming matches between families, singing and shouting from the pubs, and the constant trundle of hackney coaches pulled along by steam-powered automata. But still, that was life—the human experience laid out for all to see, and Tweed would have it no other way.

It wasn't exactly pleasant. He wouldn't romanticize it that much. But it was familiar. Comfortable.

The new world had tried to make its presence felt here. Tesla Towers dotted the landscape of the East End just as they did everywhere else in London. But the new technology never seemed to work. The towers transmitted energy through radio waves, powering nearly every piece of new technology that had sprung up in the past fifteen years, sending instructions to the thousands of new-generation automata around the city. But the technology was still in its infancy, the towers having a worrying tendency to break down, especially when it rained. (Or when it was too hot. Or too windy. Or too cold. In fact, the towers were so temperamental, those who lived in the poorer sections of the city used steam as their primary source of power, and if the Tesla Towers actually worked, it was considered a bonus.)

Tweed could see the Tesla Tower half a mile away, towering high above the surrounding buildings. But it was dark, the blinking lights that indicated a working tower, dull and lifeless.

Tweed took another deep breath. He felt better now that he had a course of action. He wasn't the kind of person to just sit around waiting for others to solve his problems. He had to be out there doing it himself. It centered him, made him feel calmer.

Tweed pulled his coat tight around his shoulders and set off.

♊

About an hour later Tweed reluctantly turned into an alley that branched off from Berners Street. He was feeling rather annoyed. Things weren't going to plan. He had gone to Carter and Jenny's house only to find it locked up with nobody at home. No help there. That meant he had to pick the next person on Barnaby's list, a man of even more dubious moral certitude than Barnaby, Jenny, and Carter put together.

Harry Banks.

And on the way there, Tweed had nearly walked right into a quicklime spill on George Street. The driver obviously moved the dangerous product around at night, thinking it safer than carting it through the daytime streets. That hadn't stopped the accident, though. Tweed only just managed to get away before he inhaled the toxic fumes.

He paused in the alley entrance. High walls hemmed him in on both sides. A single gas lamp gave off a weak glow at the far end of the lane, the drizzle forming a glowing halo around the smoky glass.

A figure lounged against the wall about halfway down the alley. He was smoking a rollup, the orange tip flaring to life every time he inhaled.

Tweed cautiously approached, making sure his hands were visible. The man straightened, his arms dropping to his sides. Tweed thought he recognized him. He'd been on the door the last few times he and Barnaby had come here. The man was whippet thin, not much to look at, but Tweed had seen him break a man's arm without dropping the cigarette permanently gripped in his fingers.

Tweed did a quick memory scan. "Marsh, isn't it?" he said.

"Who's askin'?" Marsh squinted through the smoke, studying Tweed's face. "You're Barnaby Tweed's boy, aren't you?" he said, surprised. "What you doin' here?"

"I need to see Mr. Banks."

Marsh frowned. "Where's Barnaby?"

"He's hiding behind me—" Tweed clamped his mouth shut when he saw Marsh actually lean to the side to look for his father. He sighed. No point in antagonizing the doorman. "He's not here, Marsh. Something's happened. Something bad. I need to see Harry."

"I dunno, kid. This isn't the kind of place— "

"Barnaby told me to come here if something ever happened to him." Tweed straightened up. "You know I'm Harry's godson, don't you?" He wasn't, but Marsh wasn't likely to know either way. "Come on, Marsh. It's important."

Marsh hesitated, then sighed and opened the door. "In you go, then. But don't blame me if you get your head kicked in, right?"

"I won't, I won't. Don't worry."

Tweed stepped through the door and found himself in a huge, shadowy warehouse. Sealed crates covered in oiled leather were piled up around the space. Against the far wall was a long table, and standing on either side of it were industrial-sized oil lamps casting their glow across the floor. Tweed headed toward them, stepping around the table and kneeling on the ground. He'd been here a few times before, so he knew exactly where he was going.

There was a trapdoor in the floor. Tweed heaved it up, and as it lifted away from the stone it was as though he'd opened the door onto a riot. Shouts and yells erupted from the gap, screams of anger and joy. The sound of clinking glass could be heard, and over all that the heavy clanging of metal on metal.

Tweed hesitated, wrinkling his nose at the smell of sweat and stale tobacco smoke. He'd only ever been here during the day, when everything was quiet. He wasn't even sure what Harry did here.

Lucky me, thought Tweed. *Looks like I'm about to find out.*

Tweed took a deep breath and descended the steps that led beneath the warehouse, lowering the trapdoor behind him.

The stairs led to a secondary floor space about half the size of the warehouse above. The smoke-filled room was packed with men and women, all of them facing inward, craning over each others' shoulders to get a better view of something

Tweed gently pushed a sweating old man aside, distastefully wiping his hand on the man's shirt after he'd done so, and saw that the focus of everyone's attention was a boxing ring inside of which fought two automata. As Tweed watched, one of the automata stepped forward and swung its clenched fist, connecting with its opponent with a loud clang. There was the screech of scraping metal and a burst of sparks showered into the fetid air. The automaton stumbled back a step, then braced itself and launched forward with both arms swinging. They connected against the first automaton's chest and head, a furious onslaught that had Tweed watching in astonishment. Not only because he'd never seen one of the metallic constructs move so fast, but also because they weren't supposed to be able to do that at all. Fighting was impossible for automata, their internal programs filled with fail-safes to stop such behavior. It was one of the reasons the public had eventually accepted them into society, the knowledge that they couldn't attack or fight.

The first automaton fell back against the thick wires that squared off the boxing ring. It raised its forearms in at attempt to fend off the blows, but the furious barrage kept coming.

The cries of the punters grew louder, screams of outrage and anger mixing with shouts of encouragement and drunken joy.

Tweed searched the floor space, wondering where Harry Banks would be. He noted the heavyset men lounging around the walls, their eyes on the crowd instead of the match, ready to step in should anyone get out of hand.

Tweed found his eyes drifting back to the boxing match. There was something bothering him about it, something not quite right. It wasn't just the fact that the automata shouldn't be able to fight, it was something else. Their movements were slightly off. Not much, but enough that a keen observer could spot the difference.

They didn't move like constructs. They moved . . .

A slow smile spread across Tweed's face. He was surprised no one else had figured out the truth by now. His gaze slid over the screaming, sweating masses, the crowd wavering on the razor edge of hysteria. *Then again*, he thought contemptuously, *maybe I shouldn't expect anything else.*

Tweed shoved his way through the crowd, aiming for a door he'd spotted against the far wall, the only other door in the room. The heavyset man leaning against it straightened as Tweed approached.

"Tell Mr. Banks that Barnaby Tweed's son is here to see him."

The man didn't move, except for his brows, which contracted slightly to shadow his eyes even more than they already were.

They stared at each other. Tweed was about as tall as the man, but he was under no illusions as to who would come off worse if the man decided to attack. Various insults and wittily clever disparagements flitted through his mind, but he clicked his tongue in irritation and reluctantly forced them aside. Now was not the time for such things.

"Please?" he said.

The man's eyes wrinkled slightly as if he was trying to smile without moving any other muscles in his face. "Didn't hurt, did it, lad? Manners don't cost a thing. You remember that. Piece of advice me old mam used to give me. One moment please."

The man disappeared through the door, reappearing a few moments later and nodding Tweed through.

Tweed stepped into a room that took up the second half of the lower level. It looked like it was used mainly as a workshop. Benches lay everywhere, covered with spare parts for automata: glass valves, copper tubing, and wiring. In fact, it looked similar to Tweed and Barnaby's living space.

But that was all background detail. What really captured Tweed's attention as he entered the room was the second boxing ring that took up much of the floor space.

Tweed walked slowly forward, his eyes on the scene in front of him. Two men were strapped into metal frameworks that followed the contours of their bodies. Every time they moved there was the briefest of pauses, then pneumatic hisses and blasts of steam burst from the rigs as their instructions were carried through to the heavy metal frames. As Tweed watched, one of the boxers, a dark haired man who looked like he had been fighting all his life, lashed out and landed a blow on his opponents face. The framework caught the blow, but the other man still staggered backward and fell to one knee.

There was a surge of volume from the room behind him. Tweed had thought it had to be something like this. The movements of the two men in front of him were being transmitted to the automata outside. But none of the punters would know that. They would think they were watching an illegal automaton fight.

"Evenin' boy," said a quiet voice at his side.

Tweed spun to see Harry Banks standing next to him. The man barely came up to his chest, his lank, black-grey hair parted down the middle so precisely that Tweed could count his dandruff flakes. But he was a familiar face to Tweed, something he hadn't realized he'd needed to see until right that moment.

"Hello, Harry," he said. He took a deep, shaky breath. "Barnaby said I should come to you if things went wrong."

"And he was right," said the old man. He tilted his head back and squinted up at Tweed. "Come on then. Let's have a chat, eh?"

They sat down in old, tatty chairs and Tweed filled Harry in on the events of the night. The boxing match finished while he told his story, the boxers climbing out of their rigs and limping away to clean up. Soon, only he and Harry remained in the workshop.

When Tweed mentioned Professor Moriarty, Harry pushed himself to his feet and paced nervously away, one hand playing with his lank hair. He turned and walked back.

"You're sure it was him?"

"Well, I *think* so. I mean, they looked like the descriptions that are floating around. Hadn't really believed the stories up till now, though."

"Oh, they're not stories, lad. It's really him. Seen him with me own eyes."

"But what does he want with Barnaby?"

"No idea. But I think we can both agree it won't be good." Harry flopped back into his armchair.

"Well?" asked Tweed.

"Well what?"

"Will you help?"

"*Help?* What is it you want me to do?"

"Help me find Moriarty," Tweed replied. "Find out where he's hiding out."

Harry shook his head. "No chance. I'm not risking coming to the attention of that man. You do *not* want him as your enemy."

"You mean you're scared?"

"Oh, yes," said Harry. "I thought I was making that clear. *Everyone's* scared of Moriarty, boy."

Tweed got to his feet, his face cold and angry. It looked like Barnaby had been wrong about Harry.

But before Tweed could go anywhere, Harry raised his hands in the air.

"Relax, sonny. I'm not saying I won't lend a hand. Just make sure you keep my name out of it."

Tweed forced himself to calm down. He nodded. "Fine. Of course. If that's what you want."

"It is. There's someone I know of who might be able to help. Calls herself Songbird. She's the only one who knows anything about this gang. Word is she's been collecting information on them."

"Why?"

Harry shrugged. "Don't ask me."

"So what do I do?"

"Go home. I'll make contact and see if it's even in the cards."

"And if it is?"

"I'll get word to you."

CHAPTER FIVE

Octavia arrived at the abandoned workhouse along the Thames two hours after midnight and one hour before the meeting was to take place. It was the best time for keeping appointments such as this. For one thing, she was absolutely sure her father would be asleep, and also, the streets were at their quietest between then and dawn.

She hadn't been sure she'd even come. Not after what happened last night on the bridge. But Harry Banks's note had said it was important, that it had something to do with the professor.

How could she say no to that?

She took up her position in an abandoned guard's shed right on the lip of the embankment, about fifty feet from the workhouse. She could hear the water of the Thames at her back, rolling up against the stone wall ten feet below her. Octavia made sure her hair was piled up beneath her dirty cap and that the brim shadowed her features.

Then she settled down to wait.

Half an hour later there was movement on the street. A figure walked out of the alley alongside the workhouse. He paused and looked both ways along the embankment. It looked as if her contact had arrived early to check out the meeting place. Sensible.

Octavia leaned forward to get a better look through the empty window frame. The figure was tall, with unruly black hair. He wore a long black coat, and as he turned to survey the street, revealing his pale, sharp-featured face, Octavia frowned in surprise.

The figure in front of her looked to be about the same age as she was. How odd.

He glanced up at the high workhouse walls, then turned in a

slow circle until his eyes fell on the cramped shed in which Octavia hid. His eyes lingered.

Oh, dear.

Octavia moved back until she was swallowed up by the shadows. It didn't do any good, though. The figure started to walk toward her. Octavia whipped out her black scarf and wrapped it around her lower face so only her eyes were visible, and even those were hidden beneath the peak of the cap. She had already charged her Tesla gun. It was safely hidden in her pocket, easily within reach.

How did he know she was in here? She hadn't made a noise, she was sure of it.

The boy stopped three paces away and put his hands in the pockets of his coat. Octavia waited but he didn't say anything, just stood there waiting. She felt her irritation start to rise. He was putting her on the back foot here, and she didn't like that. *She* was supposed to be in control.

Neither said anything for some time. Eventually, the boy cleared his throat and asked, "Busy night?"

Octavia hesitated. "What?"

The boy nodded at the guard's shed, then glanced around the deserted street. "Lots to guard here. Have to keep an eye out for all those criminals out to steal empty buildings."

Octavia's mouth dropped open. Was he . . . was he making *fun* of her?

"The meeting was supposed to be in the warehouse," she snapped.

"That's what I thought. And yet here we are."

"I don't have to be here, you know," said Octavia.

The boy stared thoughtfully into the distance, then nodded. "My apologies. It's been rather a long couple of days. Let's start over, shall we? My name's Sebastian Tweed. I don't suppose there's much point in asking your name? Only, I always find it better to know who I'm talking to. Breaks the ice, so to speak. No?"

Octavia didn't answer. She was still trying to figure out what to make of this Sebastian Tweed fellow. He was decidedly odd.

"I thought not," he said. "The reason I want your help is that my father has been kidnapped and Harry Banks seems to think you are the person to help me."

Octavia nodded, then realized he couldn't see her in the darkness. "Harry mentioned masks?"

Tweed turned toward her. "Masks, yes. Old-fashioned smoke masks. And odd weapons. Tesla-powered, if I'm any judge. I've never seen anything like them before."

Octavia felt the excitement in the pit of her stomach. Tweed's descriptions matched Moriarty and his gang. The one's who had taken her mother. But still, she had to be sure.

"I'll need a description of the masks," she said.

The boy reached inside his coat and pulled out a folded piece of paper. He hesitated. "May I?"

It took Octavia a second to realize he was asking if he could come closer. "Yes. Pass it through."

Tweed stepped forward and passed the paper through the window. She leaned down and opened the shutter of a small lamp at her feet and glanced over the detailed sketches, her eyes stopping on the drawing of Moriarty, that strange insect-like mask. She remembered it well, the light glinting from the glass eyes as he grabbed hold of Octavia's mother and dragged her into a carriage . . .

She shook herself and glanced up. "You're a pretty good artist," she said absently.

"I know. I've studied anatomy, the masters, techniques of sculpting, medical encyclopedias—"

"I was just paying you a compliment," Octavia cut in, "not asking for details."

"Ah. I see." He nodded at the paper. "Do you think you can help?"

"I don't know. I won't lie to you. I've been trying to track down Moriarty and his gang for a year now. They're . . . hard to pin down."

She looked at the sketch again. *What is your plan?* she wondered.

"You must have some information on them."

"Oh, I do."

"Will you share it? Perhaps we can join forces, pool our resources?"

Octavia gave a small laugh. "I don't think so. I don't work with amateurs."

"Of course, of course. How silly of me. I totally understand. Nothing worse than working with a common layman. You never know how he'll mess everything up, yes?"

Octavia hesitated. She wasn't sure if Tweed was making fun of her again or not. He was very difficult to read. "That's right," she said.

"Then how will I contact you?"

"Harry. He'll pass on anything I find."

Tweed opened his mouth to reply. Then he frowned and looked up.

"What—?" she began.

She didn't get a chance to finish because at that moment something screamed out of the night sky, leaving a long trail of smoke in its wake. The object smashed into the roof of the workhouse with a crash of splintering tiles.

Tweed's eyes widened and he lunged forward, throwing himself through the door of the tiny guardhouse.

As he did so the workhouse exploded with a thunderous, ear-rupturing roar. The building disintegrated into a huge orange fireball, fragments of brick and splintered glass tearing lethally through the air. A vision-distorting wave of hot air burst through the wooden slats of the hut, knocking Octavia's cap from her head. She squeezed her eyes closed against the heat, but when she opened them again she saw a roiling, burning wall of flame rolling rapidly toward them. Tweed yanked her away from the window. She had a second to register his face, noting that he looked strangely calm, and then the concussion hit them, picking up the hut and flinging it into the air. Smoke and fire engulfed them, swirling around the cabin. Octavia fell onto Tweed's legs, then was flung against the roof as the hut turned end over end.

There was a heavy splash, then water poured through the gaps in the wood. The explosion had thrown them right out over the embankment and into the Thames.

At least that took care of the flames, she thought, as the icy, dark water flowed around them.

Octavia swam through the door before the shed started to slip below the surface. Bits of wood and material from inside the workhouse hit the water with hisses and splashes, giving off tiny wisps of steam.

Tweed was ahead of her. He swam about twenty feet downstream and used the rusted ladder bolted to the embankment wall to haul himself out of the water. Octavia climbed up after him, her teeth chattering uncontrollably as she fumbled with the rungs. What had happened? Had Tweed led Moriarty to them?

Tweed leaned over the ladder, holding out his hand to her. Octavia ignored it and pulled herself back onto dry land. They both stared at the burning warehouse. The walls had been reduced to rubble by the explosion. Fire raged through the gutted interior, flinging bright red sparks into the night sky. Octavia could feel the heat from where they stood.

"Looks like you were followed," said Tweed.

Octavia whirled to face him. "Me? Think again, mister. I've been doing this for a long time, you know. I'm *careful.*"

Tweed raised an eyebrow at her. "You've been doing this for a long time? You look like you're fourteen years old!"

Octavia's hand went to her face. Her scarf had fallen off in the water. She sighed. Too late to do anything about it now. "I'm seventeen, actually."

Tweed shrugged, as if her age was of no importance to him. "Does that change anything?" he asked, nodding at the fire.

"It means we have to be more careful. You especially. They must know where you live."

"No one followed me," he repeated. "Believe me, I'd know."

"So you think it was totally random that someone fires some kind of missile at the building we were supposed to meet in? How could they know—?"

She broke off as something occurred to her. She saw the dawning realization on Tweed's face as he thought the same thing.

"Harry Banks," he said.

Octavia nodded. "Looks like it." She thought for a moment. "I'll kill him."

"Violence is not usually the first method I turn to," said Tweed. "I find it betrays a weak mind. But in this case, I might make an exception."

"I—" Octavia saw something over Tweed's shoulder. "Oh, *bother*," she said. "That's not good."

A group of figures had emerged from the alley to the rear of the ruined workhouse. Even from this distance Octavia could see the blue spark of electricity arcing around the hat of one of the figures. The tallest of the group, Moriarty, shouted instructions at the others, pointing in Octavia and Tweed's direction. Octavia fumbled for her gun, but it wasn't there anymore. It must have fallen out of her pocket in all the excitement.

"Run?" said Tweed.

"Run," Octavia agreed.

CHAPTER SIX

They sprinted along the embankment, trying to put as much distance as they could between themselves and their pursuers. Tweed glanced over his shoulder as they ran. At least it was easy enough to spot them coming. Even from this distance he could see the flickering blue light arcing around the top hat of the one he'd come to think of as "the Gibbering Man."

Tweed frowned, trying to get a good look at him. The odd little man wasn't simply running, but loping along on all fours with occasional leaps into the air, moving like a chimpanzee Tweed had once seen at a circus.

That's a bit . . . disturbing.

Tweed turned back to face front. As he did so the man released a high-pitched howl, followed by his odd, gibbering laughter, which echoed around the empty dock.

The girl turned her head at the sound, glancing at Tweed with eyes that glinted with excitement.

Odd. Tweed would be the first to admit he had limited experience with the opposite sex. Most of his interactions had been with friends of his father's, and they weren't what you would call "sophisticated." Salt of the earth, true enough, and he wouldn't hear a bad word said against them, but they *were* slightly . . . rough. But from what he'd gathered from books and plays, girls didn't usually look happy when being chased by gangs of insane killers.

Another thing Tweed couldn't help noticing was that the girl's eyes were very large. Was that from her mother's side? Her father's? Normally, he would have been quite interested in asking her about that—studying the science of heredity was one of his hobbies—but he thought that perhaps now was not the best moment for such questions.

And then she did something quite extraordinary. She *grinned* at him. Then she turned her attention back to the path ahead.

"Are you drunk?" he shouted.

She glanced back at him. "*What?* No. Don't be absurd." She grinned again. "Why? Are you offering?"

Tweed opened his mouth to respond, but the girl put on an extra burst of speed and pulled away from him. Tweed put his head down and caught up with her just as they arrived at the eastern end of Thames Street.

"This way," the girl said, turning right. "We can double back along Russell then onto Trinity Street. There's a church there. People."

Tweed saw her plan. Their pursuers might look scary in their masks, but they couldn't exactly walk around in public with them on, could they?

The problem there was that they might just decide to kill everyone, like they did at Samuel Shaw's house.

"No," he said firmly. "I've seen what they do to witnesses. We need to hide."

The girl hesitated, indecision plain on her face. Finally, she nodded and they ran across the wide road and into Isambard Wharf. There were lots of buildings there, huge factories and storage sheds built flush with the water's edge so that supplies could be unloaded onto the dock for the building of Brunel & Company's airships.

Tweed ducked behind one of the brick storage sheds. The girl joined him, trying to take the spot closest to the edge so she could peer around the corner. Tweed frowned at her.

"Do you mind?" he whispered fiercely.

"Not at all," she said, kneeling down and slowly slipping her head around the corner to check for pursuers.

Tweed sighed. How tiresome, he thought, leaning over her to get his own look. As he did so there was a flash of blue-white light. He and the girl jerked their heads back just as a stream of lightning flew past the building and hit up against the double doors of a factory behind them. The doors exploded inward, flying off the huge iron hinges and spinning into the dark interior of the massive building. A strange metallic taste filled Tweed's mouth as he stared at the empty doorway.

"We should probably try to avoid getting hit with that," he said, "if at all possible."

"I agree."

They moved back along the wall of the building until they came to an opening. Tweed ducked inside, noticing for the first time the tracks that had been laid into the cobbles at his feet. He checked along the embankment and saw the tracks headed into the distance, but with secondary lines veering off into each of the warehouses and sheds that occupied Isambard Wharf.

Inside the shed, the floor was cut by a deep rectangular gouge that let the waters of the Thames inside, allowing crates and supplies to be more easily unloaded from ships.

"So," said the girl. "Thoughts?"

"More than you can possibly imagine. Here. Help me with this."

Tweed hurried to the back of the shed, where a large cart rested on the tracks. He felt around the sides for the brake lever and yanked it back. Then he started to push it forward. It was heavier than he thought. The thing barely moved.

"Come on, then," he said. "Give us a hand."

There was a low chugging sound, then the container lurched forward, yanking free of his hands. Tweed straightened up. The girl stood on the other side of the track, watching as the flatbed chugged around the bend in the track and out through the open door.

"Steam power," she said.

"Well, yes, obviously," said Tweed, brushing his hands together.

The girl's eyes widened. "Oh. You didn't think we should be on that, did you? I personally thought that would be an atrocious idea, so I didn't bother to ask, but it strikes me how you may have thought that was how we should escape."

"Don't be absurd," said Tweed, striding to the door and peering after the cart as it picked up speed. "It was a diversion."

The girl joined him. The cart was over two hundred yards away by now. As they watched from the shadows their pursuers came sprinting into view, running after the cart.

The two with the identical smoke masks came first. Then came the man with the two discs that shone light directly into his eyes. The Gibbering Man came next. He stopped, then raised the metallic weapon he carried. A burst of lighting shot out of the metal tube and arced through the air. But it didn't get far, grounding into the metal tracks instead, crawling and sputtering across the line. Tweed and the girl quickly shifted their feet to make sure they weren't touching the metal. The Gibbering Man cursed, then shoved the metal weapon into a holster on his back and set off after the others.

The girl waited for a moment, then got ready to move. Tweed grabbed her by the arm. She whirled to face him, but Tweed hastily raised a finger to his lips and gently inclined his head outside.

A moment later, Moriarty strode into view. He walked with his hands behind his back, the tails of his long black coat flaring out behind him like a cloak.

They waited until the cart veered around the far end of the huge factory, the masked figures scurrying after it, Moriarty taking a more sedate pace. Then they slipped outside and moved quickly back along the wall to their original hiding place.

Tweed looked back the way they'd come. It was a lot of open ground. They'd have to move fast if they wanted to get clear.

Then he frowned, hearing a distant putt-putt sound growing louder. The cart was coming around the factory, already heading back in their direction.

Which meant their pursuers would be coming back as well. They'd never make it to cover in time.

The girl grabbed his arm and they ducked through the still-smoldering doorway of the factory just as the cart sped around the corner and shot past them, leaving behind a cloud of steam.

"They're going to figure out it's empty any minute now," said the girl. "I suggest we hide."

They turned and moved deeper into the building.

The front room was a greeting area, with comfy sofas and a small table on one side of the room and a huge mahogany desk on the other. Unfortunately, the tasteful decoration had been somewhat ruined by the lightning gun. One of the front doors was now embedded in the rear wall of the room, while the second had smashed into the base of the desk, shattering the dark, polished wood.

There was only one exit. They hurried forward and pulled open the door.

As it moved inward, Tweed felt the swish of air against his face. A cavernous space opened up before them. He stepped forward and found his eyes drawn up.

And up. And then up some more, all the way to the roof some three hundred yards above him.

Tweed tore his eyes away from the distant roof. The factory floor itself took up the entire half-mile length of the building. Glass-enclosed lanterns were spaced every few yards along the wall, the tiny circles of orange light they gave off almost completely useless in the vast, shadowy workshop.

In the center of the factory floor, supported by huge iron girders coated with flaking red paint, was a massive, unfinished passenger zeppelin.

Only half of the airship had been covered with material, the metal framework of the second half left visible for all to see. The ship looked half naked, as if they had interrupted it in the process of getting dressed.

"Plenty of places to hide in here," said Tweed. "Come on."

To their right a set of stairs lead up to a gantry that circled the factory. There were more gantries bolted to the walls, giving access to every level in the factory all the way to the roof. Tweed ran up the stairs, but his footsteps clanged on the metal grating. He paused, then decided to just keep on going. There was less chance of being seen at the top.

They clambered up the stairs until they arrived at the top, then moved quickly along the suspended grating. Tweed kept looking over his shoulder as they ran, fearing that he would see the silhouette of Moriarty stretching across the floor, attracted by the noise.

About halfway along this walkway was the first of many ladders that led into the interior of the zeppelin's structure. From here Tweed could see long metal grills criss-crossing inside the airship, linked together by long planks of wood for use by the builders as they constructed the airship. To their right was a long, glass-fronted control room.

"In there?" the girl suggested, inclining her head to the control room.

Tweed craned his head all the way back. "Up there," he said.

At the very top of the airship skeleton, a platform hung from the roof of the factory. The platform looked about thirty yards long, and it hung from a system of pulleys that allowed it to move the entire length of the factory.

"You're crazy," said the girl.

"Why? If they come up here the first place they'll look is in the control room. But you can barely see that platform."

It was true. The platform was painted black, blending in with the shadows around the roof. Tweed had only seen it because he was thinking of hiding on one of the scaffoldings that had been erected inside the airship's skeleton.

"You first, then," said the girl. "And if you fall, don't grab for me on your way down. This is your idea. You don't have to take me with you."

Tweed climbed up the ladder and ducked beneath the curved metal of the zeppelin's frame. There was a paint-spattered plank of wood at his feet. Another was laid across it. The planks made up a temporary floor, crisscrossing each other so that the builders could easily move to any section of the zeppelin they wanted to. About ten feet above his head was a second level, identical to the first.

He moved carefully along the wood until he arrived at a ladder, then climbed to the next level. There was another floor of criss-crossed planks above him. He checked over his shoulder to make sure the girl was managing. She stood directly behind him, impatiently gesturing for him to move ahead. He supposed he shouldn't be surprised. From what little he'd seen of her she didn't seem the type to linger at the back of the line.

Tweed climbed another five levels before they arrived at the very top of the airship. A short distance away he could just make out a rope ladder dangling from the edge of the platform.

He was about to move toward it when he felt the girl's fingers curl around his wrist. He turned and saw her staring down at the floor.

Tweed leaned to the side and grabbed hold of the metal frame, peering back to the factory door. Far below him he could see the tiny worms of electricity dancing around the Gibbering Man's top hat.

The tall figure of Professor Moriarty walked into view. He looked around for a moment then pointed. The Gibbering Man lifted his gun, and a burst of lightning shot from the tube and wrapped itself around the set of stairs, arcing and spitting as it crawled and leaped along the metal grating.

The lightning died away. Smoke drifted sluggishly into the air. A second later the same thing happened on the next level, then the next and the next, all the way to the top. Tweed could see the control room through a gap in the scaffolding, and the blue-white light crawled and spat across the floor and walls inside. If they had hidden in there they'd be dead.

Tweed felt a breath of air on his ear.

"Excuse me," the girl whispered. Then she leaned past him and gently pried his hand away from the metal strut he still held onto. She gestured for him to follow, guiding him along the wooden walkway until they stood in the center of the zeppelin.

A moment later the lightning burst and exploded all around them, arcing up the metallic skeleton of the airship, crawling, spitting, sparks flying, the smell of burning tin heavy in Tweed's nostrils. Their eyes reflected flashing white light as they stared in awe at the electricity arcing up to either side and meeting above them, a cage of deadly energy.

The only thing that saved them was the wooden plank on which they stood.

Tweed couldn't tear his eyes away. The noise was intense, unsettling: staccato barks and cracks of energy. Lightning arced straight down from the top of the airship, grounding itself in anything conductive. Tweed shuddered, realizing how extremely dead he would be right now if the girl hadn't removed his hand.

A few moments later the lighting flickered and died away. Smoke filled the air, and occasional tiny crawling worms of light flashed and disappeared.

Tweed swallowed nervously, then pointed at the wooden platform above them. The girl nodded and they moved toward it, using the smoke for cover. Tweed grabbed the rope ladder tightly and held it for the girl to climb up, then he followed after her and collapsed onto the wooden platform. He could hear sirens in the distance.

Tweed stared up at the roof of the factory, no more than twenty yards above him. Then he rolled over to find the girl peering over the edge.

"They've gone," she said. "Ran when they heard the sirens."

Tweed nodded and closed his eyes.

"We should probably stay here for a while," she said. "I don't really feel like answering the police's questions."

"Fine by me," said Tweed.

They were both silent for a while. Finally, Tweed sat up and prodded the girl's foot.

"Have I earned the right to ask your name yet?" Tweed asked. "'Songbird' just sounds so . . . *fake*."

The girl frowned. She stared at Tweed, then sighed. "Fine. My name's Octavia. Octavia Nightingale. My mother . . . I used to sing her songs. She called me her little songbird. Before . . ." She trailed off and shook her head sharply so that part of her fringe fell forward to cover her face.

Tweed waited for her to carry on, but it soon became apparent that she wasn't going to. He leaned forward to try to catch a glimpse of her face, but she turned her head away.

What had he done? He'd obviously said something to upset her. Should he apologize? Ignore it? He wasn't very good at this kind of thing.

What would Barnaby do?

He thought about it, then leaned forward and hesitantly patted her on the head. "There there," he said awkwardly. Then he added, "Buck up."

Octavia turned her head slightly to look at him with a baffled look on her face.

Then she burst out laughing.

"What?" said Tweed.

"*You!* Patting me on the head like that. I'm not a dog, you know."

"Oh." Tweed thought about this and nodded. "I see your point. Sorry about that. I'm not very good with other people. Never had a lot of time for socializing. I much preferred reading, really." He frowned thoughtfully. "I've been told that spending my formative years with my nose buried in a book may have made me a bit . . ."

"Odd?" said Octavia.

"No—"

"Disturbed?"

"No—"

"A bit . . . mental?"

"*If* you will let me finish. A bit . . . socially awkward around people I don't know. Which brings me back to the Songbird thing. It's seems that I've offended you somehow. Your mother . . . did she die?"

"What? No! At least, I don't think so." She sighed. "The truth is, I don't know. My mother works for the *Times*. About a year ago she started looking into the reports that Moriarty had returned to London. He obviously didn't like a reporter snooping around, and one night he and his gang turned up and just . . . took her away."

"Oh," said Tweed. "I'm sorry. Seems we're in a similar position, you and I."

"So it would seem," said Octavia. "That's what all this Songbird stuff is for. A way to keep my identity hidden. I've been gathering any information I can on Moriarty, hoping I'll stumble onto something. Maybe find out where he's hiding."

Tweed nodded thoughtfully. "Octavia Nightingale, I have a proposition for you."

"Sorry, I'm not that kind of girl."

"What? Oh, I see. Yes, most amusing. No what I want to say is: My father, your mother—both kidnapped by Moriarty and his gang. We can join forces, pool our resources. You can be my assistant and—"

"I *beg* your pardon? I'll be no such thing. If anything, you can be *my* assistant. *I'm* the one who's spent the last year investigating Moriarty."

"And doesn't the fact that you haven't found him yet tell you something? Because it tells me a fresh pair of eyes are needed. Barnaby trained me in logical thinking from a very young age. That's what this situation needs. Logic. Clear-headedness. Not brash emotion, running off willy-nilly after every little lead."

Octavia stood up. "You, sir, are a buffoon. I have never ran anywhere 'willy-nilly.' Nor do I ever intend to. I can think just as logically as you."

"Then what's our next move?"

"I . . . well, I hadn't thought of that yet."

"I have," said Tweed. "And if you apologize for calling me a buffoon I'll tell you."

Octavia folded her arms across her chest. She narrowed her eyes at him. "Fine," she said eventually. "I'm sorry I called you a buffoon."

"Thank—"

"When it's entirely clear to anyone who spends even the smallest amount of time with you that you are, in fact, a hedge-born canker-blossom!"

Tweed opened his mouth.

Then he shut it again. Even he had to admit, that was a damned fine insult.

CHAPTER SEVEN

T weed eventually dozed off, and Octavia decided to let him sleep. She could still hear sirens coming and going, so she didn't think they should move yet anyway. It would be safer to wait a couple of hours.

She studied him as he slept, his mouth slightly open as he snored loudly. He certainly was an odd one, nothing at all like anyone she'd ever met. She'd only known him for a few hours, but he seemed all right, as far as she could tell. Slightly annoying. But all right. He displayed a strange mixture of arrogance and naivety, something Octavia hadn't thought possible up till now. One usually canceled out the other, but in Sebastian Tweed, the two existed side by side.

Octavia eventually dozed off in the early hours of the morning, waking some time later to find Tweed staring at her intently.

He jerked back when her eyes opened, looking quickly away. He got to his feet, sending the platform swaying back and forth, and clapped his hands together. "Right. Plans to make, Nightingale. Things to do. People to see. Well, I say 'people,' but it's really only one. And he smells odd, so don't get too close to him."

Octavia blinked and yawned, taking in this verbal stream. Then she frowned. "Hoi," she said.

"Yes? What?" he turned to face her.

"What were you staring at me for? While I was asleep. It's not polite."

"Isn't it? Sorry. To answer your question, I noticed that the two sides of your face are not symmetrical. I was trying to see the difference."

"I beg your pardon? My face is *perfectly* symmetrical."

Tweed shook his head. "No one's is. Yours is very slight, don't worry. Far from a deformity. I *did* notice that one eye is ever so slightly larger than the other, though." He leaned forward as he talked, then apparently realized what he was doing and quickly straightened up. "But it's barely noticeable." He gestured to one of the windows in the roof. The light outside was the grey of early morning. "The first workers will be here soon and I don't want to have to explain the door. Or the blackened metal everywhere. Shall we?"

୭୧

They walked for about three miles or so along the embankment, heading away from docks and into the actual city proper. Hansom cabs pulled by automata jounced past on their right, using the slow lane reserved for them. Omnibuses chugged by in the faster lanes, clouds of steam billowing from their chimneys into the grey morning air. Rush hour was approaching, and even the bluest of skies would soon become hidden behind London's permanent dirty cloud cover.

The soot and steam and dirty smoke from the thousands of vehicles coated everything, turning London into something out of a gothic painting, as if rendered in strokes of black and grey. The city had tried many methods of keeping the buildings clean, most involving small, animal-like automata that spent their lives scrubbing brickwork, but they needed to draw power from somewhere, so they just ended up contributing to the problem.

"Where are we going?" she asked. "Shouldn't we get to Harry Banks? Ask him just what on Earth he was thinking?"

Tweed stopped walking, a frown on his face. "I forgot about Harry. We should do something, yes. I don't think we should be quite so open about it, though. If he did sell us out then what's to stop him from pulling a gun on us and just handing us over to the professor?"

"But he might have information about the gang."

"Possible, but I don't think it's likely. Harry's a small-timer. You'd know that if you've dealt with him. I think he saw an opportunity and he took it."

"So we're just going to let him get away with it?"

"On the contrary. I think we should make him suffer. I just don't know if now's the best time."

"So if we're not going to see Harry, where are we going?"

Tweed pointed at a building across the street. "There."

Octavia turned and looked to where he was pointing. She knew the red-brick building. Everyone did.

It was New Scotland Yard.

"You won't find anything there," she said. "I've already asked them."

"Oh? Who did you speak to?"

Octavia shrugged. "Someone at the front desk. I showed them my *Times* card, but they said they didn't know what I was talking about."

"Ah. Well, they won't, will they? I have a feeling certain people higher up won't want word of Moriarty and his gang getting out into the public domain. Professor Moriarty, back from the dead? No one will be too happy to hear that. But there are ways and means."

"Are you saying you could do better?"

Tweed nodded. "Yes. But don't feel bad about it. It's just that I happen to know someone."

Tweed led her across the road and into a side street, nodding at any helmeted policemen he passed. They seemed to know him. As they passed beneath a concrete arch that spanned the street, she leaned closer to him.

"Do you come here often?"

Tweed looked briefly uncomfortable. "Ah, yes. I do, actually. They think I work in the records room."

"Why on Earth would they think that?"

Tweed paused in the street and looked around to make sure no one was listening. "My father was a bit of a . . . a criminal. A con man."

"What?"

"So am I, I suppose. He taught me, brought me up doing it. Lately he's been pretending to be a psychic and charging people money to talk to their dead relatives. I started coming here to find out what I could about the marks."

"That's horrible," said Octavia, pulling back slightly.

"I know. That's what *I* told him. I wanted to stop. I came here to try to find something that would give them peace. To make them really think they *were* speaking to their lost ones. And before you say it, I know that doesn't make it better, but it . . . it *helped* some of them."

"Is that what you tell yourself? That you *helped* them?" said Octavia angrily.

"No, yes . . . *No.* Look. I know it's wrong. I was trying to find a way to give them what they were hoping for."

"That doesn't make it right!"

"No, but it makes it *less wrong* . . ." He hesitated. "Listen, you don't know me. You don't know the life we've had. You can't judge me on what I've told you. Sometimes you have to do things to survive. Or haven't you ever experienced that?" He stepped back and stared at her. "Actually, probably not. You're rich, yes?"

"Why do you say that?" snapped Octavia.

"Your clothing. I noticed that scarf you had wrapped around you last night. It was a cheap cut of material, but the thread was black silk. And your hair. You've tried to hide it with . . ." he leaned forward and sniffed. Octavia recoiled slightly. ". . . coal dust, but the natural luster is there. You can't hide it. Expensive soap. Healthy diet. So, there it is. I understand you disapprove, and that's fine. So do I. Just realize that's not all I am."

Without waiting for a response, he turned away and moved quickly up the steps.

"Wait."

He turned at the top of the stairs. He looked as if he feared she was going to say something else. She wanted to, but what *could* she say? He already said it was wrong. Her telling him the same thing yet again wasn't going to make a difference.

"I have to get back home," she said instead. "My father is hardly ever around but I should be there in case he looks for me. I'll tell him I'm working for the paper for the next few days. That should give me some leeway. Plus, I need to change. Don't think I'll get in looking like this." She fingered her tatty clothes. "Will you be here later on?"

Tweed nodded. "I'll be in the old records room, downstairs. Find me there."

He straightened up, all signs of unease gone in an instant. Octavia watched him stride into the building, walking as if he owned the place. She shook her head. She'd never seen such a mixture of awkwardness and confidence in one person. He disappeared inside New Scotland Yard and Octavia hurried back through the dim, early morning streets until she saw a hansom cab. It was an old-fashioned one, pulled by a horse and driver.

"Let's see your money, first," said the old man.

Octavia bristled, but then remembered what she looked like. She quickly fished out a coin from her pocket and handed it over. Then she climbed inside and gave the driver her address.

Octavia managed to sneak back into the house and wash up without drawing any attention to herself, although, admittedly, she had no idea if anyone was even *in* the house at the moment. The rooms were silent, the curtains still drawn. Her father had probably been up late again, working on his catalogs for the museum.

Octavia had spent a lot of time letting it be known she preferred to be left alone, and because she had recently completed her studies to her father's satisfaction, he acquiesced. He had even given up complaining about her spending her days at the *Times*. At first he'd been horrified that she was even thinking about following in her mother's footsteps, but she had told him in no uncertain terms that that was exactly what she was going to do, and nothing he could say would change her mind.

What did he think she would do with her life? There was no way she was going to simply marry some gentleman and start raising his children. That might be the height of ambition for other girls her age, but that life wasn't for her.

At midmorning, when her father still hadn't risen from bed, Octavia retired to her room and dressed in tweed trousers, a white shirt, and a tailored jacket. The look was inspired by Ada Lovelace, the writer and one-time business partner of Charles Babbage. The range of clothing had even been named after her.

It was a testament to the woman's influence. Lovelace was now eighty-four years old and still going strong, running Ada, the computing company she set up to compete with Babbage. The Ada machines were a new generation of analytical computers. Designed to be beautiful, not bulky like the Babbages were. Streamlined and simple to operate. Not many people used them yet, but their elegant designs were starting to gain popularity, especially amongst the Progressives.

The clothing was becoming all the rage amongst the younger ladies around London, and Octavia was very grateful. The tailored clothing was so much easier to move around in than skirts and corsets. Another reason that Ada Lovelace was a personal heroine to Octavia.

Octavia reached beneath her bed and disconnected the second Tesla gun from where it was charging. She slid it into her left pocket, thinking she would have to buy another one now to replace the gun ruined from its dip in the Thames. She didn't like only having one.

Octavia closed her bedroom door and slipped from the house, taking a deep breath of freedom as she did so. She hailed a passing automaton pulling a carriage behind it. The automaton was an old model, its face featureless except for two rectangular eye slits. Octavia climbed inside and leaned forward.

"New Scotland Yard!" she shouted in a clear voice. These old automata had problems with their hearing mechanisms. It was why no one really used them for anything other than pulling coaches.

The automaton took her through the busy streets, passing horses pulling hackney coaches and slow-moving omnibuses snaking their ways around corners like steam-driven caterpillars. She noticed that someone had vandalized the automaton, scratching rude pictures into its metal casing.

The cab stopped outside the red-brick building of New Scotland Yard. Octavia slotted the correct change into the automaton's casing then hopped off and headed up the stairs and through the front door.

She mimicked Tweed's confident walk. She'd liked that walk when she saw it earlier. It made him look like he belonged. Unfortunately, her stride faltered slightly as she passed into the main offices of the station. It was chaos. Bobbies hurried everywhere, some pinning their blue cloaks on as they left the station, others taking off helmets and flopping down before badly cluttered desks. Shouts and conversations buzzed around her as people struggled to be heard above the mayhem.

A large central desk raised on a dais dominated the room, behind which were four policemen trying to deal with the crowds vying for their attention.

Octavia decided not to ask anyone here where the old records offices were. They would probably just kick her out. Instead, she slipped along the wall and down a corridor, walking aimlessly, poking her head into offices and rooms as she went.

Tweed had said the room was downstairs, as was the records room at the paper. Records were always stored in cramped, dimly lit rooms that no one else wanted to use.

She found the stairs and descended. A faded sign on the wall told her which way to go, and she followed its directions. The passageway she found was dark. No gas lanterns, no candles. Nothing. Her footsteps echoed on the creaking floorboards as she walked to a black door at one end.

She hesitated, then pushed it open, only to be confronted by an automaton slightly shorter than she was. The construct's face had a mask on it, carved to resemble one of those disturbing ventriloquist dummies. The wide eyes stared at her, the clacking mouth opening and closing as if it wanted to bite her.

"Hold," she commanded. The construct's mouth stopped moving. "Give me space." The automaton responded to her commands and moved back and to the side, the huge eyes moving to stare at her as it did so.

A moment later she came face to face with another odd sight: an ancient man about the same height as the construct, with wild white hair that burst from his scalp like dandelion fronds. A thick, bushy beard hid half his face while two rheumy eyes glared at her.

"Who're you? What you want?" he demanded.

"A little respect will do for starters," said Octavia.

The man's eyes widened. "Whassat now? Respect? Ye want respect? I've worked here nigh on fifty years, Missy, I give no one respect."

"It's fine, Bertie. She's with me."

The man immediately changed his demeanor. His face crinkled

into a smile, and he turned and bowed as a tired-looking Tweed approached.

"I thought you didn't give anyone respect," said Octavia.

"Exceptin' Mr. Tweed here. He's a good'n. Clever." He tapped his head. "Has brains in here, you know."

"As opposed to having them somewhere else?"

Bertie frowned. "Whut?"

Octavia sighed. "Nothing. So, may I enter?" she asked.

"Aye, in you come, then. But no funny stuff, you hear?"

"Bertie, I think I can promise you without a shadow of a doubt that there will be absolutely no 'funny stuff.'"

Bertie narrowed his eyes suspiciously, then stepped aside so Octavia could enter. She looked around the dim chamber. This wasn't just the Archives. It seemed as though the room was used as a storage room for everything that was unwanted upstairs. Ten automata stood up against the wall, all of them with ventriloquist dummy masks tied to their heads.

The room was stacked with row upon row of floor to ceiling shelves, the shelves themselves filled with labeled drawers. Tweed led her to a desk littered with loose paper and leather-bound files. He pulled up a second chair and slumped into the one he must have been using all morning.

Octavia sat down. "Any luck?"

Tweed glanced over her shoulder to make sure Bertie wasn't in hearing range. "Nothing," he said in a frustrated tone of voice. "I've been over every single attack and murder over the past year. Do you realize how much work that is? I haven't found one single official mention of Moriarty, or his gang, or the strange masks they wear. Nothing."

Octavia frowned. "How is that possible? We know it happened. We've seen it with our own eyes. You saw them murder those people only two days ago."

Tweed leaned toward her. "Harry said he thought the police were trying to keep it hush-hush. That they don't want word to get out because of the panic it would cause. He may be right."

Octavia shook her head. "They couldn't just ignore it, could they?" She looked around the dilapidated room. One of the automata walked past with a jerky gait, pulled open a drawer, and took out a long box of files. It then took the box to a desk pushed up against the wall, where Bertie was busy working.

"There must be other records. Kept somewhere else. You know. Sensitive stuff? Top secret?"

Tweed looked slightly disappointed that Octavia had come up with that suggestion. "I was coming to that," he said testily. "I asked Bertie about it. He says there's another records room upstairs, for restricted files. I've been coming here for five months now and it's the first I've heard of it."

"So, how do we get in?"

"That's the hard part." Tweed slid a piece of paper across the desk. Octavia picked it up and scanned it.

"It's a requisition form," she said.

Tweed nodded. "I got it from Bertie's desk when he wasn't looking. If someone needs records from upstairs, Bertie has to formally request them. It needs to be approved and signed off by a senior officer."

Octavia slumped back in her chair. "We're never going to get that. Can't Bertie just ask?"

"No. He doesn't know I have an ulterior motive for coming here. He thinks I enjoy it, enjoy helping him." A look of guilt slid across Tweed's face. "Thing is, I *do* enjoy it. All the records and stuff. And Bertie's fine when you get to know him. But . . ."

Octavia understood. "You don't want him thinking you used him."

Tweed nodded.

"So we somehow need to get one of the inspectors of New Scotland

Yard to approve a request for any files they have regarding Moriarty and his gang? Files they have stored in their top secret records room because you reckon they don't want anyone knowing about them. Is that about the gist of it?"

"That's the gist of it exactly." Tweed grinned. "And now that you're here, we can put my plan into action."

Octavia studied his eager face. Why did she suddenly feel so worried?

CHAPTER EIGHT

Tweed had always been proud of his plans. He was *good* at them. For enjoyment he used to read about the crimes happening throughout the world and would then lie back on the couch and come up with alternate ways of carrying out the robbery, the investigation, the murder, *whatever.* And invariably, he would come up with a better way of doing it.

The point was, he thought himself quite clever.

So he was slightly disappointed with what he'd come up with to try to get a signature out of one of the senior officers. Admittedly, he'd only had an hour or two, but still. It wasn't witty. It wasn't clever. Barnaby would be very disappointed. He could just imagine him shaking his head. "For shame, Tweed. I taught you better than that, didn't I?"

"Let me get this straight," said Octavia. "You want me to distract a police inspector by getting all hysterical, and then you'll get him to sign the form, which you will cunningly—and I use the word advisedly—conceal beneath another form so he won't know what he's signing. Is that right?"

Tweed flushed with embarrassment and glanced over his shoulder to make sure Bertie wasn't listening.

"I know, I know. It's not brilliant, but—"

"You're being too kind," said Octavia. "I think it's very, very far from being brilliant."

"Fine. It's *far* from brilliant. But can you come up with anything better? We can't forge a signature. We can't break into the records room. We can't just bluff our way in. It has to be done properly."

"I suppose you've got a point," said Octavia reluctantly.

"Then you'll do it?"

"I didn't say that." Octavia leaned back in her chair, draping one arm over the back while studying Tweed through narrowed eyes. "Tell me, do you think the only way I can distract a man is by acting hysterical? Is that what you think of women? I'm surprised you didn't just tell me to undo a few buttons and flash my cleavage at him. Would you like me to do that, Sebastian Tweed? Hmm?"

Tweed swallowed nervously, locking his eyes fiercely on Octavia's. *Don't look down*, he ordered himself. *Do. Not. Look. Down.*

He wasn't used to girls speaking to him so plainly. Actually, he wasn't used to girls his own age speaking to him *at all*. Truth to tell, it was entirely possible Octavia Nightingale was the first girl his own age he'd actually had a proper conversation with. When he rescued Barnaby he'd be having some severe words with the old man. What had he been thinking, keeping him from socializing with others his own age? It was a whole level of knowledge he was deficient in. He *hated* that.

"Of course not," he said. He hesitated, then leaned toward Octavia. "And just so you know, I don't think women are the weaker sex. I don't think men are stronger, or cleverer, or any other number of ludicrous beliefs some men hold. As I may have mentioned before, the female influence in my life has come from a number of rather . . . *bohemian* friends of my father's. And not a single one of them was a wilting wallflower. I may not know much about girls my own age, but I know that women—" he stared up at the ceiling for a second while he tried to order his thoughts, then looked down again— "women are every bit as capable as men at being devious, clever, wonderful, stupid, surprising, sad, brilliant and—" he waggled his fingers—"*whatever*." He grinned and raised a finger into the air. "But I'm also aware that many others of my gender don't share my enlightened views. Which is why I suggested the plan."

He stopped talking, suddenly realizing he'd gone on a bit of a speech. He looked up at his finger, then lowered it. The sound of slow clapping echoed from the far corner of the room. Tweed glanced over Octavia's shoulder to find Bertie on his feet applauding.

"*Brava*, young sir," he said. "Always knew you were a good 'un. My mother'd love you, she would. Disguised herself as a lad and went off to fight in the war when she was sixteen, she did."

"Yes, thank you, Bertie," said Tweed. And when Bertie carried on applauding, he added. "Please stop clapping, Bertie. There's a good chap."

Bertie winked at him, then sat down again. Octavia stared at Tweed with an odd, calculating look on her face.

"What?" he asked.

"Nothing. You just . . . *surprise* me, that's all."

"Oh. Good. Surprising people is much better than being boring, don't you think? Can't abide boring people. Now, shall we be off?"

ᑫᑫ

Tweed decided to look for an inspector called James McLeod. It wasn't that he was the most senior officer, or the friendliest, or even the stupidest. Just that Tweed had spoken to the man once or twice before when McLeod had ventured into the archives looking for records, so it would make the ruse more believable.

Tweed also knew where his office was, which made it a lot easier than wandering around the building looking lost.

He sat down on a bench in the hallway just around the corner from the inspector's office, carefully arranging the papers. The top piece was a standard office supplies requisition form from the archives. Tweed had found piles of them lying around. But he had neatly folded the bottom half of the form underneath and laid it over the top of the form he *really* wanted signed, the request for information from the high security records room.

He had used a tiny amount of glue to stick the pieces of paper together. Not much, just enough to hopefully hide the seam. He held it up and looked at it critically. It would never work. He could still see the join just above the empty spot marked for a signature.

Tweed sighed. Nothing for it, though. There was no other plan forthcoming. Not in the amount of time they had.

He stood up and arranged his shirt into untidy folds, twisting his suspenders around to give himself a scruffier appearance more in keeping with someone who worked in the archives.

He slumped his shoulders, mirroring the defeated posture of the terminally employed, and halfheartedly knocked on the door.

"Come!" barked a Scottish voice.

Tweed pushed the door open, bowing and bobbing into the room in the same manner Bertie assumed when talking to his superiors. Subservience and groveling. A combination guaranteed to get people underestimating you.

MacLeod's office was tiny. Just enough room for a set of wooden filing cabinets, a chalkboard, and his black-painted desk. The man himself sat squeezed between the desk and the back wall, wreathed in a cloud of pipe smoke. He squinted at Tweed through the haze. That was handy. Perhaps the smoke would obscure the subterfuge.

"What is it?" asked McLeod. "You're Bertie's helper, yes? The records boy."

That's right, thought Tweed. Keep thinking that. I'm just the records boy.

"That's right, sir. Bertie sent me up, if it pleases you." *Careful, Tweed. Less of the country farmer routine.* "He asked if you'd sign this," said Tweed, waving the paper through the air, stirring up the smoke so that it moved sluggishly around the desk. Tweed leaned over the pile of books and placed the paper down, just out of reach of McLeod.

"What is it?" asked McLeod, leaning forward.

"Requisition form, sir. For more ink."

McLeod was just leaning forward to read the form, plucking his pen from the holder, when Octavia stormed into the room.

"I demand to see the inspector!" she shouted, slamming a hand down on the desk.

Tweed and McLeod blinked at her in surprise. Surprise that was certainly not feigned. *This is how she distracts someone with hysterics?* thought Tweed.

"Erhm, I'm the inspector, young lady. What can I do—?"

"Don't you 'young lady' me! I'm a member of Her Majesty's free press."

She flashed a small piece of card before them both, waving it under their noses. Tweed moved his head back to get a clearer look. It was a *Times* identification card with Octavia's photograph on it. Tweed was impressed.

"I demand to know what's being done about this outrage."

McLeod and Tweed exchanged bemused glances.

"What outrage is this?" asked McLeod. "Forgive me, I've been working on a case—"

"Hiding away from reporters is more like it!" snapped Octavia. "And don't pretend you don't know what I'm talking about. I am, of course, referring to the forced eviction of the poor on Finch Street. Just in time for the visit of the Tsar Nicholas II. Trying to pretend London doesn't have any slum problems? For shame, Inspector."

"Madam, I assure you, I have no idea what you are referring to. The Metropolitan Police does not take part in any form of slum clearances, I assure you."

"A likely story." She paused and looked at Tweed with an expression of disgust. "I'm sorry, but who is this . . . this *boy*?"

Tweed bowed. "Just a humble records assistant, madam," said Tweed.

"Can you please deal with him so we can discuss this properly?" said Octavia to McLeod.

"Um . . . of course." McLeod turned his attention to Tweed. He actually felt a bit sorry for the man. He wasn't a bad sort, as far as he could tell.

"What was it again?" asked the inspector.

"Just your signature here, sir," said Tweed, leaning over and pointing at the form, keeping his hand down over the join of the two papers. "For Bertie. Ink and stuff. Supplies."

"Of course, of course. Bertie." McLeod hastily scrawled his signature on the paper. Tweed whisked it away before he could look any closer.

"Thank you, sir. And good luck." Tweed turned and bowed at Octavia. "Madam, don't worry. I'm sure you'll find a husband someday."

Octavia's superior smile faltered. "I beg your pardon?"

"It's just, I saw you weeping in the hallway earlier on. Heard you talking to one of the tea ladies about how your fiancée had left you because—now what was it you said?—because he thought you a crushing bore with the spiky personality of a hedgehog. Horrible thing to say, madam. Horrible. As I say, I'm sure you'll get lucky someday. And if not, it's not the end of the world, eh? Spinsterhood is still an . . . acceptable alternative. Lots of free time to play with cats, I imagine."

Tweed scurried from the room before he burst out laughing. The look on her face! Tweed was sure he was going to suffer for it later on, but oh, it was worth it.

꧁꧂

It turned out getting into the restricted records room wasn't the hardest part of the plan. The hardest part was actually finding the crime reports he was looking for once he was *in*.

The door was answered by a young man with spectacles so thick his eyes looked about three sizes too big. When he saw the signed form, he nodded Tweed in and returned to his desk against the far wall.

The room was about half the size of the archives downstairs, but a lot more modern and a *lot* cleaner. It looked more like a library in one of the toff's houses where Tweed and Barnaby did their cons: posh leather chairs, mahogany reading tables, wood-paneled walls, and the clerk who kept a watch over it all from his desk.

Tweed didn't have any idea where to start. The walls were lined with wooden filing cabinets with strange codes and numbers stamped onto the drawers. He pulled one open at random and flicked through the files before closing it again with a sigh. It looked as if he would just have to ask.

He approached the clerk and cleared his throat. "Excuse me. Inspector McLeod asked me to bring him the file from the Knightsbridge attack. Two days ago? One of the victims was a man named Samuel Shaw."

The clerk tutted at Tweed as if he had caused him an immense amount of pain, then opened a thick ledger on his desk and ran his finger down the entries. He looked up.

"Cabinet X-3. File, Twenty-eight October, number fifty-six." Then he nodded at a cabinet over Tweed's shoulder.

Tweed hurried over to it and pulled the drawer open. He flicked through the files, resisting the temptation to see what other events were deemed so secret they couldn't be stored with the public police records. He found the October twenty-eighth separator, then flipped through until he found number fifty-six. He pulled out the file and took it over to one of the reading desks and sat down with his back to the clerk.

About ten minutes later he got up and asked the clerk for a piece of paper and a pencil, then wrote down a list of numbers and names. He took the paper and visited another fifteen filing cabinets, pulling out the documents and jotting down everything he thought he might need.

ଡ଼ୡ

Sebastian Tweed was furious. It took a lot to make him angry. Testy, he could do quite easily. Rather enjoyed it, actually. Sarcastic? Easy. Arrogant? Again, it came naturally. But to make him truly angry took a lot of doing.

"*Fifteen* deaths!" he hissed at Octavia as they strode along the late afternoon streets, wending their way through the end-of-day pedestrian traffic. "Fifteen murders committed by Moriarty and his gang. And what have they done? Nothing!"

"But . . . I don't understand," said Octavia. "If they know it was Moriarty, if they know these killings are linked, why don't they do something about it?"

Tweed stopped and waved his arms in the air. "They *don't* know! It took me half an hour to realize they were committed by the same people, that they had the same M.O. It would take the police the same amount of time, if they could be bothered to check. But they haven't! Someone marks the files as restricted and hides them away before anyone can even view them."

"But why?" pressed Octavia.

"Harry must have been right. Fear. It's the only answer that makes sense. They don't want it getting out that Moriarty's back. They're scared of the panic it would cause."

"So they're just letting him swan around London killing whoever he wants?"

"The deaths are spread out over the past few months. I'm sure if they all happened within days of each other Scotland Yard would have to do something. As it is someone just files away the cases and hopes it all goes away." Tweed held up his finger. "I am not a happy person, Octavia Nightingale."

"Er . . . I can see that. Which is why I'm not going to take you to task for that terrible joke in McLeod's office."

"Oh. Yes." The finger came down. "Sorry about that. Seemed funny at the time."

"Oh, it was. Funny, I mean. It was all I could do to stop from laughing."

Tweed squinted at her. "Really?"

"Really. I do have a sense of humor, you know." Her face clouded over. "I got that from my mother."

"Ah, yes. Thanks for reminding me. Here." Tweed fished inside the jacket he'd retrieved from Bertie's archives and pulled out a file. He handed it to Octavia.

"What's this?"

"The restricted file on your mother. I thought you might want it." Tweed turned and started walking again, hopping aside just in time to avoid being hit by a man on a motorized penny farthing as he put-putted along the pavement.

"Hoi! On the road, granddad." Tweed gave the back of the penny farthing a kick as it went by. The wheel wobbled, and the driver fought to regain control as the huge wheel bumped off the curb and onto the street, narrowly avoiding a collision with an oncoming omnibus.

"Quite a woman, your mother," said Tweed as he carried on walking. "Human rights crusader. Investigative reporter. Did you know she was the one who broke the Ramases case? What am I talking about? Of course you know. I—" Tweed became aware that he was talking to himself. He paused and turned to see Octavia still standing where he'd left her, pedestrians parting around her like a rock in the ocean. He hurried back.

"What's wrong?"

"Do you know how many times I asked to see this file?" she asked. "They would never even admit they *had* a file. Always said they couldn't talk about it. Weren't allowed to."

Tweed clapped his hands together. "There you go then. It's all yours. Consider it a gift. Or if you don't like gifts, a favor. Something you can repay me for later."

Octavia opened the folder and scanned the contents before she reluctantly closed the file, folded it lengthwise, and put it in her inside pocket.

"Those men," said Tweed thoughtfully. "In those files. The ones who were murdered over the past few months by Moriarty. They're connected to each other."

"How?"

"Every single one of them was some kind of computing engineer. Whether it was a machinist, a Babbage programmer, a Babbage builder, a punchcard programmer. They're not just linked by the fact that they were killed by Moriarty. They're all linked because they have something to do with computing, something to do with Babbage's analytical machines."

They resumed walking again, heading for where Tweed had parked his steam carriage. He had slipped out of the archives earlier that morning, fetching it from where he'd left it last night before his meeting with Octavia.

"Did they work for Babbage & Company?" asked Octavia after a while.

"No. They were retired."

"What, all of them?"

Tweed nodded. "All over the age of sixty."

"But *did* they work for Babbage & Company? Or did they have their own company?"

"Don't know. It didn't say in the reports."

Octavia nodded thoughtfully. Then she flashed a brilliant smile at Tweed. "I have a plan," she said.

oq

"So?" said Octavia. "Are you suitably impressed?"

They had just left the Companies Registrar offices, where Octavia had accessed public files about shareholders in businesses, using a Babbage machine to input the names of all their victims. Two minutes later she was given the name of a company that all fifteen of the victims had been part owners of.

"Moderately so," said Tweed.

Octavia stared at him.

"Fine. I am *very* impressed. Well done. Spiffing job. We now know all the victims were part owners of—" Tweed snatched the piece of paper from her hands—"United Analytics. What does that—?"

He frowned, scanning the page.

"What?" asked Octavia.

Tweed quickly pulled out the list of names he had made back at New Scotland Yard and compared it to the list of the owners of United Analytics.

There were two shareholders in the company who weren't in the police files.

Which meant they were still alive.

CHAPTER NINE

It was dusk when they arrived at the house of Henry Meriweather, the first of the two names from United Analytics that didn't appear in the police reports.

The early autumn evening was chill; wet, brown leaves flicked and gusted through the air, bringing with them the first hint of winter. Octavia shivered as she stared up at the double-story house. Obviously, the company had done well for its owners, because the house was in a leafy, well-kept street, with red-brick houses and immaculate, if small, gardens. Tesla power was available here. She could tell by the yellow-white glow shining from the windows. Gas lanterns had a singularly different look about them. In fact, the Tesla Tower itself could be seen from the street. It heaved up into the clouds, red and orange warning lights flickering on its bulbous crest to warn away passing airships.

It looked as if they were out of luck, though. Henry Meriweather's house was dark and silent, the only house on the street without some kind of light burning inside.

Tweed hurried along the short path and knocked firmly on the door. No answer. Octavia pushed the doorbell, hearing the long ring echoing inside the house.

Still nothing.

Tweed glanced warily around the street then took a long leather wallet from his inside pocket. He chose two pieces of thin metal, got down on his knees, and inserted them into the lock.

"What are you doing?" whispered Octavia, glancing quickly around to make sure no one was approaching.

Tweed paused, looking at her in surprise. "He could be lying dead in there. Or injured. We need to see if Moriarty's been here yet."

Tweed turned back to the lock, then stopped and frowned up at her again. "After all we've done since yesterday, *this* is what you're concerned about?"

Octavia pursed her lips. He had a point.

A few seconds later there was a slight clicking sound. Tweed put the lock picks away and pushed the door open, then straightened up and slipped inside. Octavia followed after.

She closed the door behind her and looked around. They stood on a small landing. In the dim light filtering through the window she could see that the floor was tiled with a mosaic pattern. There was a set of stairs to her left.

"I'll check upstairs," she whispered.

Tweed nodded and poked his head around the first door in the hallway. Octavia left him to it and hurried upstairs. Three rooms opened off the second floor landing. The first was what looked like a guest bedroom, with a single bed and a small table. The second room was an office, but it looked unused. An empty desk, empty bookshelves. Hmm. Octavia was beginning to wonder if anyone actually lived in this house.

The last door opened into the main bedroom. There was a large double bed, but it had been stripped of sheets and bedding. Octavia hurried over to the cupboard and pulled open the doors. Empty.

She closed them again and looked around in frustration. He wasn't here. Coincidence? Or had he found out what was happening to his old business partners and decided to take a long holiday somewhere far away?

She left the room and headed downstairs. Tweed was waiting in the corridor.

"Anything?" he asked.

Octavia shook her head. "He's not here. No clothes in the room, no sheets on the bed."

Tweed nodded. Then he smiled. "Still. Least we didn't find a decomposing corpse lying on the floor. So that's something, yes?"

"I . . . suppose?"

"Right. What's the last name on the list?"

Octavia didn't have to check it again. She'd memorized it. "Jonathan Ashdown. Ann Street."

Ann Street was not a residential road. It was an alley of offices that opened off from Wellington Place.

Octavia and Tweed paused at the entrance. Two benches had been placed beneath a small tree in a little quadrangle about halfway along the length of the alley. Gas lamps reflected off the damp cobbles. *It looks quite pleasant*, thought Octavia.

Night had fallen. Most businesses had closed up, and people were making their way home or, in the case of the pub right behind them, warming themselves in front of a welcoming fire. Octavia could hear the raucous laughter, could see the movement and cheer behind the windows.

She heaved a sigh and pulled her jacket tighter about her. "Shall we?" she asked.

"No," replied Tweed.

Octavia frowned at him. He stared intently into the alley. "What—?"

"Sshh."

"Don't tell me—"

She didn't get a chance to finish. Tweed's gloved hand flashed out and clapped across her mouth. Her eyes widened in outrage. She was about to tear his hand away and give him a piece of her mind when he turned to her and put a finger against his lips—much as she'd done back in the airship factory—then he slowly pointed into the alley.

Octavia's eyes swiveled to the side. At first she saw nothing. Then, at the far side of the alley, where it fed into Apsley Road, she saw a slight movement.

Someone was hiding in the shadows.

Octavia and Tweed moved closer against the wall. Had the figure spotted them?

"Do you think it's one of them?" she whispered.

"Not sure. I can go ask if you like."

"Nobody likes a smart aleck, Tweed," she snapped.

"Is that so?" said Tweed, distracted, still peering into the alley. "Is that why you have no friends? Can you smell that?"

Octavia frowned, then sniffed. She *could* smell something. Very faint, just a hint on the damp autumn breeze.

Smoke.

A moment later a door to one of the buildings in the alley flew open and banged against the wall. Two figures stepped outside, wreathed in a billowing cloud of black smoke.

It was two of Moriarty's gang, the ones with the long smoke masks that fell to their chests. They turned and hurried along the alley, heading toward the figure waiting in the shadows. As they approached, he stepped into the light.

It was Moriarty.

The three held a brief conversation, then Moriarty nodded and the three turned toward Apsley Road.

"We need to follow them," said Tweed urgently.

"What about Ashdown?"

But Tweed didn't answer. He was already running, heading toward the other end of the alley where Moriarty and his goons had vanished. Octavia hurried toward the building that was on fire. She coughed and tried to wave the smoke away.

"Hello?" she called.

Nothing. Octavia crouched down. There was no smoke at this level. That was good, wasn't it? It meant the fire hadn't taken hold of everything inside. She also couldn't feel much heat from where she was.

Octavia hesitated, glancing over her shoulder at Tweed. He was still peering around the corner of the alley. He must be trying to see what kind of vehicle Moriarty was using so they could search for it later on. He couldn't exactly be flying his airship through the streets, could he?

Octavia hesitated for a second, then took a deep breath and ran into the house at a low crouch. Her movement caused the smoke to swirl and eddy around her head, drawing it down from the ceiling into the clear band of air she moved through. Octavia swore and slowed her movements, trying to make sure she didn't disturb the thick, black smoke any more than she had to.

The air was already heavy in her lungs. She coughed and ducked her head even lower, trying to draw clean air into her body. She saw an open door up ahead and glanced inside. It was a storeroom filled with wooden filing cabinets and stacks of old furniture. She turned back to the corridor and paused, trying to see where the smoke was actually coming from, but she couldn't see. It was growing thicker, the band slowly dropping down to fill the corridor. It was clear she didn't have much time. She pushed open the next door. A sitting room. Nothing of interest.

There was only one more door, at the end of the passage. As Octavia drew closer she saw that this was where the smoke was coming from, streaming out from the gaps around the door. Octavia struggled to breathe. Her eyes were streaming, turning everything into a blur. She covered her mouth and put her hand to the door. Then she jerked it away with a cry of pain. The door was burning hot.

But she had to check. Ashdown might be in there. Might be injured. She used her foot to push down the door handle—

—and she was thrown bodily to the ground, landing on her back with a grunt of pain. Octavia heard a loud roar. She looked up in surprise and saw a long, billowing stream of flames roiling along the ceiling, followed by thick, cloying black smoke. Stunning heat wrapped around her face, drying her mouth and eyes, stealing away her breath. She winced, closing her eyes and looking away.

Something pulled at her. She cracked her eyes open and saw that it was Tweed, dragging her away from the room. She pushed herself onto her hands and knees, crawling along the passage. She glanced over her shoulder, but all she could see were flames roaring out from inside the room, crawling up the door frame. There was no way anyone could be alive in there.

The noise grew louder as they made their way to the front door, a frightening crackling sound that surrounded her on all sides. The ceiling was engulfed with fire, the angry flames crawling down the walls. Octavia was astounded at how fast it moved. Twenty seconds ago the passage was smoky but still breathable. Now it was an inferno.

Octavia couldn't see anything except smoke and fire. The heat pressed down on her from above, driving her to the carpeted floor. She ran her fingers frantically along the burning walls, knowing she just had to keep going straight ahead to get out. The smoke had draped across the whole hallway like a deadly curtain. She didn't know which way she was going.

Then she saw the smoke swirl as it was sucked outward. The door! She staggered into a crouch and lunged forward, bursting out of the house, sucking in great gasps of cool, refreshing air.

She felt hands under her arms. "Come on, Songbird," said Tweed hoarsely. "Time to breathe later. We have to get after them."

Octavia coughed out more smoke and straightened up. She wiped her streaming eyes, squinting back at the house. Flames were visible in the windows now. As she watched, one of them exploded outward, showering the alley with shards of glass. Flames roared out of the empty frame, reaching up into the sky.

"Come on," Tweed shouted.

She turned to see him hurrying back along the alley to where he'd parked the steamcoach when they arrived. She sprinted after him and climbed up into the seat just as he pumped the lever that sucked air into the boiler. A shrill whistle burst from behind them, and Tweed quickly yanked on a release valve. The carriage lurched forward, trundling out across the cobbles of Wellington Place.

"Did you see them?" she asked.

"'Course I did. They're in a horse-drawn hansom."

"Horse-drawn? Rather old fashioned of them."

Tweed steered the carriage around a corner. As he did so, Octavia saw a group of five automata running toward the alley. They were painted red and yellow, but the paint was old, dull and chipped, and covered in smoke stains. They were much larger than normal automata, about ten feet tall, with huge bulbous backs that contained a chemical used to douse fires. Their æther cages were hidden away, reinforced so as not to get damaged by the heat. They contained the souls of firemen who now served the city in death, their widows and families paid a monthly salary.

At least the fire won't spread to the other houses now, thought Octavia.

Tweed turned right at the end of Wellington Place, moving onto the busy traffic of Arbour Street. They spotted Moriarty straight away. There weren't many horse-driven carriages nowadays. They were used mostly by the Traditionalists, who refused to have anything to do with modern transport, or the extremely rich, who used horses in a pathetic attempt to be different or eccentric.

The thickening mist had slowed the traffic in the steam-driven lanes, a lucky thing because it would have looked odd if Tweed drove his steamcoach at the same pace as Moriarty's carriage.

The automata pulling carriages had lifted the plates covering their æther cages, allowing the white light of the trapped souls to illuminate the way forward through the dark and mist, the glow sending a cone of hazy light out in front of them. Moriarty's carriages had lanterns hung above the driver's seat, the bouncing of the wheels causing the lights to swing wildly.

They followed Moriarty onto Commercial Road, then onto Fleet Street and into the Strand. Octavia glanced out at Trafalgar Square as they passed, her attention drawn to the massive brass statue of Sir Charles Babbage that had been erected in the square twenty years ago. In one hand Sir Charles held a tiny gear between his finger and thumb, and with his other he was plucking a star from the sky. The plinth on which his statue rested was surrounded by eight different automaton designs, ranging from the very first prototype to the most modern version.

The statue was four times the height of Nelson's column, and had become the focus of hatred for those opposed to the rapid state of change in their society. Every couple of years the Traditionalists tried to destroy it, and every couple of months it was defaced with ever-increasingly imaginative insults.

Only last week there was a riot in the square, one of the worst London had experienced in a decade. It was rumored to have been started by the Traditionalists' new leader, someone vehemently opposed to Babbages and automata. The government was trying to crack down on the Traditionalists, saying they were spreading sedition and discontent. Octavia thought this was the wrong move. By marking them as dangerous, the government was actually giving the Traditionalists more power, instead of just dismissing them as crackpots who wanted to live in the past.

The traffic slowed as it moved through Charing Cross, then Moriarty's carriage turned into Whitehall. Octavia felt a glimmer of unease at this. She and Tweed shared a puzzled look. Why would Moriarty be heading into the political hub of the city? He would certainly draw attention to himself if anyone saw him in that ludicrous mask he wore. Designed to strike fear into the hearts of his victims, yes, but not exactly inconspicuous.

But the carriage went even deeper into Whitehall. The Thames was now on their left as they drove onto Parliament Street. The traffic thinned out drastically here, so Tweed had to slow down so they wouldn't be spotted.

They passed Downing Street, then turned left onto Bridge Street, where Tweed quickly braked and pulled over to the side of the road. The gothic buildings of the Houses of Parliament dominated the skyline to their right, the huge, brightly lit structure towering over the River Thames. The new, nearly completed Clock Tower could just be seen through the mist, a dim, shadowy outline towering above Big Ben, reaching high into the sky.

Below the lights of Westminster Bridge Octavia could just make out the orange lantern hanging from Moriarty's hansom swinging slowly to a standstill.

"They've stopped," said Octavia.

Tweed glanced at her. "Amazing powers of observation there. Pity you didn't use them earlier."

"What are you talking about?"

"You almost got yourself killed back there!"

Octavia blinked at him in surprise. She'd thought he was being a bit silent as they followed Moriarty, but she'd put that down to him concentrating on the chase. Was he *angry* at her?

"It wasn't something I intended, I assure you," she said.

"But you must have felt the heat on the door. Why would you do something so stupid?"

"What are you *talking* about? Of *course* the door was hot. The house was on fire. What else did you expect me to do? He might have been alive in there."

Oddly, Tweed looked disappointed. "Ah. So you *didn't* know."

"Know what?"

"Backdraft. Common occurrence. Heat in an enclosed space causes a buildup of pressure. When that pressure is released, it explodes outward."

"So, let me get this straight. You were angry at me for doing something you thought was stupid. And now you seem angry—or at least disappointed—that I didn't *know* what I was doing was stupid. Have I got that right?"

Tweed turned away and stared through the mist.

"You really are incredibly hard to understand, Sebastian Tweed."

"Look." Tweed inclined his head forward.

Octavia leaned forward next to him and could just make out a hunched figure walking from the direction of the Houses of Parliament, heading toward Moriarty's carriage. He used a walking stick to aid his movements.

Tweed watched this for a moment, then leaped from his seat and crawled through a small opening into the back of the carriage. Octavia turned to see what he was doing.

Tweed pulled up a cushion on one of the chairs in the messy space. He reached inside the base of the seat and pulled out something metallic. He wound it up and dropped it onto a workbench, then moved away to do something else. Octavia's eyes widened, because stretching and unfolding its legs on the workbench was a small silver and brass spider.

Octavia fell instantly in love with it. She climbed through the opening and into the cramped quarters, getting up close to the construct. It was beautifully designed. The thin, elegant legs were the work of a master craftsman. There was even faint decoration carved into the metal. The head of the spider was carved to resemble the creature it was based on, with a lens dominating the center of the head. As she watched, the lens closed, then opened. The spider scuttled toward her.

Octavia turned to find Tweed seated before some kind of machine, staring into a cloudy sepia viewing glass. She saw her own face displayed in the glass.

"It's magnificent," she breathed. What she wouldn't give for something like this. It would make her work so much easier. "It must have cost a fortune."

"Not really," said Tweed. "I made it."

Octavia fought unsuccessfully to keep the surprise from her face. She looked at the spider then back at Tweed. "You?"

"Yes, me."

"*You* made this?"

"Yes."

"*All* of it?"

"Yes. Why do you keep asking me the same question?"

"I just didn't see you as . . . being good with your hands, I suppose."

"I'm *very* good with my hands," said Tweed, offended.

"Sorry. How does it work?"

"Ah, well, the programming was mostly done by a friend of mine. Stepp Reckoner."

"Stepp . . . ?"

"Reckoner."

"Stepp Reckoner?"

"It's not her real name, 'Songbird.'"

"Well, *obviously*."

Tweed finished adjusting something on the machine. "Right. Ready to go."

He swung the back door of the carriage open. The spider scuttled off the workbench and hopped outside. Tweed pulled the door shut and moved back to the viewing glass. Octavia joined him, watching as the glass showed an image of wet cobbles moving rapidly beneath the spider's feet.

"Joking aside," she said reluctantly, "that thing really is a marvel. You should apply for work as a Babbage designer. Actually, scratch that. A *Lovelace* designer. That thing is definitely elegant enough. Who taught you?"

"Barnaby," said Tweed. "He taught me everything."

"Careful," said Octavia suddenly. "It's going to hit the old man."

Tweed turned a small dial on the machine in front of him. The spider stopped moving forward, but the old man carried on walking until he arrived at the carriage. Tweed gently nudged the dial and the spider scuttled forward, perching underneath the hansom as the man rapped on the door with his cane.

"Good evening, Lucien," said a crackly voice. Although it was crackly, Octavia could tell it was a strong voice. She couldn't imagine it coming from the old man. It had to be Moriarty.

"No it isn't. It's a foul evening."

"Please yourself. Do you have what we need?"

"Of course. His current favorite route takes him through St. James's Park every night."

"Good."

"He starts his walk about midnight. You have to do it tonight, so I have enough time to prepare for the state banquet. I hardly need to say this, but the assassination has to go *exactly* as planned. Any deviation means the Ministry will be suspected. I can't have that." The old man—Lucien—smacked his cane angrily on the ground, raising a small splash of muddy water that peppered the spider's lens, causing the image to blur into nothingness. "I despise leaving this so late, but the damned fool changes his route every week. Had to make sure he'd stick to it."

"Don't worry. Everything will go smoothly."

"Good. Farewell, then."

They still couldn't see anything on the viewing glass. Octavia leaned forward and stared out the front of the carriage and saw Lucien walk slowly back into the Houses of Parliament.

"Why is a politician meeting with Professor Moriarty to talk about assassination?" she asked. "That can't be good."

"Is the coach still there?" asked Tweed.

Octavia shifted her gaze. The hansom was moving forward now, heading across the bridge to the east side of the Thames. "He's moving! Quick, can't you get that spider onto the carriage? It can show us where he's going."

"I'm *trying*," said Tweed.

Octavia glanced at the screen and saw that it was still blurry from the muddy water. Tweed spun the dial, causing the unclear image to leap and judder. She realized he was trying to get the spider to leap onto the carriage without actually being able to see what he was doing.

Then the image froze, shook violently, and turned black, accompanied by a metallic crunching sound. Tweed cursed and pushed himself up, bumping his head in the process. He cursed again and rubbed his head.

"Damn thing got itself run over," he said.

He scrambled back through to the front of the carriage and pumped the lever to get a good head of steam going. But the lever moved too easily. Tweed swore for a third time and sighed.

"Throw some coal in the boiler, will you?"

Octavia stared at him. "You mean we can't follow them?"

"Not unless you want to get out and run, no."

Octavia glared across the bridge in frustration. She was actually considering it. They couldn't just let them get away like this! They had to keep Moriarty in sight. He was the only link to her mother. And to Tweed's father.

"Forget it," said Tweed, as if reading her mind. "You'll never be able to catch up."

"But we're just letting them get away! They're our only lead."

"Not quite," said Tweed. "We know they're going to be at St. James's Park at midnight tonight. We can find them there."

Octavia thought about this. "All that talk about assassination. Do you think they were talking about assassinating Meriweather? Perhaps they found out where he was hiding."

"I . . . don't think so," said Tweed. "The way they were speaking, talking about the banquet . . ." He stared out the window, a worried look on his face. "Octavia, the only banquet I know about, the one *everyone* is talking about, is the state banquet at Buckingham Palace for Nicholas II."

Octavia's eyes widened. "You think they're gong to assassinate the Russian tsar? But why?"

Tweed shrugged. "I have absolutely no idea. But if Nicholas Romanov is assassinated on British soil, I think it's fair to say there will be a lot of *very* angry Russians. The way things have been between our countries, who knows what will happen."

"War?"

"Possibly." Tweed sighed. "Come on, let's get going. I need to introduce you to some very close friends of mine."

CHAPTER TEN

T he carriage lurched to a stop outside a well-appointed, three-story house just off Regent Street. A cloud of steam wafted forward, surrounding the carriage and cutting off Tweed's view. But not before he saw the lights in the windows. He felt a surge of relief. They were back.

"Who lives here?" asked Octavia.

"Carter Flair and Jenny Turner."

"Carter Flair?" said Octavia dubiously.

"Not his real name," replied Tweed. "He's a thief and a con man. Carter Flair is just the name he uses between jobs."

"Ah. More of your father's friends?"

"Yes. And if it weren't for them, we wouldn't be in this mess."

"What do you mean? Can't we trust them?"

"Oh, yes. We can trust them. But the only reason I went to Harry Banks was because they weren't home."

He climbed out of the carriage and rapped sharply on the door. A minute later is was opened to reveal Carter Flair, peering at Tweed and leaning against the door frame. His short frame was wiry; he had lost a lot of weight since Tweed last saw him. His dark hair was just long enough to look untidy, or if styled correctly, dashingly unkempt. He looked Tweed up and down, then turned languidly to call over his shoulder, "Darling, there's a waif at the door." Carter leaned forward and squinted over Tweed's shoulder. "And he appears to have kidnapped a young lady. A *pretty* young lady."

At these words a woman appeared from one of the rooms opening off from the corridor. She had short red hair, untidy and spiky. Tweed grinned at her. Jenny had never been one to care what others thought, and her new look certainly reflected that. She wore men's clothes: tweed trousers, a large, baggy shirt, and a waistcoat three sizes too large.

"Darling!" she exclaimed.

"Yes?" said Carter.

"Not you. I'm talking to the *true* love of my life. Young Tweed over there." She glanced over Tweed's shoulder. "You'll have to fight me for him, girly."

Octavia raised her hands in the air. "You're welcome to him."

Jenny winked at Tweed. "Playing hard to get, is she? Don't worry. Your natural charm will win her over."

Tweed tried his best to ignore the snort of amusement from behind him.

"You two are in serious trouble," Tweed said.

Carter straightened up and looked at Jenny. "I knew your disreputable past would catch up with us some day. What's she done?"

"I came looking for you yesterday. You weren't here."

"Oh. We were at dinner," said Jenny, linking arms with Carter. "Then dancing, then robbing a few rooms at the Grand. It was very romantic, wasn't it, dear?" Jenny kissed Carter on the cheek.

"Her birthday," said Carter. "Sort of a tradition. Dinner, dancing, robbery. What did you want with us?"

"Barnaby's been kidnapped," said Tweed.

The look of playfulness on Carter and Jenny's faces dropped in an instant. Jenny pushed Carter back into the house, then ushered Tweed and Octavia inside.

"Come on. In. In," she said, waving her hands impatiently at the two of them. "Through there," she said, pointing to one of the rooms. "Go."

The admittedly small amount Tweed knew about relationships and how couples related to each other he had learned from Jenny and Carter. He'd known them as long as he could remember, and even from a truly early age he'd been aware of one thing: The two were madly in love, and would *always* be madly in love. They teased, they bickered, they insulted each other, but it was always lighthearted. It was how they showed each other they cared.

He'd once asked Barnaby about them and he said they were childhood friends who grew up on the same street. When Carter was eighteen he was caught trying to steal the money clip off a politician and was sent to Millbank Prison. When Jenny heard about it, she broke him out, but only after getting him to reveal his true feelings for her.

They got married three months later and had been together ever since.

Tweed always felt himself relax in their presence. The joking, the merciless jibes, the banter, it was all done from a place of love, a place of warmth, and that warmth filled their home. Tweed came away from his visits with them feeling energized, open to the world, ready to take on whatever life had to offer.

When Tweed finished telling them everything that had happened, Carter and Jenny exchanged glances.

"I'll kill that Harry Banks," said Jenny, standing up and pacing furiously up and down. She stabbed the air with an imaginary blade, yanking it up as if gutting someone. "Slit him from balls to throat. I always said he was a bad 'un. Didn't I?" She pointed her imaginary knife at Carter.

"You did. I can't quite remember *when*, but I'm sure you did. Positive."

"You know who they saw, don't you? Who this Lucien fellow is?" said Jenny to Carter.

"Lucien Mcallister. The head of the Ministry."

"Exactly. One of the—if not *the*—most powerful men in the Empire."

"But why would the Ministry be dealing with a criminal like Moriarty?" asked Tweed. "Aren't they a government department?"

Carter snorted. "The very fact that you think government departments wouldn't deal with criminals shows just how young you are, dear boy." He paused, seemingly trying to gather his thoughts. "The Ministry is the *shadow* the government casts. Understand? Governments can change, but the Ministry is constant. Who is it that greets the new P.M. as he walks through the door of Number Ten Downing Street? It's the head of the Ministry."

"The Ministry . . . deals in information," cut in Jenny. "They trade it, horde it. Guard it like treasure. People say they're the real power behind the Crown. The real power behind the *government*."

"Imagine a pyramid," said Carter, interrupting again. Jenny frowned at him. "The Ministry is at the top, yes? Then *way* at the bottom are the Crown and the government."

Tweed frowned. "Where are we?"

Jenny laughed. "We're in the mud below the pyramid. No, *beneath* the mud. In their eyes we're the germs and disease that fester in the stagnant water that makes the mud."

"It's said they started out as a department of spies for Queen Elizabeth I," said Carter. "And with every successive coronation they gained more and more power. There were rumors the Crown wanted to curtail their power, so the Ministry backed Cromwell in the Civil War."

"Any discoveries, anything that could possibly be used to aid the Empire, is taken to the Ministry," said Jenny. "The thing is, despite what Carter says, not *everything* they do is wrong. It was the Ministry that recruited Nikola Tesla. They saw his inventions and realized he could be a huge boon to us. I mean, it's because of him we have airships, that automata can now be shrunk down to the size of a mouse."

"Pff," scoffed Carter. "The Ministry is evil, and nothing you say will ever change my mind." Carter leaned forward. "The Ministry is *above* the law," he said earnestly, "and because of that they are to be feared. Their only remit is to ensure the security of the Empire. How they do that, who they have to kill to achieve that, it means nothing to them. Understand? They use Tesla's research to create weapons that can rip a man in two. No one dares to speak out against them. No one dares act against them."

"But they have Barnaby!"

Jenny sat down next to Carter. "That's what troubles me. Barnaby was always careful. Cautious. He's not stupid enough to do anything to draw the attention of the Ministry. So why do they want him?"

"You say he was definitely alive?" asked Carter.

Tweed nodded.

"Then there's still hope. Remember that. If the Ministry wanted your father dead, he'd be dead. They need him for something."

"Which means he'll probably be locked away somewhere," said Jenny.

"It's too much of a coincidence that it happened now," said Tweed. "Surely it must have something to do with this assassination they were talking about."

"That's what worries me. That your hunch is correct and they really do plan on killing the Tsar." Jenny stared thoughtfully at the ceiling. "I hate to say this, but I wonder if we wouldn't be better off contacting the police."

"There's no point," said Tweed. "They're burying anything to do with Moriarty."

"That makes more sense now," said Octavia. "We never understood why the police would do that. But Lucien must have given the order to suppress any information to do with the gang. If he's working with Moriarty he's not going to want the police investigating them."

Tweed nodded in agreement.

"What if Barnaby somehow found out about their plans?" said Carter.

"Then why not just kill him?" said Jenny.

Tweed waved his hand in the air. "There's no point in thinking about that. Not now. We don't have enough information. We deal with the facts. It seems the Ministry has Barnaby, and if he's still alive he'll be locked away somewhere. We have to find out where."

A thoughtful silence descended over the drawing room. Then Octavia straightened up.

"My mother," she said.

Tweed turned to her. "What?"

Octavia's face was alight with excitement. "Don't you see? This adds weight to my mother still being alive. She was investigating this gang. Maybe she found out about the connection with the Ministry. Maybe they have her in one of their prison cells as well!"

Jenny and Carter exchanged uneasy looks.

"Honey," said Jenny. "How long has your mother been missing?"

"A year."

"A year in a Ministry cell . . . that's enough to break the strongest of men."

Octavia drew herself up, clenching her fists. "My mother is *not* the strongest of men. My mother is the strongest of *women*. And if they didn't kill her she would make sure she stayed alive to get back to her family." She took a deep breath and let it out slowly. "Do you understand?"

Jenny nodded slowly. "I understand," she said softly.

"So the Ministry has Barnaby for some unknown purpose," said Tweed. "*And* Octavia's mother," he added, before she could say anything. "It seems Moriarty and his gang are doing their dirty work. Or at least they're doing *Lucien's* dirty work." Tweed stared thoughtfully at the ceiling. "Does anyone know where these Ministry prisons actually are? Can we get to them to find out if they *are* really being held there?"

"*No one* knows," said Carter. "Or at least, if they do they're not talking. The cells are inside the actual Ministry buildings. But no one knows where the Ministry *buildings* are. Secrets within secrets."

"But we'll ask around," said Jenny. "We'll call up favors, round up our contacts. Someone must know something."

Tweed nodded. "And see what you can find out about this Lucien as well. Barnaby always said to find as much as you can about your enemy. We need to know who he is. What he stands for."

Jenny clapped her hands together. "Ooh, look at Tweed getting all grown up and masterful. Isn't he sexy?"

Tweed flushed slightly. "Jenny . . ." he implored.

She grinned at him. "What? I'm just proud to see little Tweed all grown up. And *ever* so commanding."

Carter got to his feet. "Right. Obviously, time is of the essence. Darling, you take our West End contacts. I'll canvas our more dubious friends in the east of our fair city. What time is it now?"

Jenny took out a pocket watch from her waistcoat. "Nine."

"Good. Plenty of time. We'll meet back here at dawn." He leaned forward to giver her a kiss. Jenny grabbed him before he could pull away and turned the quick peck into a passionate embrace. Tweed flushed red and averted his eyes.

"Aw, look," he heard Jenny say. "He still looks away when we kiss. Isn't that sweet?" Tweed, staring out the window into the night, felt warm fingers on his face. He turned and was surprised to find Jenny's lips on his. She held the kiss for a brief second, then pulled back with a smile.

"Loosen up, darling. Don't *ever* take yourself too seriously."

She strode out of the room. Tweed watched her go with a bemused expression on his face. A second later he heard the slam of the front door.

"Don't even *try* to figure her out," said Carter, shrugging into his jacket. "*I've* never been able to. Make yourselves at home. There's food in the kitchen, whatever you need. See you later."

He left the room and the front door slammed for a second time.

"Interesting friends you have," said Octavia.

"Indeed," said Tweed, getting to his feet in an attempt to hide his embarrassment. "We should get some food. Prepare ourselves for tonight."

ᴗᴗ

An hour later, Tweed was seated on the window seat in the front room, staring into the night. The fog was much thicker now, grey-white tendrils that he could clearly see scudding past the yellow sodium glare of the street lamps. A horse-drawn trundled past, the wooden wheels spraying up streamers of muddy rainwater.

How did Octavia do it? Her mother had been missing for over a year, yet she still had faith she was alive. Barnaby had only been missing for two days and already Tweed was finding it difficult to stay positive.

Barnaby had always trained him to rely on logic, and logic told Tweed that if Moriarty hadn't killed Barnaby back at the house, then they needed him alive. But for Tweed, knowing this in his head was a thousand miles away from believing it in his heart.

And the doubt was getting to him, eating away at him. It shouldn't *be* there. His mind had always been in charge, but now he felt it was letting him down. It wasn't strong enough to control his emotions, his fears. And it *should* be. After all, the mind conquered all.

So why was it not conquering this?

"Are you all right?"

Tweed turned to find Octavia standing in the door to the front room. He shrugged, then nodded. "Yes. No. I'm . . . not sure." He turned back to the window. He hated this! It was weakness. Lack of control. His father was alive. He *knew* that. Why couldn't he *feel* it?

He saw Octavia's reflection in the window as she approached.

"You're allowed to feel scared," she said softly. "He's your father. It's understandable."

"You don't understand. I'm *not* allowed. I was raised to control my fears. To take emotion out of the equation. Emotion clouds judgment. It makes . . ." He trailed off, trying to formulate what he felt into words.

"Makes you human?" said Octavia.

"No," snapped Tweed. "It makes you *weak*. Emotions take control. They dominate your life. Making decisions based on emotions is wrong . . ."

Again, he trailed off.

"I think your *father* was wrong," said Octavia softly. "Emotions are what let you *enjoy* life. They're not . . . irritations to be brushed away. You can't look at the beauty of a sunset logically. You have to feel it. I mean, what goes through *your* head when you see something beautiful?"

Tweed thought about it. When was the last time he even noticed something beautiful? He was rather shocked to realize he didn't know. He couldn't remember. Or he simply spent so much time in his head that he didn't notice.

"Do you truly believe your mother is still alive?" he said, ignoring her question. "After all this time?"

"I do. I *have* to. It's what keeps me going."

"But *how*? How do you do it?"

"You can't break everything down into patterns and logic, Sebastian Tweed." He saw her reflection turn away, then pause. "Sometimes you just have to have faith and *feel* life. *Experience* it."

CHAPTER ELEVEN

An hour before midnight.

The fog was thick and cloying as they left the house. It drifted against Octavia's face, wafting before her eyes like lace curtains undulating in a breeze. It deadened the air, turning what was a chill night into something clammy and oppressive.

They climbed into Tweed's steamcoach. He pulled out into the street with a slow, lurching movement that only gradually picked up speed. Octavia watched him pump a lever, twist knobs, and smack pressure valves as he tried to coax some momentum out of the machine. She thought they'd be better served with a couple horses pulling them along, but she kept her thoughts to herself. Tweed seemed to have a fondness for the vehicle. He'd only be offended if she said anything.

He took them onto Regent Street, then turned right into Piccadilly, moving through the slow-moving traffic until they reached Saint James's Street. Octavia knew from past visits to the park that St. James's Palace was somewhere off to her right, but she couldn't catch a glimpse of it in the murky fog.

Tweed stopped his carriage alongside the fence to St. James's Park. They disembarked and moved through the gate that led directly onto the Mall, the long stretch of walking ground shaded over with elm and lime trees. Octavia had been here a few times in the past with her mother and father. The park was a favorite spot for picnics, and the massive lake that took up most of the grounds was used for skating every winter. Octavia could almost smell the roasting chestnuts and taste the drinking chocolate costermongers sold along the shore.

She wondered if she would ever feel as happy as she had then. So free of worries.

She sighed unhappily, then turned to Tweed. He hadn't said much since their conversation back at the house. Octavia wasn't sure why this was, so she had just let him be. Maybe he just needed to sort things out in his head.

"It must be about half an hour before midnight now," she said, looking left, then right. She couldn't see much of anything. There were lamps placed every twenty feet or so along the Mall, but the fog made it difficult to see anything. Octavia was rather pessimistic about tonight. They might not even be able to see what was going on, never mind warn whoever it was that they were in trouble. Moriarty might be no more than ten feet from their position and they'd never even know it.

"We should probably just take up position halfway along the lane," suggested Octavia. When no response was forthcoming, she turned to face Tweed. "What's going on with you?"

Tweed blinked at her. "Sorry? What?"

"You haven't said a thing all the way here. Where are you?"

"Um . . . Up here. Thinking." He tapped his head.

"Yes. Well, I think we can both agree that you spend rather too much time up there." Octavia tapped his forehead hard with her index finger. He jerked back, looking at her with an affronted expression on his face.

"Oh, don't look like that. I think I'm figuring you out, Tweed. You like to think of yourself as oh-so-rational, oh-so-clever. You like to think you've got everything figured out, that you can deal with anything so long as you just think about it long enough. But you can't. You're no different from the rest of us. Trying to figure life out as we go along. That's called *living*, Tweed. You do it out here—" Octavia gestured around her—"not up here." She tapped her head.

"Now, I would appreciate it if you would get your act together and ready yourself for what lies before us. Because I, for one, do not wish to be toasted to a crisp with one of those Tesla weapons. Yes?"

Tweed stared at her with wide eyes for a moment, then nodded. "Yes."

"Splendid," said Octavia. "Now, I suggest that tree over there." She pointed to a huge elm just to their right. The trunk was thick enough that they could hide behind it and keep an eye on the lane while still being close enough to the exit in case they needed to make a quick escape. "What do you think?"

"I think it's as good a tree as any," said Tweed, moving toward it.

Octavia watched him go until he was almost swallowed up by the fog, then hurried after him. She rounded the trunk to find him leaning back against the bark.

"You'd better not be sulking," she said to him.

He blinked at her in surprise. "I'm not sulking. I'm pondering."

Octavia let him ponder all he wanted while she peered out from behind the tree, keeping an eye on the just-visible lane that stretched the length of the park. She was surprised at how many people were out at this time of night. She saw an old couple out walking their dog. She saw four tramps ambling along in tatty clothing. Two of them drank from bottles and had a slight stagger to their walk. One of them was talking to himself, mumbling about the youth of today having no respect. The fourth was slightly better dressed than the others, so much so that he was approached by a woman wearing a low-cut top that directed eyes straight down to her cleavage.

"Lookin' for a good time, squire?" she asked the man.

He turned to her in surprise. Octavia could just make out the figures through the mist. He bowed low. "Madam, I am already having a good time, I assure you. The attentions of one such as your good self while no doubt increasing my enjoyment of the evening air will leave me feeling empty as my purses. In short, I have not the money."

The prostitute waved her hand at the man in irritation and walked off. The tramp chuckled and disappeared into the mist.

Octavia fished around in her jacket and pulled out her pocket watch, flicking it open. "Almost midnight." She closed the lid with a sharp click and looked around uneasily. "What exactly are we going to do to stop Moriarty?"

Tweed pulled something out of his coat pocket and held it up to her. It was a weapon similar in style to her own Tesla gun, but rather more basic in design.

"Where did you get that?" she asked in surprise.

"Carter's house. Hopefully I won't have to use it, though."

They waited some more. Tweed shifted impatiently from foot to foot, rustling the grass. Octavia tried to ignore the sound, instead focusing outward, listening for anything that sounded out of the ordinary.

Like a scream.

The sound pierced the night, coming from off to their right. Octavia and Tweed exchanged glances, then set off at a run trough the trees, ducking beneath low branches that loomed suddenly out of the fog.

The scream echoed through the night again, much closer now, then the sharp crack of a gunshot cut it off.

Octavia slowed slightly, pulling her own Tesla gun out of her pocket. They moved more cautiously, trying to stay off the fallen leaves.

Octavia peered through the fog to her left and saw a familiar-looking black carriage. Moriarty. She stopped behind a tree and peered out. Tweed joined her. A woman lay on the ground—the woman Octavia had seen earlier on talking to the tramp. Her chest was covered in blood, her sightless eyes staring upward.

Octavia heard a scuffling sound from the other side of the carriage, then two figures staggered into view. One was Moriarty. He still had the mask covering his face. The second figure was tall and distinguished, dressed in a smart suit with a black overcoat and scarf.

The tall man had Moriarty's hand in a tight grip, trying to keep the gun Moriarty held away from his face. The two men staggered back and forth, each trying to wrest the weapon away from the other.

Then Moriarty shoved forward. The man slipped, his back leg giving way. Moriarty used his weight to drive the man to the ground. As he did so, they both swung around so that Octavia and Tweed could get a close look at the victim.

Tweed gasped in surprise. Octavia felt her mouth drop open in shock.

The man Moriarty was attacking was none other than Sir Arthur Balfour, the Prime Minister of Great Britain!

Balfour flailed with his hands as his attacker leaned over him, and he grabbed hold of Moriarty's mask. He dug his fingers in, obviously trying to go for the eyes. Moriarty jerked his head away, and the mask was pulled from his head.

His back was to them, so Octavia couldn't see his features, but Balfour could. He stared up into his attacker's face, his eyes widening in shock. That moment of distraction was all Moriarty needed. He yanked his gun hand free and swung the weapon hard against the Prime Minister's temple. Balfour's head jerked hard into the ground and his body went limp.

Moriarty let go of his victim and stood up. He knocked on the carriage door, and a second later two of his gang came around the side and grabbed the Prime Minister's unconscious body, lifting it into the carriage. Moriarty stepped into the center of the path, looking around to make sure no one had witnessed what had just happened.

Octavia was able to get a close look at his lean face. She noticed the eyes first, sharp and piercing, taking everything in. Then the hawklike nose and square chin, the dark hair swept back from his wide forehead.

Octavia blinked, not quite believing what she was seeing. She turned to Tweed, and by the shocked expression on his face, he was thinking the exact same thing she was.

The man standing before them wasn't Professor Moriarty at all.

It was Sherlock Holmes.

Octavia felt Tweed grip her arm, pulling her back into the trees. Octavia hesitated, doubting her own eyes even though she was actually standing there. Surely it couldn't be him. It simply couldn't. Sherlock Holmes had been dead for over four years.

Then Holmes turned away, watching the two men throw the body unceremoniously into the carriage. As he did so, Octavia saw that the right side of his face was hideously scarred, as if it had been burned in a fire.

Tweed's fingers dug painfully into her arm. Octavia grimaced, trying to pull away, but he wouldn't let go. She finally tore her eyes away and turned around.

Only to find the fog behind her glowing with a pale blue light.

The light grew stronger and a second later the Gibbering Man stood before them, twitching and jerking. Electricity zipped around the strange top hat. The fog hissed as it touched the blue light. Octavia smelled burning tin. The Gibbering Man reached up and touched something on his hat, grinning at them while he did so, and the lightning shot around even faster, leaping and sparking when it hit the copper wire at the front.

He held up the metal tube and slowly licked it. Then he pointed it at them.

Tweed slowly raised his hands in the air. The Gibbering Man grinned even wider, his lips twitching every time the electricity jumped into the air.

Octavia tensed, raising her own hands. But when they were halfway up, she suddenly dropped them and pulled the trigger on her Tesla gun. A bolt of blue lightning zipped through the mist and hit the man's top hat. It flared brightly, a blossom of white light. The electricity coruscating around the metal frame spat and jumped erratically, the lightning searching for a place to ground itself. It crawled rapidly over the rim of the hat, writhing across the Gibbering Man's face.

He screamed in pain. The electricity arced into his mouth and danced across his eyes until they glowed blue, two unearthly orbs shining in the night.

He turned and ran. But he didn't get far before the electricity started crawling over the strange contraption on his back. There was a hiss, a strange burping sound, and a second later the Gibbering Man exploded.

Bits and pieces of him flew through the air, slapping wetly against the trees. His top hat whirred through the fog, spinning straight at Octavia. She jerked away, the lethal projectile missing her by inches. As she did so, she saw Sherlock Holmes striding toward them, peering into the fog.

Octavia shoved Tweed and they both staggered into the fog as a shot rang out behind them. It hit the tree right next to her. Fragments of bark spun painfully into her cheeks.

Octavia grabbed hold of Tweed's hand as they sprinted through the trees. They had to stay together. If they became separated now it would be the death of them. She heard Sherlock Holmes and his men running after them, their heavy footfalls echoing across the ground. Trees loomed out of the fog, appearing only an instant before they had to duck to avoid the branches. Whereabouts were they? Close to the gate? She had no idea. The fog was so thick they could be running in totally the opposite direction.

A moment later, Tweed yanked her to a stop and pulled her behind a huge tree. His face loomed close to hers and he put a finger to his lips.

Quiet.

The running footsteps came closer. Octavia could just see around the trunk, and she saw Holmes dart past, his face a twisted scowl of anger. She swallowed nervously as he vanished into the fog.

Seconds later the other two with the smoke masks lumbered past. Then silence.

They waited, then Tweed pried his hand loose from hers. She released it, embarrassed. She hadn't realized she was still holding it.

He pointed behind them then moved quietly away. Octavia followed. They crossed the Mall, then slipped quickly through the gates and into Tweed's steamcoach.

They exchanged glances. Octavia could see the same feelings reflected on Tweed's face that she was experiencing herself.

Confusion, puzzlement . . .

Fear.

CHAPTER TWELVE

T weed paced back and forth in one of the rooms at Carter and Jenny's house, absently chewing his fingernails. The floorboards creaked rhythmically as he moved.

One, two, three, *creak*, four. Pause. Turn. One, *creak*, two, three, four.

The single candle he'd lit cast a dim glow throughout the room, his hulking shadow growing and shrinking every time he paced.

He felt confusion. A great deal of confusion. And he *hated* that. It meant he didn't understand something. That things were out of his control. *Another* thing he hated. Not being in control meant that the unexpected could happen. And the unexpected was . . . well, it was unexpected, wasn't it? That was the point.

Time to put all that teaching Barnaby gave him into action.

It was Holmes who had been going around London murdering engineers. *Not* Professor Moriarty.

Why?

That was the big question, wasn't it? Actually, no. The big question was why had he feigned his own death? But that wasn't something Tweed could possibly deal with just then, so he pushed it aside.

So. Why was Holmes doing this? That was the question that needed to be answered. Were the engineers he'd murdered criminals? Traitors? Was it possible that Sherlock Holmes was working undercover for the Crown? That could explain his association with Lucien and the Ministry.

But no. What was he thinking? He and Octavia had just witnessed Sherlock Holmes attacking and kidnapping the Prime Minister of Great Britain. That wasn't the work of a good person. That was the work of a villain. He was involved with the Ministry, yes. But they weren't working on the side of law and order.

So: Sherlock Holmes had been murdering the retired engineers, seemingly on the orders of Lucien, the head of the Ministry.

Why? Was it related to something the engineers were working on? Was there any way to find that out? That was something to follow up on tomorrow. There might be a clue there.

Tweed stopped pacing and stared at the wall.

Something was missing. Well, a *lot* was missing. Obviously. But Tweed couldn't fathom the connection between Sherlock Holmes, the Ministry, his own father, the murdered engineers, and the kidnapped Prime Minister.

Tweed realized something else.

They would have to go to the police with this. As soon as word got out tomorrow, the country would be in chaos. People would want to know what was going on.

They had to report it. It was their duty. But they had to do it without being recognized by anyone who might have seen them at the Yard. Best thing would be to write out what they had witnessed and drop it on someone's desk. At least then New Scotland Yard would know. Whether they believed it or not was a different matter entirely.

Tweed yawned. It had to be three in the morning now. He had dropped Octavia off at her home before coming here, but she'd said she was coming back at the crack of dawn. So he should probably get his head down for a few hours. He was no good to anyone with his brain all muzzy from lack of sleep.

He flopped down onto the bed, the springs squeaking loudly in protest, and closed his eyes.

He was asleep in an instant.

ꙮ

The next morning, Tweed was seated in the front room when he heard a knock at the door. He finished writing the last sentence describing what they had seen the previous night, then put the pen down and rose from the desk.

It was Octavia. Tweed blinked at her as he opened the door. She wore her long black hair down. It framed her pale face and neck in a manner he found . . . distracting.

"Look at this!" she said, thrusting something into his face.

Tweed stepped back so he could focus on the object she was holding. It was a newspaper. *The Times.*

Tweed blinked and searched the headlines, expecting to find reports of the kidnapping of the P.M.

Except it wasn't there.

The front page story was about the Tsar of Russia and the talks that were taking place between their two countries. There was another mention of the state banquet to be held at Buckingham Palace in a few days. There was even a grainy photograph of the Tsar grinning at the camera.

Tweed snatched the paper from Octavia and flapped it out. He scanned the rest of the front page. Nothing.

"Is this today's paper?"

"Of course it is."

Tweed scanned the page again. "There's no mention of the P.M. in here at all."

Octavia stepped inside and closed the door. "Oh, there is," she said over her shoulder. "Page four."

Tweed opened the paper, and there it was: an article about the Prime Minister touring the building site of the new Clock Tower before its completion next month. He was to be there at eleven today.

Tweed had one last look over the paper. Just to make sure they hadn't missed anything. "This doesn't make any sense," he finally said. "We weren't mistaken, were we? It was definitely the P.M.?"

"Definitely," said Octavia. "I've seen enough pictures of him during my time at the paper."

Tweed dropped the paper on the side table. "I suppose we should pay a visit to the new Clock Tower then."

They arrived just before eleven. The unfinished tower thrust up into the sky, more than double the height and three times the thickness of the now puny-looking clock lurking in its shadow.

"Poor old Ben," mused Octavia, as they moved along the street, passing reporters and curious onlookers. "It's only a clock. It's not as if it's obsolete."

"Doesn't have to be obsolete. Bigger and better. That's the Empire's motto," said Tweed.

"Bigger, certainly," agreed Octavia. "Better? Not so sure."

Tweed glanced at her in surprise. "Are you a Traditionalist?"

"Not at all. But I understand them. I don't see the point of technology for technology's sake. If the clock's working, why change it? And if a human can do a job just as well, why build a computing device to do it?"

"To see if they can?"

"Exactly. And that's the problem. I mean, what was wrong with the old clock?"

Tweed looked up. Each of the new clock faces was square, over fifty feet along each side. They were made from glass so that you could see the inner workings of the mechanism, could see the brass cogs and gears as they turned and diced up segments of time. It was said there would be a permanent staff of specially constructed automata whose job it would be to make sure the Clock Tower stayed clean and functioning.

"Sorry, but I kind of like it," he said. Then he frowned. "Why am I apologizing? I *like* the bloody thing. I think it's going to be magnificent."

"That's because you have no taste," said Octavia. "Or style. It's not your fault. It's what comes from being raised in an all-male household."

"I resent that," snapped Tweed. "I have lots of taste. And I'm *incredibly* stylish. This coat is a collector's piece, you know."

"Yes," said Octavia, "you can tell. It belongs in a museum."

Tweed straightened up and pulled his jacket tight across his chest. "You, madam, are a . . . a *buffoon!*"

That didn't have quite the effect Tweed wanted. Octavia burst out laughing. "A buffoon, you say?"

Tweed turned haughtily away. "That's right."

Octavia grabbed him by the shoulder. "Wait, don't walk off. What about a scallywag? Am I a scallywag as well?"

Tweed pursed his lips. "Right now? Yes. You are."

Octavia laughed so hard that she snorted. But that didn't stop her. She hung onto Tweed's shoulder, head hanging down as her back heaved and trembled with laughter. She suddenly looked up.

"What about . . . What about a dollymop?"

Tweed frowned. "I wouldn't go *that* far."

She sniggered. "A strumpet?"

Tweed sighed. "No."

"A flap dragon?"

"N—What does that even *mean?* You just made that up!"

"I did not!"

"You did! There's no such thing as a flap dragon." Tweed shook her off his shoulder and headed toward the spot where the journalists had started to congregate.

"What about a flax wench?" he heard Octavia call. "Do you think me a flax wench?"

Tweed didn't answer. He was reasonably sure that wasn't a real word either.

The journalists were putting away their flasks filled with coffee and tea, straightening up with their notebooks out and their pencils sharpened. As Tweed approached he noticed a tall, brass automaton standing dead center in the group.

"Have you finished now?" he asked Octavia when she joined him.

She wiped the tears from her eyes. "Yes. I have. And thank you. I haven't laughed that hard in . . . well, for a long time."

"Then it's my pleasure. Now what's that for?" he asked.

She glanced at the construct, her lip curling in disdain. "A perfect example of what I'm talking about. That's the *Financial Times* showing off. It'll record the words of whoever speaks and then go back to the offices where a secretary will transcribe them for the paper. People are saying the editor has asked Babbage if he can create a program that will enable it to pick out the important bits and write them down itself. I mean, what's the point? All they're doing is putting a journalist out of a job. The thing must have cost more than ten years' salary of the man he replaced."

Tweed and Octavia squeezed their way through the crowd, ignoring the grumblings and complaints. Beyond the cordon was the building site. Rubble, bricks, and metal girders had been shoved into slightly neater piles to accommodate the P.M.'s visit. Scaffolding crisscrossed all the way up the new tower. Tweed squinted up against the light drizzle that had started to fall and could just make out the top of the structure. It was difficult to see the clock face from down here, but that was only because he was so close to the tower. From any other point in London, the view of the new clock would be magnificent.

The journalists all straightened to attention. Tweed glanced forward and saw movement from the blackness beyond the huge arched doorway leading into the tower. He could see figures moving, walking into the light.

The Prime Minister came first.

Tweed frowned, staring hard at the man. He had to be an impostor, surely? It was the only solution.

And yet . . .

And yet, as the man approached, it was obvious to Tweed that it wasn't an impostor. It really was Arthur Balfour. His features, his hair, his mustache, his clothes. It was him.

So what had happened? Had he escaped? But then why was there no mention of the kidnapping in the papers?

The Prime Minister approached a small dais that had been set up for his use. He stepped up onto it, smiled, and nodded at the journalists.

Tweed stared at him. From this close to the man, Tweed noticed certain things. Things that didn't add up. The Prime Minister's eyes seemed to glaze in and out of focus. Every now and then the man seemed to fall under a momentary cloud of confusion, as though he didn't know where he was. He would blink, look around, then stiffen and pull himself together. He also moved awkwardly, favoring one of his legs, as though he'd suffered a leg wound recently that hadn't yet healed.

Concussion? From the blow to the head?

The P.M. was surrounded by a gaggle of followers. Some of them looked at him with respect: those who worked on the clock. Others checked diaries and timepieces to make sure he was running on schedule: those who worked for him.

He cleared his throat and straightened up.

"This is a new world we are living in. We all know that. We are moving forward, heading toward great things. Who knows what the next ten years will bring? The next twenty? No one can predict such things. All I know is that we live in exciting times. And the Traditionalists—those who stand against progress—have no place in these times. You cannot live in a constantly evolving city like London and eschew progress while enjoying the benefits of Babbage and Lovelace's technology. Doing so makes you a hypocrite."

The P.M. surveyed them all with a serious look, then he broke into a proud smile.

"I have been very impressed with what I've seen here today," he said. "The design and construction of the new Clock Tower, next to the sadly outdated and now sadly misnamed Big Ben, shows the world just how far the British Empire has progressed in such a short space of time. Both towers stand as symbols, one of the old way of life, and the other of the future."

The P.M. smiled and shook hands with someone who looked like an architect. Then he shook hands with the people in charge of the actual construction of the tower. Reporters shouted questions at him, but he merely held up his hands in a placating gesture.

"Forgive me. I must go. I am already running late for my talks with the Tsar of Russia. And before you ask, the talks are indeed proceeding well. I foresee a future of mutual prosperity between our two countries." He smiled, then moved away with his advisors, heading toward the Palace of Westminster.

The reporters started to disperse, drifting into small groups as they chatted about what Balfour had said.

Tweed looked at Octavia. "What do you think?"

Octavia shrugged. "You tell me."

CHAPTER THIRTEEN

There was a note waiting for them when they got back to Carter and Jenny's house. Tweed glanced it over then handed it to Octavia.

Darlings,

Have found someone who is willing to talk about Lucien. It wasn't easy, I can tell you that for nothing. You owe me, darling boy. You owe me big. Now, just prepare yourself. The man is a wee bit on the rough side. He claims to have once worked for the Ministry, but managed to escape. He's since gone "underground" as he puts it, attempting to stay out of sight The only reason he eventually agreed to speak to you was because we said you were going to kill Lucien. So just go along with it, yes? Carter and I will see you back here later.

Loves and smooches,

Jenny

P.S. I suppose I really should tell you where to meet him, yes? That probably would be helpful. Trafalgar Square. Beneath Babbage's statue. Said he wanted somewhere public. Two o'clock. Don't be late. His name is Horatio.

Octavia read it over again. "She's . . . unique, isn't she?"

A small smile tugged up one side of Tweed's mouth. "One of a kind," he agreed. He glanced at the clock sitting on the mantelpiece. "One thirty. You ready to go or do you need to be somewhere else?"

Octavia handed the note back to him. "*Please*," she said. "Do you honestly think you're going to get rid of me now? Besides, my father spends all his time at work. If I went missing it would take him a day or two to notice."

Tweed's small smile came back again, ever so briefly. In fact, it was so brief Octavia wondered if she'd imagined it.

He shrugged. "Oh well. It was worth a try."

ॐ

The weather was turning foul by the time they reached Trafalgar Square. The temperature had dropped and Octavia's breath clouded in the grey afternoon air. She shivered, pulling her tweed jacket closer about her frame.

They soon arrived at the statue of Charles Babbage. Its base was a solid block of stone, forty yards on each side. Octavia always thought it odd that people worshipped him so much. Yes, he was an inventor, but the way people spoke of him, you'd think he was royalty or something. Everyone seemed to have forgotten the horrible things he'd done, like getting the Babbage Act passed, a law that banned all street musicians. He couldn't stand them, so he just used his influence to stop them.

Certainly Ada Lovelace saw him for what he was. She left his company over twenty years ago to start up her own business. And even though most people still used Babbages, it was her Ada computing devices that were fast becoming the new thing.

There was a bearded, tired-looking man slouched against the base of the statue. She stopped a few feet away from him, unsure if he was even their contact.

"Are you . . . Horatio?" she hesitantly asked. Tweed caught up with her as the man lifted his head and stared at them suspiciously.

"Never heard of him," he said.

"Jenny sent us," said Tweed. "I'm Sebastian Tweed. This is Octavia." The man narrowed his eyes. He glanced over their shoulders, then checked around the square. Only when he was satisfied no one was watching did he struggle to his feet.

"You're the ones who want to kill Lucien."

"Well . . ." began Octavia.

"That's us," interrupted Tweed. "Bastard kidnapped my father. I want him back. If I have to kill Lucien to do that I will."

Horatio nodded his head thoughtfully. "Right," he said. "The good news is, if your father wasn't killed outright, they want him for something. The Ministry doesn't do anything without a reason. So if he was still alive when he was taken, chances are he's still alive now."

Octavia glanced sideways at Tweed and saw relief flood his face.

"'Course, his body could have been dumped somewhere and no one's found it yet. 'The Thames is a deep river,' as they say."

"What can you tell us?" asked Octavia.

Horatio's eyes flicked to Octavia. He looked her slowly up and down. "Follower of Lovelace are you?" he said, taking in her clothes.

"Admirer, not follower," she said. "There's a difference."

"Is there? One leads to the other, in my opinion. Anyway," he said abruptly, "you want information, yes? Well, the first thing you have to do is forget what you think you know about the government, about the Ministry, about the *Crown*. Because the Ministry is all these things. They are the puppet masters. Their job is to make sure the British Empire does not fall, and they do not care how many are killed to see this goal through."

Horatio paused to look around Trafalgar Square once again, then he jerked his head, indicating for them to follow him as he turned and shuffled away from Babbage's statue.

"What did you do for the Ministry?" asked Octavia, hurrying to catch up.

"I worked down there." Horatio stamped his foot on the ground. "I was a Mesmer." He squinted at them. "Know what that is?"

"Sort of. We've heard stories. I mean, everyone has."

Horatio waved his hand in the air. "Probably all wrong. The Ministry likes to put false information out there. Keeps people confused." Horatio looked thoughtfully at them. "I'm going to tell you stuff now that could get you killed. It's secret, understand? Once you know, you're going to be in danger. From the Ministry. From Lucien."

"We're prepared to take the risk," said Tweed.

Horatio nodded. "Fine. About a hundred years ago, the Ministry started looking into spiritualism and mesmerism. The head of the Ministry back then was convinced it was real, that they could harness the powers of the occult. Over the course of the years, the Ministry sought out those with the gift and inducted them into their ranks. These agents were called Mesmers."

"What did they do?" asked Octavia.

"They spoke to the dead," said Horatio simply. "They cast aside the veil to communicate with the deceased."

Octavia thought about this. She knew constructs were powered by human souls, yes, but she never saw the soul in the sense of a complete person. She'd always just thought of the souls as a power source, a disembodied energy like . . . like the sun.

"Problem was, the dead are actually incredibly boring. Very confused. Like an elderly relative you've sent to the workhouse. They don't even really know they're dead. Just going on about Mavis from down the street not returning the sugar bowl, or cousin Graham marrying that trollop from Manchester." Horatio paused and turned to look at them both. "Quite a disappointment, I must say."

Horatio paused at the curb, his hand held out to flag down an automaton-pulled hansom. It stopped next to the curb and Horatio whispered to the construct, then nodded at Tweed as he climbed in. "Take care of that, will you, pal?"

Tweed paid the fare and climbed in, sitting next to Octavia. They both stared expectantly at Horatio as the cab pulled into the traffic. In such closed confines, Octavia couldn't help noticing Horatio's smell. A mixture of sweat, tobacco, and vinegar.

"So, the Ministry had put all this money into researching spiritualism, the power of the mind, the occult, mesmerism, all that stuff. See, they wanted psychic spies, agents who could use their minds to assassinate an enemy from the other side of the world. Didn't work, though. Least, not while I was there. They're probably still researching it. Hundreds of thousands of pounds, decades of work. And what do they find when they make their first significant breakthrough? When they can finally talk to the dead? Well, nothing much really. They couldn't tell us anything we didn't already know. No glimpses into heaven or hell. No sightseeing in the afterlife. Nothing."

"What did they do?"

"What do you think they did? Experimented. Kept going. The Ministry had the best engineers in the Empire. The best psychics, the best occultists. Some of them were off chasing ghosts, others trying to read the minds of foreign kings, but the Mesmers, they started to study the human soul. They wanted to see if they could measure it with science. If they could quantify what makes us human.

"That's stupid," said Octavia.

"Is it? You may say so. Others certainly did. But that didn't stop them. They tinkered, and fiddled with . . . well, I won't say 'volunteers,' but let's just say the prison population dropped quite substantially around this time."

Horatio blinked and gazed out the window, watching the London streets drift past. He sighed.

"Eventually, they managed to take an actual soul out of a body. They had no plan. They looked on themselves as pioneers. Knowledge outweighed ethics."

"How did they do it?" asked Tweed.

"With the help of something called the God Machine, a contraption the Mesmers built with the help of Ministry engineers. How it worked was, a Mesmer strapped himself and a 'volunteer' into the God Machine. The Mesmer's mind and body became one with the device, and over the course of twelve hours or so he extracted the soul of the volunteer and stored it in an æther cage—similar to what you find on automata."

"Did the subjects die?"

"No, they didn't. Which in itself is interesting, don't you think? They were alive, but empty shells. No mental activity, no thought. Just basic bodily functions. The Mesmer could then reverse the process, placing the soul back in the body, and the subject could walk away from it all, no harm done. The only drawback was that a Mesmer had to imprint himself onto his subject. It was like a permanent bonding. Once a Mesmer had connected with an individual, that bond was final. No other Mesmer would be able to work with that soul. We never figured out why that was."

"We?" said Tweed sharply.

Horatio paused, chewing the inside of his lip. Tweed got up from his chair and leaned over the suddenly nervous man, his hands resting on the cab wall on either side of Horatio's head.

"*You* did these things?" Tweed said.

"No! I *was* a Mesmer, but I didn't do any of that. God's truth! That was all before our time. Anyway, I left, remember? When I saw the kinds of things Lucien wanted us to do, I ran as fast as I could. There was no way I was going to be a part of it."

Octavia gently laid a hand on Tweed's arm. He clenched his jaw, staring intently at Horatio. Octavia tightened her grip slightly. Tweed breathed in, then pushed himself back and sat down.

"There's worse to come, so save your outrage till later," Horatio went on. "Taking souls from bodies was just the beginning. Once they could do that, they got more inventive. Taking souls out of *two* bodies, and trying to swap them over. That didn't work, though. The bodies rejected the foreign souls as if they were some kind of virus. But—and here's where they got even *more* imaginative—if the soul of one person was utterly destroyed, then a foreign soul *could* be inserted into this now-empty host. So for one of these soul transplants to work, the original soul of the receiving body had to be destroyed first. This job fell to a group of maligned Mesmers, those who weren't very good at anything else. They became known as Reapers."

"That is just . . . ungodly," whispered Octavia.

"Yes. I agree. But without the Mesmers doing what they did, we wouldn't have such powerful automata wandering around today. When they were first built, there was no way they were practical. They needed huge computing devices to control them. To make a single automaton work, a Babbage the size of a sitting room was needed. And the construct had to be connected to the machine by huge wires. So what happens? One of the Mesmers working with the souls wonders what would happen if the soul of a newly dead person was put into the casing of an automaton.

"You know how that went. The souls took over the automata. It was able to move them around, to obey simple instructions. Yes, they had the intelligence of a three year old, but so what? They were free of the wires now, free of the Babbages. I'm not defending the Ministry, but all that came about because of their experiments. Hell, they're the ones who actually funded Babbage in the first place, so you can say the Ministry is responsible for just about everything in our society—good and bad."

"But those automata are already becoming obsolete," said Octavia. "The ones powered by Tesla are the new wave."

Horatio waved his hand in the air. "Not obsolete. *Affordable.* The soul-driven automata will never go away. They do what they do, and they do it well." Horatio smacked his hand against the cab. "Look at us now! Being ferried around by one of them. But you mentioned Nikola Tesla—again, something the Ministry is responsible for. He was headhunted by Lucien. Brought over to Britain. And it's because of him we have this mysterious wireless transmission of energy that nobody seems to understand. So again, all that progress, and all of it came from these Mesmers playing around with human souls. Not ethical, I'll grant you, but do you, do *any* of us, have the right to say it was a hundred percent wrong? How many lives have been improved? How many lives *saved*, because of what the Ministry did?"

"You sound like you're on their side," said Tweed.

"I'm not. I had to get out. I knew that if I stayed there much longer I'd come to think that the greater good was the most important thing. More important than *people*. I'd seen it happen, and I didn't want to be like . . ."

Horatio trailed off, his eyes cast downward. Finally, he looked up at them. "The Ministry is cloaked in shades of grey. There is no black and white. Everything can be explained. Everything can be justified if you try hard enough. I just couldn't live like that."

The cab trundled to a stop. Horatio opened the door and climbed out. Tweed followed next, then Octavia stepped out onto the ground.

She looked around. They were in a rundown area, a small side street with three-story buildings hemming them in on either side. To her left, about thirty feet away, the side street fed into a busier road. People walked past, as did automata, carriages, and cabs.

But in this side street they were alone.

She frowned at the trash: old newspapers, sodden and sticking to the curb; pieces of old fruit crates, smashed to pieces by bored street children; all now turning black with rot.

"Why are we here?" she asked, turning her attention to Horatio.

The man stood before a wall. "Because I want to show you something. Follow me."

Horatio took a step to the side—

—and simply vanished. At least, that's what it looked like. Octavia stepped forward and saw that what she'd at first thought was the wall of a building was actually something of an illusion. There were in fact *two* walls, one slightly behind the other. But the brickwork, and even the painted insults daubed *on* the brickwork, flowed across them both in such a way that it looked like a single wall. Anyone looking in or even walking up the side street wouldn't be able to see the gap. It was only when you turned around and looked back from the bricked-up end of the alley that it was visible.

She and Tweed entered the dark opening and found themselves in a dingy corridor. Horatio waited for them at the top of a flight of stairs.

"Come on," he said. "We have to be quick."

They followed him down the steps. There was a dim light coming from somewhere, but when Octavia looked around she couldn't find its source.

They walked for about five minutes, all the while descending beneath the streets of London. Finally, the stairs leveled out and they found themselves on a tiled platform. The dim light had a slight green tinge to it that tinted the white tiles a sickly bilious color. The light throbbed, stronger and weaker, stronger and weaker—almost as if it were breathing.

Octavia walked forward to the edge and looked down onto a set of train tracks.

"What station is this?" she asked in surprise.

"A secret one," said Horatio. "It was abandoned about thirty years ago. Never used. At least," he corrected himself, "never used by the public."

The platform was distinctly eerie. It wasn't just the light. Every station Octavia had ever been to was filled with people—angry people, happy people, rushed people, bored people—but here it was empty of life. Even the walls were bare. At all the other stations, every available space was covered with advertisements for something or other. Here there was just . . . *nothing*.

Horatio hopped of the edge of the platform and straight onto the tracks. Tweed followed Horatio, and Octavia jumped down last. The tracks receded into a dark tunnel. Octavia eyed them nervously, but she had no choice. She'd come this far, and she certainly wasn't going to show any kind of fear in front of Tweed.

Horatio led them only a short way along the tunnel before coming to stop. He folded his arms and waited for Octavia and Tweed to catch up.

"Why have we stopped?" asked Tweed.

Horatio nodded over Octavia's shoulder. She turned around to find another door, this one made of solid-looking metal. There was no handle on it, just a slightly raised panel.

"What's this?" asked Octavia.

"A way into the Ministry," said Horatio. "If Barnaby is being held by them, you'll find him somewhere in there."

Octavia's eyes widened. She stared at the door hungrily. It was possible her mother was somewhere in there, too, then.

"How do we get in?" asked Tweed.

Horatio reached into his dirty jacket and pulled out a tatty cardboard file. It was thick with papers, tied closed with an old piece of leather. He handed it to Octavia.

"What's this?" she asked.

"The layout of the Ministry compound beneath London. All twenty square miles of corridors, offices, prisons, rooms, laboratories . . . everything, really. Plus intelligence on security. You'll need that." Horatio shook his head. "It's a suicide mission, mind. But that might help you." He started to walk back along the track.

"Wait," called Tweed. "Why are you doing this? You put yourself in danger by bringing us here."

"I told you," said Horatio. "I want Lucien dead."

"No," said Tweed. "There's more than that."

Octavia could just make out Horatio smiling in the darkness. "Smart lad, aren't you? Fine. I'm helping because I used to be friends with your father, boy. The man you call Barnaby Tweed? He used to be a Mesmer. Just like me."

CHAPTER FOURTEEN

Tweed paced back and forth in the front lounge of Jenny and Carter's house. He had shoved the table and couch against the wall so he could get a good stride going while he tried to assimilate what he'd read in the file and what he'd been told by Horatio.

His father, a Mesmer.

His father, a Ministry lackey.

He couldn't understand it. Barnaby *hated* the Ministry. Hated it with a fierce passion. And now here was this Horatio fellow telling him he used to work with Barnaby *inside* the Ministry?

Perhaps Horatio was lying, but why? What would he have to gain? Nothing.

It had the ring of truth.

It would explain why Barnaby had always insisted they keep a low profile; why they never strayed from the overcrowded Whitechapel. Because Barnaby had been in hiding. All this time he had been scared the Ministry would track him down. And it looked like his fears had finally come true.

Tweed heard the front door open and close.

"Darling," called Jenny, "I'm home!"

She and Carter entered the front room, tossing jackets and scarves onto a chair. Carter glanced around at the rearranged furniture. "Not sure I like what you've done with the place, old chap."

"Never mind that," said Jenny. "Did you meet up with him?"

"Did you know Barnaby used to work in the Ministry?" asked Tweed.

Jenny and Carter exchanged confused looks.

"What on Earth are you talking about, dear boy?" asked Jenny. Don't be absurd."

"This Horatio fellow says he used to work for the Ministry, said Barnaby did as well."

Tweed went on to tell them everything they had learned from Horatio. Octavia joined them as he was doing so, adding in details he missed.

When Tweed finished, Jenny and Carter looked dazed.

"We had no idea," said Jenny. "We met Barnaby when you were just a babe. He's never said anything . . ." She frowned and turned to Carter, waving a fist in his face. "He better not have told you about this on one of your gentlemen-only pub crawls."

Carter raised his hands. "This is news to me, my love! I swear!"

Jenny narrowed her eyes and stared suspiciously at him.

"I promise! I didn't know about this."

Jenny pursed her lips and nodded. "Fine. I believe you."

"You can all talk this over with Barnaby himself, once we get him out of the Ministry prison," said Octavia. She nodded at the file in Tweed's hands. "You've been reading that thing for hours. Is it going to help us?"

Tweed hesitated. "It's . . . It's not going to be easy," he said reluctantly. "I mean, for obvious reasons, yes? It's the Ministry. They take their security seriously. Plus, we're talking about breaking into the Ministry *prison*."

"Tell us," said Carter.

Tweed ran his hands through his hair and started to pace again. He stopped and turned. "Right. Our first problem is simply getting *inside*. The Ministry has made it difficult, even for their own people. They have a Babbage terminal at every door. For an employee to gain access to the building the Babbage takes a photograph of the employee's eye and compares the iris against a detailed record stored in its database. Then the terminal reads the fingerprints of the employee, and finally, if he passes the first two tests, he has to repeat his name into a recording device so the Babbage can compare the voiceprint to one stored in its system. Only if all three of these are perfect matches will the door unlock."

The others exchanged worried glances.

"Oh, there's more," said Tweed, noting their expressions. "Everyone in the Ministry knows each other. At least by sight. The Ministry makes sure of this so that, should a stranger ever gain access to the Ministry complex, one sighting should be enough to raise the alarm.

"There are over twenty square miles of corridors, offices, warehouses, and laboratories down there. The place is a maze. One wrong turn and you could be stuck wandering around for days." Tweed held up the file Horatio gave them. "There are maps in here, but they're years out of date. Who knows what's changed since then?" He dropped the file onto the table. "Then there's the prison itself. The prison cells are buried a *mile* underground. Their positioning and shape are . . . unique."

"I don't like it when you say 'unique' like that," said Octavia.

"Neither do I. The prisons are situated in a circle around a huge central shaft. Basically a massive hole in the ground. There are a hundred levels, one beneath the other, and fifty cells on each level. The only access to the cells is by a single elevator that is operated from the top floor of the prison complex. But before we even *think* about that, we have to somehow find out which cell Barnaby is in, and check if Octavia's mother is being held there as well."

Tweed glanced over at Octavia as he spoke. He could see she was surprised that he'd thought of her mother.

"We have to find out which cells they're being held in, which means we need access to the Ministry's Babbage computing network. The problem with that is that it's all internal. The serving machines that feed the network are all situated right in the middle of the Ministry complex. So we need to somehow access the serving machines *before* we go off looking for the cells."

Tweed folded his arms, looking at their worried faces, and said, "I'm afraid we're going to need some help."

"No kidding," replied Jenny.

क्ष

"Right, listen up," said Tweed, as the four of them stood before a rundown house on Norfolk Street. "You're about to meet someone called Stepp Reckoner." Tweed held up his hands to forestall any questions. He was already dreading this. He knew it was going to end badly. "Not her real name. An alias she came up with. Stepp is the one who helped me program the spiders. She's an expert on analytical computers, on Babbages, on Adas—anything computer-related, she knows about it. But the government doesn't like that. They like to control everything about computing machines. Babbage himself isn't allowed to talk about how they work."

"And you think she can help us get into the Ministry?" said Jenny.

"She's the only one who *can*. With the amount of Babbage security we're facing, we're finished if she doesn't agree to help. But you have to be careful not to offend her. She's very . . . touchy."

"I don't see why we can't just get our old crew together and fight our way in," said Carter.

Jenny put a hand over his mouth. "Shush, dear, the grown-ups are talking."

Tweed stepped around the rusted gate hanging from its hinges and approached the chipped and damaged door. Appearances were very deceptive, however, and as he knocked, he heard the dull echo of the thick metal sandwiched between the wood.

Octavia came to stand next to him. "Are you sure about this?" she asked.

"You want to find out if your mother is in their cells, don't you?"

"Of course I do."

"And I want to get Barnaby out of their hands. But I don't think they're just going to hand him over. This is the only—"

He was interrupted as the door was opened by an eleven-year-old girl. She was thin and sickly looking, her head shaved to the scalp. She stared suspiciously at them.

"Um, hello there," said Octavia. "Is—" Octavia glanced uncertainly at Tweed—"your sister in? Or your mother?"

The girl stared scornfully at Octavia, then turned her dark, shadowed eyes to Tweed. "Who's she?" she asked in an Irish accent. "Your new girlfriend?"

"No," said Tweed. "But a friend. So behave." Tweed frowned at her. "You don't look so good, Stepp. Are you sick?"

Stepp waved his concern away and scratched her head. She turned the scratch into a tap. "This is from the lice. The rest . . . well, I've had a bit of the flu is all. What you want, Tweed?"

Tweed tried to ignore the astonished look Octavia passed between he and Stepp. He also tried to ignore the chuckling from Jenny and the rather confused questions Carter was asking her.

"Need your help. The Ministry has Barnaby."

"Then say your goodbyes and move on. No way you can get him back."

Tweed held up the file. "Ah, but we have inside information: security protocols, maps, Babbage model numbers . . . everything you need to crack the Ministry wide open."

Tweed grinned as Stepp's eyes lit with gleeful excitement. She stepped aside and swept her hand wide in a theatrical bow.

"Ladies and gentlemen—and you," she said, glaring at Octavia. "Welcome to my center of operations."

ᴘᴘ

Stepp's "center of operations" was the basement of the rather rundown house she lived in with her alcoholic father. The man was barely aware of the passing of time, never mind the fact that his daughter was one of the foremost computing mechanics—"mechs"—in London.

Tweed lounged on a tatty couch while Stepp scanned the files. Every now and then she would giggle to herself. Tweed had seen it all before, but the other three, huddled in the opposite corner of the room, looked vaguely worried.

Tweed nodded at a small viewing terminal attached to a brass and copper keyboard. It seemed to be one piece of equipment, instead of the usual separate keyboard and viewing screen. "That's new," he said.

Stepp glanced up. "Oh, It's the new Ada. Not even on the market yet. Wanted to get into it before everyone else. It's what I use when I'm cutting a system. Very fast."

"How did you get it?" asked Octavia.

Stepp looked her way. "I have someone who works in the factories. Someone who owes me a lot of favors."

"So what do you think?" asked Tweed. "Is your reputation as the best cutter in the city well-earned?"

"You know it is, Tweedy."

Tweed sighed. "What I'm asking, Stepp, is can it be done?"

"Possibly."

"Then my next question is, will you help?"

"That depends."

"On what?"

"On whether or not you agree to leave my punchcards in the Ministry serving computer when you sneak inside."

"Why would you want me to do that?"

"So I can gain direct control over their systems whenever I want to."

"Ah, I see. Then I agree."

Octavia straightened up. "Tweed! You can't do that!"

"Why not? I'm sure Stepp will be a good little girl and use her power responsibly, won't you Stepp?"

"Call me a little girl one more time and I'll chop your fingers off," growled Stepp.

Tweed sat up on the couch. "Apologies. Slip of the tongue. So, are we on?"

"We're on."

"When do we get started?"

"What's the time frame?"

Tweed glanced uncertainly at the others. Octavia shrugged.

"Tight," said Tweed. "Very, very tight."

"Then we start right now. Here's the first thing you'll need to do . . ."

ဝ၀

"I'm not happy with this!" said Octavia. "Not happy at all."

"What did you expect?" asked Tweed. "That we wouldn't have to do anything illegal? This is serious stuff, Songbird."

Tweed twitched the curtain aside and peered out the window of his steamcoach. Despite his words, he was, in fact, concerned about the instructions Stepp had given them. It had all made sense when she explained it, and as far as Tweed could tell, it really was the only way to get inside the Ministry. But still, sitting there watching the evening rush-hour traffic clog up the arteries of the city, he couldn't help but worry.

"It'll be fine," he said, though he wasn't sure who he was trying to convince. "Just make sure you're ready to do your bit."

Octavia leaned past Tweed and peered out the window. "Where are Carter and Jenny? Shouldn't they be around?"

"Oh, they are. You only see them if they want to be seen. Don't worry about them. They're good at what they do."

"Which is robbing people?"

"Exactly," said Tweed with relish. "The best in the biz. And they've taught me a few of their tricks. Surprisingly, a lot of it is about psychology, about making the mark think something diff—What?"

Octavia was staring at him in astonishment. "Are you *seriously* about to give me a lecture on the psychology of theft?"

"Well . . . not a *lecture*. More a . . . brief essay."

Octavia shook her head in dismay. "You are so odd."

"I resent that!"

"Do you deny it?"

"Well, no, but I still *resent* it."

"Just pay attention please." She nodded out the window. "Are you sure that's the right building?"

Tweed glanced across the street. The building was unremarkable. A bland set of stairs covered in pigeon droppings leading up to a black door. The building was three stories high, with small, square windows facing out onto the main street. It certainly didn't look like the main entrance to the most feared government ministry in the country.

"That's the address Horatio put down. What about him?" he added, as a well-dressed man exited the building and trotted down the steps onto the pavement. He put on a hat and lit a cigarette before walking away from the building.

"No," said Octavia. "Too smartly dressed. Too good looking. He'd be missed."

Tweed squinted at the man. He wouldn't call him good looking. Definitely average. "You think he's good looking?" Tweed asked doubtfully

"Indeed. He looks like an actor."

"Any *specific* actor, or is it simply the fact that a person gets up onto a stage and repeats lines someone else wrote for them that you find so attractive?"

"What about her?" asked Octavia, blatantly ignoring Tweed's question. A middle-aged woman was leaving the building, buttoning up a jacket against the blustery wind.

"No," said Tweed. "I'm not comfortable doing this to a woman."

They waited for another ten minutes. Finally, an extremely tall man wearing a creased suit with a—Tweed leaned forward to get a better look—coffee stain down the front of his shirt, exited the building and clattered down the steps. He bumped into a passing pedestrian, spun around as he muttered an apology, then started to move in their direction.

"Perfect," said Tweed. "Get ready with that thing."

Octavia pushed a button on a large gramophone that Stepp had loaned them. The smooth sound disc started to spin. Octavia picked up a long hose attached to the device and held the listening horn next to the open window.

"Ready," she said.

Tweed hopped out of the carriage, checking how close the man was. He walked away a few steps, then turned around as if he'd forgotten something. He patted his jacket and walked along the pavement, searching the ground. When he drew level with the carriage he paused and looked up. He had timed it exactly right.

"Theodore?" he said to the tall man. "Theodore . . . Smith?"

Smith? Really? That was the best he could come up with?

A look of surprise flashed across the man's features. He tried to step around Tweed, shaking his head as he did so.

"Theodore," pressed Tweed. "It's me. Bartholomew. How are you?"

The man finally stopped walking. "I'm afraid you're mistaken. My name is not Theodore."

"Of course it is. Theodore from Oxford. We met at that coffee shop, after the opera? We drank wine and absinthe and then your wife came and dragged you away. I bet you were in trouble, eh?"

"I assure you, sir. I have never been to the opera in Oxford. Plus, I am not married."

"Of course you are. Theodore Smith. Married to Jessie. Two children. How are the little tykes?"

"I have no children. Now if you will please let me get by . . ."

"No children? Really? But you and Jess—"

"Sir! My name is Maximilian Horton. I am *not* married. I do *not* have children. I have never been to the opera. I have most certainly never drunk wine and absinthe with you. Now, good day to you!"

Tweed smiled. "Sorry about this."

Maximilian frowned. "Sorry about wha—?"

Jenny and Carter appeared from out of the crowd of pedestrians buffeting them on all sides. Jenny smiled at Maximilian. "Max! Baby! How you been?" She grabbed his arm and stuck the needle of a syringe into his bicep.

Carter grinned at the man and supported him on the other side as he slumped into their grip. Jenny was babbling on, laughing, leaning across Maximilian to speak to Carter as they smoothly moved him to the back of the carriage. Tweed hung back to make sure no one was taking an untoward interest in them. He needn't have worried. Everyone was too busy going about their own business to take any notice of what looked like three friends laughing and chatting together.

Jenny and Carter managed to get Maximilian into the back of the carriage and pulled the door shut. Tweed hopped into the driver's seat, pulled his smoke goggles down, and set off into traffic, heading back to Norfolk Street to pick up Stepp and her equipment.

Phase one complete. Only . . . Tweed tried to count how many phases were left, then gave up after he got to ten, feeling the depression start to creep in. How in the name of all that's holy were they going to pull this off?

CHAPTER FIFTEEN

Tweed pulled the back door of the steamcoach open to find Stepp glaring at him, clutching her precious computing equipment to her chest while trying to hold the rest down with her feet.

"You drive like a drunken baboon!" she snapped. "This is delicate machinery here."

"Sorry."

The back of the carriage was rather crowded. Stepp, Jenny, Carter, and Octavia all squashed together in the cramped space, plus Maximilian curled into a ball on the floor. Tweed had to find alternate routes to their destination because the carriage wouldn't make it up any hills.

"Is he still alive?" asked Tweed.

Maximilian's knees were pushed up to his chest, his head twisted to the side as if his neck had been broken.

"He's fine," said Jenny. "Not our fault he's so tall. He'll have a stiff neck, that's all."

They climbed out of the carriage one by one, stretching cramped muscles, then pulled Maximilian out, laying him on the damp cobbles. Tweed glanced at the mouth of the alley, where it fed onto the busier street, but the nightly autumn mist had rolled in as they were driving, drifting across the streetlights and turning people into half-seen ghosts.

Stepp stopped clutching her equipment to her chest and put it on the floor, neatly rearranging everything. Then she lifted the trapdoor so the Tesla transceiver slid up from its hidden compartment. Tweed put the receiver into his ear and waited while Stepp picked up the transmitter and pushed the trigger.

"Hello? Hello?" she said softly.

It sounded as if Stepp was whispering directly into his ear. He gave her a thumb's up.

"Have you got the codes?" she asked.

Tweed patted his jacket pocket. "In here."

"Good."

Tweed reached inside the carriage and pulled out the heavy sack he'd picked up from home. He hefted it over his shoulder and nodded a farewell to Stepp.

"Good luck."

"I don't need luck," said Stepp. "I need neatly ordered numbers and reliable people." She narrowed her eyes at where Jenny and Carter were trying rather unsuccessfully to pick up the limp form of Maximilian without him folding in half. "But you, on the other hand, need all the luck you can get. I'll see you later Tweed, yes?"

Tweed nodded and closed the carriage door. Octavia was carrying a closed case that looked about as heavy as his sack. Jenny and Carter had finally managed to get Maximilian into a position that allowed them to carry him.

Tweed led the way along the wall until they came to the hidden entrance, slipped into the semi-darkness of the corridor, then took the stairs that led underground. Octavia was right behind him, and bringing up the rear were Jenny and Carter, struggling and swearing as they tried to maneuver Maximilian down the narrow stairwell without banging his head every time they took a step.

They staggered onto the concourse of the abandoned railway station, and everybody laid their burdens down on the white tiles.

"How can someone so thin be so hard to carry?" complained Carter. "He looks like he's as light as a bird."

"We should get a move on," said Octavia, picking up her box. "We don't know how many people use this entrance."

"The words of common sense are rarely welcomed, you know," said Jenny, picking up Maximilian's legs. She nodded at Carter. "Come on, then. And this time, try to do a little of the work. Leaving all the heavy lifting to your wife is, frankly, quite embarrassing."

"Embarrassing?" said Carter haughtily. "I may be many things, dear heart, but embarrassing is not one of them."

Carter lifted the top half of Maximilian and pulled him back. Unfortunately, he hadn't noticed how close he was to the edge of the platform. He stepped into midair and vanished from sight, dropping Maximilian onto the platform. Jenny swore and leaped forward, grabbing hold of Maximilian's shirt as the top half of his body started to slide over the edge.

Carter leaped to his feet. "I'm all right," he said, waving his hand in the air.

Jenny just shook her head wearily.

They maneuvered their equipment onto the track and moved into the dark tunnel, heading quickly to the metal door that Horatio had shown them. Jenny and Carter propped Maximilian up against the wall and Octavia placed the large box next to him. She winced and shook her arms, trying to loosen them up.

Jenny turned to Tweed and said, "Come on then, lover boy. You're up. What have you got hidden in that mysterious bag of yours?"

Tweed dropped the sack onto the floor and untied the string. He upended it, the contents spilling out onto the metal tracks.

He looked at the others' surprised faces. "You'll have to give me a hand with this," he said.

ॐ

Fifteen minutes later an automaton stood on the tracks. It twisted from side to side, measuring the give in the suit. Then it did a few rather limited squats. Metal plates clinked and shifted, scraping together, but even so, maneuverability was better than Tweed had thought it would be.

"I just wish you'd told us this was your amazing idea," said Octavia.

"Why's that?" asked Tweed, bending over to see if he could touch his toes.

"Because it would have given us a chance to come up with something else. This is insane!"

"Why is it insane? Barnaby built this to be an exact replica of an automaton. It's perfect."

"It *is* a couple of years out of date," said Carter dubiously.

Tweed turned to face him, trying to move like an automaton. "It's the only chance we've got. All Ministry employees are trained to recognize each other. But nobody notices automata. They're background objects. Like wallpaper."

Jenny put her arm around Tweed. "Well, I think it's a glorious idea."

"Thank you," said Tweed. "I *was* rather proud of it."

"Oh, good grief," said Octavia. "Let's just get this over with then."

She turned to the wall and opened up the box she'd been carrying, revealing the gramophone. She unspooled the hose, but instead of the receiver that had been attached to it earlier, this time it ended at a metal cone. She unfolded a small handle and wound the device up.

"Ready," she said.

Carter and Jenny manhandled Maximilian to his feet, turning him to face the door.

"Ready," said Carter.

Tweed took a deep breath, surveying the others through the tiny eyeholes that Barnaby had given the suit. He nodded.

"Ready."

Carter lifted Maximilian's hand and laid it flat against the metal panel on the door. Tweed heard a buzzing sound, and a moment later a second panel slid aside at eye height, revealing a large glass lens with a red glow in its center. Jenny and Carter both jerked aside, but Tweed didn't think they had to worry. It would be attached to the Babbage. No one else should be watching.

"Do it," he whispered.

Jenny and Carter pushed Maximilian up to the lens, Jenny peeling his eyelid back while Carter held his head in the correct position. The red light glowed brighter, pulsing into the dark tunnel.

They waited, but nothing happened. Jenny pushed Maximilian closer, pressing his nose against the actual door.

Still nothing.

"It's not working," said Octavia. "We should—"

She was cut off by the panel sliding abruptly back across the lens. The tunnel was plunged into darkness again.

The four glanced uncertainly at each other. Had it worked? Or were they about to be confronted by a gang of Ministry security?

"Do it," said Tweed.

Octavia switched the gramophone on. The sound disc started to spin. She put the needle down onto it and a crackling sound issued from the metal cone. She extended the hose and held it to the door. Tweed pointed out a tiny metal grill about halfway up, and she nodded and moved the cone directly in front of it.

A scratchy voice issued from the cone. It took Tweed a moment to realize it was his own. He winced in embarrassment. He didn't sound like that, did he?

"—really? But you and Jess—" Then Maximilian's voice interrupted his. "Sir! My name is Maximilian Horton. I—"

Octavia quickly lifted the needle from the sound disc.

No one spoke. They stared intently at the door, waiting. Tweed held his breath. He was already sweating inside the suit. He could feel it dripping down the back of his neck.

With a quiet little click, the door opened, swinging back against the wall to reveal a dark corridor. The lights flickered on, stuttering and winking from inside the protective metal cages bolted to the roof.

They stared into the corridor. The harsh light revealed brick walls and a stone floor. It looked abandoned. Like a passage you would find in an empty tenement.

"Charming," said Jenny.

Tweed moved forward, turning to the others before he stepped over the threshold. "You all know what to do?" he asked, his voice sounding muffled behind the mask.

"Do *you?*" asked Octavia, coming to stand before him.

He nodded. "I think so."

She smiled nervously at him. "Then good luck, Tweed. Don't mess it up, eh?"

"I'll try not to."

Tweed took a deep breath, then stepped into the Ministry complex. He turned around. The others stood framed in the doorway.

Then Carter saluted him and pushed the door closed. Tweed heard it lock and seal itself. There was a hiss of air, as if the pressure was equalizing.

He stared at the metal door. He was on his own now. Time to prove to everyone that he really was as brilliant as he made himself out to be.

ଚଚ

Tweed had spent most of the past couple of hours staring at automata, studying their movements, how they walked. He'd grown up with constructs. They'd always been there. But like everything over-familiar, he'd never actually *seen* them. They were just background decoration.

He reckoned he'd got the movements right though. The suit helped a lot, forcing him to move in the stiff-legged, rolling gait that all automata used, his arms swinging slightly but not bending. Then it was a matter of mastering the head movements. Constructs turned corners oddly. The head turned first, while the body still faced in the direction it had originally been moving, then once the head had turned, the body swiveled to follow. It made sense. They needed to see where they were going, so they turned their head first. Simple when you thought about it.

He clumped down the hallway, making sure to put enough weight and force behind each footstep. The caged lights lit a long passage, and it was only when he felt his upper body pulling on him that he realized it was sloping quite steeply downward, tunneling beneath the streets of London.

The passage finally stopped in front of a second metal door. He opened it a crack and peered out. Another corridor waited beyond, but this one was slightly less bare than the one he was in. Admittedly, it *did* look like the corridor of a school, with pipes angling along the upper half of the walls, and bright, unpleasant lighting. But at least the walls were painted.

Even if they were painted green.

As Tweed watched, a woman dressed in a suit similar to Octavia's walked past, checking a thick file she was holding. A moment later three men in severe charcoal suits hurried by, all whispering to each other. They were followed by an automaton carrying heavy-looking boxes, after which came another two women.

That was something at least. Tweed had had a terrible fear that there would be no automata inside the Ministry, that the note about them being used within the walls of the complex was wrong.

Right. Nothing else for it. He pushed the small button attached to the palm of his automaton costume.

"Testing, testing," he muttered.

∞

Octavia was just climbing into the back of the steamcoach when she heard Tweed's voice crackling over the speechifier built into the Tesla transceiver.

"Testing, testing."

Stepp was busy clicking away at the keys on her Ada, so Octavia picked up the transmitter and depressed the trigger.

"Octavia here. We can hear you fine, Tweed. How are things?"

"Hot," said Tweed's voice. "This suit is incredibly uncomfortable."

"Take it up with your father when you find him," she said. "He built it."

"I will. I'm about to enter the main section of the Ministry."

"Does he have the codes?" said Stepp, without looking up.

"Stepp asks if you've still got the codes," said Octavia.

"Of course I have. Tell her I'm not an idiot."

"He says—"

"I heard," said Stepp. "Tell him, 'opinions are varied on that point.'"

Jenny leaned into the carriage and picked up a satchel from the floor. She winked at Octavia and ducked back out again. Carter waved, and they disappeared into the mist.

They were going to take up position outside the Ministry building, close to where they'd kidnapped Maximilian. The satchel was filled with small bundles of explosives. If they needed some kind of distraction, they were to drive the steamcoach along the road past their hiding place. That was the signal for Jenny and Carter to plant and detonate one of the explosives to draw the attention of the Ministry to the upper floors. Octavia hoped they didn't have to do it, though. No matter how small the explosion, that kind of thing was getting into incredibly dangerous territory.

"Right. I'm going now," said Tweed's voice. "Not sure when I'll be able to talk again."

"I'll be here," said Octavia.

જ

I'll be here.

Tweed found that quite comforting, even though it wouldn't exactly be a help if he got caught.

Tweed had memorized the map. It had been easy enough, especially with all the training Barnaby had given him growing up. Who'd have thought all those lessons would actually pay off? He'd have to keep that to himself, though. If he told Barnaby he'd never hear the end of it.

Tweed walked slowly along the corridors, mimicking the speed of the other automata, praying that no one would look at him too closely. He realized he should probably be carrying something. It would make him look as if he was actually doing something, was under someone's orders. First chance he got he would pick up some papers or files.

The corridor led to a stairwell with ornate, old-fashioned banisters and wide, institutional stairs. And again with the green walls. Tweed wasn't sure what he'd been expecting from the Ministry, but it just looked like any other working office building filled with bored personnel waiting to get home at the end of the day, serious workers who thought this *was* their home, and every shade in between.

Tweed walked awkwardly down the stairs. The knees of the

costume didn't bend very well, so his rolling gait became even more pronounced. He passed lots of people, but no one even gave him a second look. His hunch had been correct. No one noticed constructs. They were tools, there to do their jobs.

Octavia's voice came suddenly over the earpiece, almost making Tweed miss his step and tumble down the stairs.

"I asked my mother once, why she married my father," she said. "Not to be nasty, just because they were such total opposites."

Tweed maneuvered around another turn in the stairs. There was no one around, so he leaned over the banister to see how far he had to go.

Quite far, was the answer.

"She said *that* was what she loved about him. He was this straight-laced young man who took her to the museum when he was courting her. She thought that was charming. Even back *then* she was different. A bit . . . wild."

Tweed clumped on, trying to move faster, wondering if there was a point to this story, or if she was just trying to bore him to death.

"But she said not once did he try and change her. Not once did he ever tell her to cover up, to dress a bit more demurely. She asked him about it, years later, and do you know what he said? He said 'Why should I want to change you? You're who I fell in love with. You can dress how you like, dance how you like. You can even flirt if you want. And do you know why I don't mind? Because I know we'll be going home together, and the poor helpless fool who has just fallen in love with you will have nothing but a memory and the knowledge that he lost something special.'"

Octavia trailed off with a sigh. Tweed was nearing the bottom now, only a few more flights to go.

"I haven't been there for him," said Octavia. "All I've been thinking about is how *I* feel, how I miss my mother. But how must *he* feel? She's the love of his life."

Tweed wanted to say something, but there were people approaching up the stairs.

"Seeing Jenny and Carter together made me think of them both, and what they used to be like. He was never . . . spontaneous. But the way he looked at my mother, with that light in his eyes . . . Everyone should have someone like that in their lives, Tweed."

Er . . . all right. He got the story. But what did she mean by that bit at the end? Did she mean that he was going to grow old alone? Or was it something else? Maybe—

Octavia's words cut into his thoughts. "And even though I've only known you for, what, two days now? I bet you all the money you have that you're analyzing my words, trying to look for hidden messages, trying to understand the logic behind the emotion."

Tweed swore under his breath.

"I heard that," said Octavia. "You need to learn to just go with the flow of things, Tweed. Stop analyzing. Stop breaking everything down so you can see how it works."

This was most unfair. Octavia had a captive audience. She could sit there and spout her theories and stories and there was nothing he could do about it. Bad form.

Octavia had trailed off into merciful silence. Tweed finally reached the bottom of the stairs and pushed open the doors.

Where he froze.

Opening out before him was a huge floor, easily a quarter of a mile across. Desks were scattered everywhere, seemingly following no pattern at all. Ministry employees scurried to and fro, hurrying between desks, moving between huddles of people talking and comparing papers and files. There were offices all the way around the walls of the huge space. Some offices had uncovered windows, while others had dark blinds pulled down to hide whatever was going on inside. Automata moved everywhere, carrying notes, boxes, files, even tea.

Large tubes hung from the ceiling. They were used by the staff to ferry sealed containers holding what Tweed assumed were orders or intelligence reports up to various levels of the building. Babbages the size of garden sheds were placed in long lines all over the room. They were covered with flashing lights, buttons, and dials. Operators sat behind viewing screens, typing and sending information and orders out to various locations around the Empire.

Tweed realized he was just standing in the doorway. He forced himself to walk into the huge room, heading straight across to the distant door. When he finally arrived he quickly yanked it open.

To find yet another room identical to the first.

Tweed actually turned around to make sure the first one was still behind him.

It was.

These areas on the maps just showed offices and work stations, but Tweed had thought it meant proper, enclosed rooms. The maps didn't say anything about them being one huge space.

He moved through the second room and into yet another one. Tweed cast his mind back to the maps. There had been ten of these spaces, hadn't there? Tweed gritted his teeth. He knew the Ministry was big, that they controlled a lot of things, but this was ludicrous.

Half an hour later, Tweed finally made it through the final room and found himself in another corridor. By then he was sweating, the moisture dripping down his face, trickling down his back. Any second now he'd start leaving a trail behind him as he walked.

Down another set of stairs he went, then through a few doors, following more passages and corridors, until he finally stood before his first destination of the night.

The programming room.

He pushed down the handle and opened the door.

CHAPTER SIXTEEN

T weed closed the door behind him and stood facing row upon row of empty keypunch machines. Each machine consisted of a chair facing a viewing screen housed in a large brass and wood cabinet bolted against the wall. A small table folded out from the cabinet, making it look like a school desk. Tweed walked forward and studied the closest one. Each desk had a long, jointed arm attached to the cabinet on the wall, with a metal card puncher attached to the end. And in the center of the desk was a rectangular frame for holding the punchcards.

"I'm in," he whispered.

ᏙᏙ

Octavia breathed a sigh of relief and handed the transmitter over to Stepp. She ignored Octavia, frowning at the screen of her Ada, her thin face illuminated in a sickly, sepia glow. Octavia had to prod her with the transmitter before she actually peeled her eyes up from the viewing screen to glare at her.

"I need to prepare all this before he goes ahead," snapped Stepp. "Give me a second." She started to turn back to her screen, then paused. "Tell the idiot to get the punchcard ready."

ᏙᏙ

"Stepp says she'll be with you momentarily," said Octavia in Tweed's ear. "She politely requests that you ready the punchcard."

Tweed looked around. Right. The punchcard. That was the whole reason this had to be the first part of the plan. The government used their own patented type of card, the only kind that could be used in their Babbages. That meant they couldn't just pre-punch a card on the outside and bring it in with them. It had to be done here.

There was a large wall cupboard behind the door. He hurried over to it and pulled, but it was locked. Typical. Tweed tried to yank it, but his automaton arms hampered his grip. He quickly undid the latches under his forearms and pulled the casing from his arms and hands. A cool breeze wafted into the rest of the suit.

Tweed took a firm grip on the door and pulled again. The stupid thing still didn't budge. He needed something to use as leverage. He looked around, his eyes falling on the arms that were used to punch the cards. That would do. He went to the nearest machine and ripped off the arm that held the card puncher, splintering the wood of the cabinet as it pulled free of its moorings. He forced the thin end of the arm into the small gap between the doors and put all his weight against it. The lock snapped and the door sprung open, banging against the wall.

Tweed dropped the arm. The cabinet was filled from top to bottom with the Ministry's unique oblong punchcards. He took one from the pile and sat down at a nearby machine, slipping the card into the frame on the desk. He didn't switch it on, as he was doing this manually. No telling who would see if he started typing instructions into a government-run Babbage.

He stared at the arm, then at the keypad to his left. The keypad was a facsimile of the actual punchcard. Whichever button he pushed, the card puncher would then punch a corresponding hole in the card. Simple.

He wondered why they bothered mounting it to a Babbage at all. It seemed pretty straightforward. What added benefit did they get from such a machine? Maybe they did multiple copies? You put a pile of punchcards in, and the Babbage did one after the other? That would only work if each card was to be exactly the same. Any variation in each card would still have to be programmed—

"I'm here," said Stepp. "Are you set?"

"Of course I am," Tweed replied.

"Good. Make sure you type in these numbers exactly as I say them."

Stepp then proceeded to recite a long series of numbers. Tweed typed each one into the machine, watching the arm move the card puncher across the punchcard and stab neat holes into the waxed material.

It took ten excruciating minutes. Every ten seconds Tweed would glance over his shoulder, convinced someone was about to walk into the room and catch him. But his luck held. He supposed it made sense. Who would need newly programmed punchcards at this time of night?

"That's it," said Stepp. "All done. You'd better get a move on, Tweed. You've been in there over an hour now."

Over and hour? So long? It certainly didn't seem like it. Tweed pulled the card from the frame and slid it into a hidden panel on his suit. Then he buckled on the arms and gloves again.

There was a thick pile of papers on a desk near the door. Tweed picked it up, then stepped back out into the corridor.

He had to head back the way he came in, moving quickly through the corridors and then through those massive open office spaces. His route took him all the way back to the fifth room. He pushed through the door, consciously forcing himself to slow down. He had to constantly fight his instinct to move faster, to get this over with. He glanced around, searching for the elevators. He spotted them over by the far wall, a line of ten grey-painted doors.

Tweed headed toward them. He really wanted this finished. The tension was starting to get to him. The back of his neck was crawling. He kept expecting a hand to clamp down on his shoulder. Or to turn around to find everyone in the room staring at him.

Not only that, but the tension of wondering if he was even going to find Barnaby was making it even worse. They were taking a huge leap of faith in their assumption that his father was even here.

Tweed pushed the button on the brass panel next to the door. He waited, staring straight ahead, trying his best not to fidget. Knowing he had to stand absolutely still made him want to move all the more. He had an almost overwhelming compulsion to lift his feet, to stretch out his ankles in an attempt to relieve the cramp.

Someone came to stand next to him. He couldn't see who, but he heard the rustle of cloth, the whisper of breath going in, the slightly wheezy, wet air coming back out. A smoker, definitely.

The elevator doors slid open. Tweed walked inside, then turned slowly around. The person followed Tweed inside: a short, overweight man wearing a tatty plaid suit, holding an accordion file very tightly to his chest.

He barely even glanced at Tweed, just turned around and hit a button. After a few moments, he turned and frowned at Tweed.

Tweed felt a rush of alarm. What? What had given him away? Then he realized he hadn't pushed a floor button. Tweed only just managed to stop himself lunging forward and slapping one of them. Instead, he moved slowly, jerkily, and depressed a button three floors below the one the man had pushed. It wasn't the floor he was going to, but he didn't want this person knowing where he was getting off.

The elevator shook and started it's jerky descent. Ministry staff entered and exited until finally it was just Tweed on his own. He pushed a button:

20

The elevator trundled down the remaining floors and opened into a dim corridor. Tweed hesitated, peering out between the doors. The corridor was older, less clinical. Upturned lights in the walls cast their glow directly onto the stained roof, leaving the lower half of the passage cloaked in shadow.

Well, that actually worked in his favor, didn't it? No one would be able to see him clearly. Tweed stepped out of the elevator. According to the maps he needed to head along here, turn there, through these doors, along this corridor . . .

He followed his own directions until he stood before a nondescript wooden door: the programming hub of the Ministry.

Interesting that it was tucked away at the bottom of the complex, hidden beneath everything. From the room in front of him the Ministry sent out secret instructions to the Babbages upstairs, which were then sent to their automata throughout the city, to agents overseas. Every Babbage owned by the Ministry, every piece of security equipment they used, the Tesla Towers themselves, they were all controlled from here.

And Tweed was going to set it on fire.

Well, not quite. He *had* suggested it, but Stepp had been horrified at the thought and had threatened to pull out of the whole operation should Tweed even bring it up again. So a compromise was reached.

He checked the opposite side of the corridor and picked one of the closest doors to the programming room. He knocked, but there was no answer, so Tweed pushed it open and peeked inside. It was filled with filings cabinets and wall-mounted shelves stuffed full of books and files. A records room. Perfect.

Tweed closed the door behind him and hastily yanked his arm plates off. He opened up the folder he carried and crumpled up the paper inside. He pulled open random drawers in the filing cabinets and tossed the scrunched-up balls inside. Then he pulled out a matchbook of Lucifers and lit one of them, touching the flame to the crumpled papers.

He waited till the paper was burning merrily, the orange light flickering up the walls, then he grabbed his arm casings and slipped back into the hall, leaving the door open.

He waited.

And waited.

Surely there had to be some sort of fire alarm. The orange glow was getting brighter, spilling out into the corridor. Smoke crawled out the top of the door, reaching up to the roof of the passage.

"The alarm is not going off," he whispered urgently.

A pause. Then, "What?" asked Octavia.

"There is supposed to be a fire alarm," he said. "It's not going off."

"Are you sure the fire took?" asked Octavia.

Tweed stared at the flames now licking up the doorframe. He could feel the heat on his face.

"I'm fairly sure the fire took," he said.

"Then improvise!" snapped Octavia.

Improvise. Right.

Tweed whirled around, yanked the door to the computing room open, and bellowed, "Fire!" at the top of his lungs. Then he darted into one of the other rooms along the passage and listened to the panicked rush of feet, the shouts of alarm, the shrieks of terror.

He poked his head around the doorframe and saw a last person staggering out of the programming room, heading for the elevators. Tweed darted into the corridor, through the door to the now-empty room, and closed it behind him.

He hoped they managed to get the fire out. This would all be a bit pointless if he actually burned down everything on this level.

He looked around. The room was brightly lit and large. All around the walls were viewing screens. Lots and lots of viewing screens. There must have been hundreds of them, all showing different images: the streets of London, various buildings, and what appeared to be hospital wards. Others, somewhat alarmingly, seemed to show images from inside peoples' houses: normal people, sleeping in their beds or shuffling about for a late-night cup of tea.

Tweed let out a long, pent-up breath.

"I'm inside," he said.

ᴘᴏ

"He's in the room," said Octavia.

Stepp took the transmitter from her and pushed the trigger down. "Right. Look for an access panel on the Babbages, something you can easily open. That will be the feeder, where they put the punchcards in. See it?"

ᴘᴏ

Tweed stood before the rear wall, looking at the long banks of machines, all of which had access panels and a little sign with an arrow pointing upward saying, "Punchcards this way up." He pulled a handle on the closest and the whole front section of the machine folded downward. As it lowered to form a sort of table in front of him, a section from inside slid toward him. It was a long rack holding hundreds of punchcards. There was a small, embossed piece of metal on the front of the rack. It said "Bethlem Royal Hospital, London Road—Chelsea and Westminster Hospital, Fulham Road."

Tweed looked back toward the viewing screens, then pulled the small lever on the front of the framework that held the punchcards. There was a shuffling sound, then a click, and the tray of cards rose up and rolled forward toward Tweed. As it did so, the viewing screens showing images of hospitals flickered and went black.

Tweed quickly pushed the small lever back and the punchcards retracted back inside the machine. The viewing screens flickered back into life.

"Um . . . there are rather a lot of machines that hold punchcards," he said. "The one I just opened only deals with spying on hospitals."

"Then look for one that deals with the Ministry security protocols," said Stepp. "That's the one we need."

Tweed started moving along the bank of machines. There was activity in the corridor, shouts, then some sort of hissing noise. A small line of white smoke curled under the door.

Right. They were putting the fire out. He needed to move faster. Tweed quickly pulled open the doors of the machines. Westminster. Downing Street. Interesting, thought Tweed. Spying on the Prime Minister? Piccadilly.

This wasn't what he needed. All these Babbages were dedicated to the Ministry spying on locations throughout London. He wondered how the people being watched would feel if they knew how their privacy was being so systematically abused. He wondered how many times he and Barnaby had appeared on these viewing screens, and whether or not Barnaby knew about them. Had his father picked their home because it was in a blind spot? That was possible. Likely, even.

Tweed finally found what he was looking for. The third bank of machines he inspected all seemed dedicated to the Ministry building itself. Tweed had a sudden, horrible thought. Had they seen him enter the building in the railway station? What if they'd seen them on the tracks and this was all a plot to get them to reveal their plan?

But . . . Tweed looked at the viewing screens on the walls. The Ministry had to be selective. They couldn't watch every single part of the building. There were likely other rooms like this one, with wall-to-wall viewing screens. But even then, nobody would be able to watch them all at once.

When he opened the fifth machine, he saw that it was labeled, "Security Protocols, Ministry House, Internal."

"Found it," he said, reaching out to pull the lever that would bring the tray of punchcards out.

"Don't touch anything yet!" Stepp shouted in his ear.

Tweed froze.

"If you disengage those punchcards all sorts of alarms will go off. Right. That punchcard you made. The sequence I gave you to imprint was the coded address for my Ada. What that means is that when you insert that punchcard inside the Ministry's security protocols, it will piggyback on their systems, transmitting everything that goes on in their security machines to me. But also, and here's the clever bit, allowing me to transmit my own instructions through that punchcard."

Stepp hadn't actually explained this part of the plan before. "Are you saying you will have complete control of all of the Ministry's Babbage systems?" asked Tweed.

"Not all of them. Just security protocols. Alarms, doors, and *prisons.*"

"That's quite . . . impressive," said Tweed.

"I know," said Stepp. "Now, there's a specific place you need to insert it. You see the little cut taken out of the edge of the punchcard?"

Tweed pulled the card out and saw what Stepp was talking about. Three quarters of the way along the card there was a small oval cut.

"You need to line that up with the ones already inside. That sequence controls the transmission of instructions. That's what I need."

Tweed bent over the machine and peered inside. He saw the little marks cut out of different places along the edges of the punchcards. Right at the back of the machine were the cards that matched the one he held. He leaned inside and lined them up.

"Got it," he said.

"Good. Now slip that card inside. It has to be the first in the sequence, so all instructions transmitted into the machine come through my card first."

Tweed stretched forward with both arms and leaned inside. He flicked gently through the punchcards, then slid the new one inside at the front of the queue. He patted it down until it was perfectly in place, then closed the door on the Babbage.

"Done," he said, straightening up. "Is that it?"

Octavia's voice came over his earpiece. "You've just snuck into the Ministry, used one of their machines to program a dummy punchcard program that hijacks their security systems, managed to embed it into their machines without being noticed, and you say 'is that it?'"

Tweed opened his mouth to reply, but Octavia cut him off.

"But since you asked, no it isn't it. You still have to get down to the prison level, remember? Now get a move on."

Tweed grinned and shook his head. He eyed the automaton arm panels lying on the floor. He was really coming to hate this suit. Nothing else for it though. He strapped them back on, then glanced around, making sure he had left no evidence of his presence.

He cracked the door open, and could hear lots of movement coming from the room across the way, but there was no one in the passage. There was a lot of smoke, though. He quickly slipped into the corridor and retraced his footsteps to the elevator, jabbing at the button to call it back. Chances were someone was going to get suspicious about that fire. He needed to get to the prison level as quickly as possible.

The elevator arrived. He stepped inside and let the doors slide closed again.

"I'm in the elevator," he said. He leant over and inspected the panel on the wall. There were two floors below the one he was on: 21 and 22. He pushed 22, but nothing happened.

"Stepp, time to do your stuff. I need access to floor 22. I'm in elevator . . ." he looked around and saw a small panel screwed into the wall next to the roof, ". . . six."

"Hang on," said Stepp's crackly voice in his ear. "Just testing all this out."

Tweed's stomach twisted as he waited for Stepp to do whatever it was she needed to do. What if it didn't work? After all this?

"Right," said Stepp. "Try it now."

Tweed licked his lips and stabbed at the button. The elevator lurched and started to descend.

"I suppose I should see if Barnaby's even logged in their system," said Stepp.

"Yes, that would be a good idea," said Tweed. "And don't forget to search for Octavia's mother as well."

"I won't, I won't. It's all she's been going on about."

"Hey!" came Octavia's distant voice, still discernible even though she wasn't holding the transmitter.

The prison level was fully automated, so no chance of anyone seeing him. Tweed unclipped the automaton mask and took a huge gulp of fresh air. He took the arm panels off again and wiped his face with his shirt. It didn't do much good. The shirt was soaked through with sweat.

The elevator juddered to a halt. The doors slid slowly open and Tweed found himself staring out into a black metal corridor. The change in appearance was so marked he froze for a second, surveying everything. Small white lights traveled the length of the passage, shining upward and reflecting from the dark walls. The floor was made from smooth grey concrete.

"You're absolutely sure there are no people down here? That it's all automated systems?"

"That's the beauty of having a government that worships technology," said Stepp. "They like to take humans out of the equation. Now be quiet while I search for your dad."

Tweed stepped out of the elevator, stepping over a stain on the floor that looked worryingly like old blood. If he remembered the maps correctly, this level was built like a wheel. This elevator was one of ten that stood in a circle, and the corridor in which Tweed stood was one of the spokes that met at the hub of the central prison shaft.

He hurried along the passage, waiting to hear Stepp's voice again. Hoping it would be good news.

"Hmm," said Stepp.

"What?" snapped Tweed. "Don't you dare say 'hmm' to me, Stepp. I don't want to hear it."

"Calm down. There's no Barnaby Tweed listed here, but someone *was* brought in the night your dad was kidnapped. I think they used a false name."

Tweed breathed a sigh of relief. "What do I do?"

"Head on over to the shaft. Time to rescue your dad."

CHAPTER SEVENTEEN

Stepp typed a few more things on her Ada, then she turned and treated Octavia to a huge smile.

"Octavia."

"What?" asked Octavia suspiciously.

"Am I correct in assuming you can drive this thing?"

"Uh . . . I haven't driven this one, but I *can* drive steamcoaches. Why?"

"Well, here's the thing . . . just check that boiler will you, make sure there's coal in it?"

Octavia used the metal poker to open the boiler door. It was half empty so she filled it up with coal.

"Good. Now just make sure there's enough steam power available."

"Why—?"

"Please? I'll explain in a moment."

Octavia clambered through to the front of the carriage and started pumping the lever to work up a head of steam.

"Good," said Stepp. "Now, the thing is—and don't panic, yes? I anticipated this—the thing is, you know how I piggybacked the Ministry systems and gained access to their security protocols?"

Octavia nodded.

"What that means is that we, and by we I mean this Ada machine, is putting out a very unique signal, a signal that is not supposed to exist outside of that room Tweed was just in."

"Stepp, what the bloody hell are you trying to say?" shouted Octavia, exasperated.

"What I'm trying to say is that the Ministry can track our location, that they will try to shut us down . . ." Stepp's eyes widened slightly and she nodded out the front window. "And here they come now."

Octavia whirled around to see about ten men in black suits sprinting directly toward them.

She let out a yelp and shoved the brake in, mashed down the gear to put the carriage into reverse, and released the steam valve. The carriage lurched backward, jouncing and bounding over the cobbles. Octavia ducked her head, trying to see through the tiny window at the back of the carriage. She collided with a set of dustbins, sending them flying into the air with a terrific clatter, and burst out of the alley directly into traffic.

Octavia yanked up the brake, juddering to a stop. An automaton pulled up short, narrowly avoiding smashing into them. To her left, a driver yanked hard on a horse's reigns to avoid colliding with them. The horse reared up, kicking the air and whinnying loudly while the driver shouted and swore at them. Octavia peered through the front window. The Ministry goons were about halfway down the alley.

One of them stopped running and pointed at her. She heard a loud bang, and the front window suddenly sported a hole with cracks radiating from its center.

"They're shooting at us!" she exclaimed.

"Yes, they tend to do that when they're annoyed. Now get us out of here! We need to keep moving."

Octavia shifted gears and lunged forward into traffic, bumping another automaton out of the way. It veered to the side, struggling to keep its cab upright.

"Sorry!" she shouted at the panicked occupants. "Emergency!"

She weaved into the line of traffic, ignoring the blaring of horns and shouted insults. She glanced over her shoulder but couldn't see any sign of their pursuers. They had lost them. For now.

A second, curved corridor intersected the dark hallway Tweed was using. He turned left into it and kept walking. The circular corridor passed other dark passages like the one that led to the elevator; the other spokes of the wheel.

Tweed eventually came to a door on the right side of the passage. He tried the handle but it was locked.

"Stepp?" he said. "I need access to the prison shaft. Can you open the door?"

There was a pause, then, "Uh . . . sure thing. Just . . . hold on a second. Have it done soon."

Tweed frowned. Why did Stepp sound so distracted? And what was all the noise in the background?

"Everything okay out there?"

"Yes, yes, everything is perfect. Why do you ask?"

"Uh, you just sound a bit . . . *off.*"

"No, no. Just concentrating. Here you go."

The door in front of him clicked open. Tweed felt a waft of air against his face, and got the impression of a vast space opening up before him. He stepped forward, finding himself on a huge circular balcony, the floor of which was about twenty feet wide. Separating the balcony into two halves was a bank of Babbages that traveled all the way around the circular gallery.

Tweed walked to the safety railing, his feet echoing loudly in the vast space. He gripped the cold metal and looked down.

The empty shaft was about a hundred feet across. It receded below him into distant darkness. All the way down he could see multiple levels, each with its own balcony and railing that circled around the circumference of the shaft. He counted forty such levels before giving up. Each of them was made up of wall-to-wall prison cells. Bright white lights shone from hidden alcoves, illuminating the metal and steel of the clinical prison, haloes rebounding from the polished surfaces.

The scale was just . . . immense.

A steady breeze blew up against Tweed's face. In the center of the shaft was a steel pillar. About halfway down, Tweed saw an articulated arm that held a brass cage over the empty void.

"Stepp? There's some sort of arm with a cage attached to it that ferries people down to the cells. Can you call it up for me?"

There was a burst of static, then a shout of, "Not that way! You're heading back toward them! Turn around!"

Tweed frowned. "Songbird? What's going on?"

"Songbird is a bit busy right now," said Stepp. "Give me a moment and I'll get you moving."

"*Stepp*! Tell me what's happening!"

"Uh . . . nothing big. Just that the Ministry is tracking the signals I send into their systems, so we have to keep moving around a bit. That's all. *DUCK!*"

Tweed heard a loud bang, a bang that sounded very much like a gunshot. "Stepp," he said, worried. "You still there?"

"Still here. *No, not that way. Next time just run them over! I don't care if you don't want to kill someone, I don't want to get shot!* Hey, Tweed, let me just get this . . . Yes, I see where you are. Here you go."

The articulated arm below Tweed suddenly drew itself in, pulling the cage close to the shaft, then it slid smoothly up the pillar. The arm spun to Tweed's side of the balcony where it extended the cage directly at him.

The safety railing Tweed leaned against had little chain links that could be unfastened. He unclipped them and stepped into the cage, pulling the trellis door closed.

"I'm on the elevator."

No sooner had he said the words than the cage swung around and slid downward, the air rushing past Tweed's face. He held on to the door as the arm dropped down ten floors and stopped directly in front of one of the prison cells.

Tweed swallowed nervously, staring at the metal door in front of him. Was this it? Was Barnaby inside that cell?

He opened the cage and undid the chain, stepping on to the metal walkway. There was a panel about halfway up the door. Tweed gripped the handle and slid it aside, revealing a book-sized hole that opened directly into the cell.

There was a man sleeping on a bed shoved up against the wall. His back was facing Tweed, but he recognized that long grey hair anywhere.

He almost sobbed with relief. After all he and Octavia had been through. All the fear, all the uncertainty.

And here he was. Still alive after all.

"Barnaby," Tweed whispered.

Nothing.

"Barnaby," he said again, louder this time.

Barnaby stirred in his bed, his head tilting slightly as if he thought he was hearing things.

"Get up you fool. I'm here to rescue you!"

Barnaby whirled around and fell out of his bed. He scrambled to his feet and stared at Tweed in amazement. Tweed had never seen him look so shocked. Under any other circumstances, it might have been amusing.

Barnaby hesitated, then moved slowly forward, as if worried Tweed might vanish before his eyes.

"Tweed?" he said, not even trying to keep the shock from his voice.

"The one and only," said Tweed with a grin. He couldn't help it. He didn't think he had ever managed to surprise the old man the way he had right now. It was rather a glorious feeling.

"What are you doing here?" whispered Barnaby furiously. "How did you get in? Why—never mind. Sebastian Tweed, I *order* you to leave this installation. Right this minute. Do you hear me? Get out!"

Tweed's grin faded. Interesting reaction. He had expected grati-
tude. Happiness. Relief. *Pride*, even. Not what appeared to be anger.

"Well, good to see you too," he said.

"What? Yes, yes. Of course it's good to see you. But you're in
danger, you fool. Flee. At once."

"Do you realize how hard it's been to get in here? If you think I'm
leaving without you, you're clearly more insane that I ever thought.
Hey," he said into his transmitter, "how about unlocking his cell?"

"I'm *trying*," said Stepp. "In fact, I've been trying for the past five
minutes."

Tweed frowned. "Problem?"

"Not sure. The locks aren't responding. Just . . . let me
concentrate."

"Who are you talking to?" asked Barnaby

"Stepp," said Tweed.

"You've got *her* involved? Tweed, she's only twelve!"

"Eleven. But I needed her help. Jenny and Carter are here as well.
And while we're at it, why the *hell* didn't you tell me you used to
work for the Ministry?" demanded Tweed.

Barnaby froze. He stared at Tweed, his face going slack. He
stepped away from the door. "How did you find out?"

"Jenny and Carter tracked down someone named Horatio. Said
he used to work with you. Is it true?"

Barnaby sighed, rubbing his hands over a face that looked suddenly ten years older. "Aye, son. It's true."

"Why didn't you tell me?"

"It was in the past! That wasn't who I was anymore. I wanted to
move on, leave that life behind me." He sighed. "How much do you
know?"

"Horatio told me about the Mesmers. About the Ministry's
experiments with human souls. How that led to the automata."

Barnaby laughed bitterly. "That's not even scratching the surface. Horatio left before the bad stuff happened." He nodded at the lock. "This going to take long?"

"I have absolutely no idea. That's Stepp's department."

Barnaby nodded. He started to pace in the small cell. "The head of the Ministry is a man named Lucien. He used to be my boss."

"We know about Lucien," interrupted Tweed. "We also know Sherlock Holmes is working for him. That he's the one who took you."

Barnaby waved a hand in the air. "That's not Sherlock Holmes. Well, it is, but not *really*." Barnaby sighed. "Lucien. It all comes back to Lucien. He's been in charge of the Ministry for over five decades now, using it to gain power, to push his own agenda. Lucien was always obsessed with science, with seeing just how far we could . . . *prod* nature. Give it a helping hand." Barnaby ran his fingers through his hair. "About forty years ago, Lucien heard about the work of a man named Viktor Frankenstein. This doctor—if you can call him that—was . . . *meddling* with nature, trying to create life. When Lucien heard of his research he became obsessed. He thought Frankenstein a visionary. He sent a team of agents to Europe to steal the doctor's research." Barnaby paused in his pacing. "You understand, I'm not just talking about *normal* research here. Frankenstein was experimenting with *reanimating* corpses, with creating stitch-work people. He succeeded too, if rumors are to be believed.

"But this wasn't what Lucien wanted. He wanted much more. He devoted all of the resources of the Ministry to this work. He extended the research, took it in new directions, took it way beyond what Frankenstein originally intended."

Barnaby stopped pacing and moved closer to the door. "He *grew* people, Tweed. He created simulacra, perfect copies, brand new human beings from nothing more than a piece of skin, or a clump of hair."

Tweed's hands fell from the door. He stared at Barnaby in amazement. "He *created* human beings?"

"Quicker than nature could," said Barnaby. "A thirty-year-old man could be grown in five years. Tweed, this was nothing short of a miracle."

"A miracle? Barnaby, that's not a miracle, that's an abomination! The way you speak, it's as if you think it's a good thing."

"I don't! Least, not now. But Tweed, when I first saw what could be done, I'll admit, I got caught up in the process. I . . . I was part of the team. It was my job."

"And what did these things do? These simulacra?"

"Nothing. That was the problem. They were utterly empty, nothing more than living, breathing vessels. Expensive dolls. They didn't move, didn't speak, couldn't understand anything that was said to them." Barnaby came even closer, so that only his eyes were visible through the gap. "They had no souls, Tweed."

"Then what was the point? You should have destroyed them, burned the research. Barnaby, what you did . . . it goes against nature."

Barnaby sighed. "I know that, son. Now. But at the time, we were caught up in the process of discovery. We were breaking new ground!"

"What happened next?'

"Lucien got creative," said Barnaby. "The experiments with inserting human souls into automata had already been going on for some time. It was a separate field of research, handled by another branch of Mesmers. But one day Lucien came into our lab with a new plan. He wanted to see if we could pull a soul from a living person and insert it into one of these simulacra. He wondered—he *hoped*—it would do the same for them as it had done for the constructs. You see, if the simulacra were already soulless, then they shouldn't reject the new souls being inserted into them. That was the theory."

"And?" pressed Tweed.

"It worked. We took the soul of an old man—sick, dying—and using a device called the God Machine, we inserted it into a simulacrum."

"My God," breathed Tweed.

"Lucien was ecstatic. He had, for all intents and purposes, discovered the secret of immortality. He saw a new world order. No longer would anyone have to die. They could simply purchase a simulacrum and hire the Ministry Mesmers to transfer their soul into a new, younger copy of themselves. Actually, I say no one would have to die, but I should say the *rich* wouldn't have to die.

"Lucien made sure he was one of the first. He took tissue samples and stored them away for growing a duplicate version of himself. Then he ordered me to imprint on his soul."

"Why you?"

Barnaby shrugged. "I was the Ministry's best Mesmer. Lucien didn't trust anyone else."

"So what happened next? Actually, hang on." Tweed tried the door but it was still locked. "Stepp? Getting a bit worried down here."

◑◐

Octavia grimaced as she was flung hard against the door. She spun the steering wheel back the other way, bringing the rear of the steamcoach back onto the road. "Sorry!" she shouted to the screaming pedestrians who scattered in every direction.

She could hear Stepp talking to Tweed behind her. "I don't know what's going on. My data says the locks should be on these protocols, but I can't find them anywhere. They're buried away behind a lot of numbers. Just give me some time."

Octavia peered ahead through the cracked window at the front of the carriage. She was rapidly coming up behind a slow-moving steamcoach. She swerved to overtake it, then had to brake suddenly to avoid smacking into the back of a hansom cab. This was impossible! She craned her neck out the window, searching the streets behind her. The æther cages of automata glowed in the night. There was no sign of the Ministry goons, though. Maybe they were clear . . .

As she searched the street, three steamcoaches sped around the corner behind them. The carriages were identical: black, low to the ground, and sleek. They reminded Octavia of the pictures of sharks she'd seen. They weaved through the traffic, heading rapidly toward them.

"Stepp. Load that boiler with as much coal as it'll take! Oh, and *hold on!*"

Octavia pumped the lever furiously and darted around the hansom. She veered back so she was directly in front of it, hoping the cab would obscure her from view. She needed to get off the main road and find somewhere to hide. She didn't think she'd be able to outrun those carriages.

She turned into the first side street she came across. It was a dark, unlit alley. But she could see traffic on the opposite side. She gave the carriage everything it had, speeding between brick walls with only inches to spare on either side. At one point, she hit a hole in the street, veered slightly, and sparks exploded along the side as the carriage scraped the wall.

A moment later she burst out of the alley. There was a screeching to her left, and the sound of crushing metal, but Octavia couldn't afford to look. She had come out directly next to one of the Ministry carriages. How had it got there so fast?

She looked out the side window, locking eyes with the Ministry driver. Octavia glanced ahead, then bit her lip and turned the wheel sharply to the left, crashing into the side of the black carriage. Octavia turned the wheel again, pushing the Ministry carriage across the street. Then she quickly spun the wheel and moved back into the road.

The Ministry goon looked ahead. He tried frantically to turn, but he was too late. His carriage smashed straight into a street lamp, the metal pole crushing the front of the steamcoach.

Octavia smiled to herself. Not bad.

"If you do that again," shouted Stepp from the back, "I will personally climb up there and tear your face clean off!"

Octavia's smile faltered.

🙢🙠

"A report was sent to the Queen," said Barnaby. "At first, there was much excitement. Tissue samples were taken from all the royal household. Plus samples were taken from people of national interest, just in case they were ever needed. Sherlock Holmes, for instance. Darwin, Alexander Graham Bell . . . even Oscar Wilde."

"Why were you taking all these samples? Did all these people want to live forever? Truly?"

Tweed shrugged. "I don't know. Probably not. Queen Victoria certainly did. She was most keen. But then she found out about the earlier experiments into soul transplants. Horatio must have told you about this. Where the Mesmer reapers destroyed human souls so they could insert alien ones into the body? She was utterly horrified at this. She thought they had sentenced these destroyed souls to some kind of eternal damnation. And the more she thought about the creation of simulacra, the more she didn't like it. She didn't think it was our right to do this. Just because we could, she said, it didn't mean we *should*."

"Wise words."

"She ordered an immediate stop to the simulacra program and

the destruction of all the specimens. Obviously, Lucien was not happy with this. Outwardly, he did as he was told, but he managed to hide away some of the simulacra he was growing and carried on his research in secret."

"And no one knew? No one was suspicious?"

"Possibly. But remember, Lucien was head of the Ministry. He *was* the Ministry. He could do what he wanted."

Barnaby paused. "And then came the day we all remember. The day Sherlock Holmes fell over Reichenbach falls. Dr. Watson retrieved his body, you know. He was still alive—barely. Brain damage and the like. He wasn't going to last long. Lucien ordered him brought back to England where he made me imprint on the great man's soul and withdraw it from his body.

"Holmes's body gave up the struggle the next day. But his soul was stored away in an æther cage with the simulacrum Lucien was growing."

Barnaby sighed.

"Not long after that, Lucien came to me with a new research mandate. He wondered if it would be possible to *duplicate* souls. To make copies of them."

"Why?" asked Tweed, surprised.

"That's what I said. Lucien would only say that he was following orders from on high, from above even the Queen."

"And who was that?"

"I still don't know. Regardless, we worked for many years. The God Machine was rebuilt and upgraded. Lucien renamed it the Lazarus Machine. He found it amusing to cast a biblical name on what he saw as the triumph of science.

"Finally, we got to the state where Lucien wanted to test it for real. On one of the souls he had in storage. He picked Sherlock Holmes."

"And you just went along with this?" Tweed could barely believe what he was hearing. The things Barnaby had done—it was as if he were hearing about a different man entirely.

"No, I didn't. At least not at first. But Lucien knew my weaknesses. Just think, he said. If we are successful, where could it lead? Imagine ten Sherlock Holmeses protecting the nation's interests? No crime would go unsolved. And why stop at ten? Why not Sherlock Holmes simulacra in every district and police station? A hundred of them, a *thousand* of them, all watching over London, over Britain.

"I argued, of course. 'What of the Queen?' I asked. 'And who is she,' demanded Lucien, 'to stand in the way of scientific progress? It is not her right. These discoveries have already been made,' he said. 'They cannot be undone. It is our duty to follow the research through to the end, to make sure it is done responsibly. Only *we* can do that. Only the Ministry has the facilities to make sure these experiments are done in a humane way. The Queen argues that doing this is against the will of God? But how could we even *make* these discoveries had not God allowed us to?' This was Lucien's argument. 'We started it,' he said. 'It is the will of God that we finish it.'"

"And that was all it took to convince you? Some petty moralizing?"

"Don't take that tone with me. I argued! Of course I did. 'What if God only allowed us to make these discoveries so we could see we were moving too fast?' I asked. 'What if we are meant to realize that discovery for the sake of discovery is not *progress*, but rather arrogance of the highest degree. That we are like children *pretending* to be God.'"

"But still you gave in," said Tweed.

"Yes." Barnaby sighed again. "The truth is, Sebastian, a part of me wanted to see if we could succeed.

"So what happened?"

"It turned out I was right to be wary. I duplicated Holmes's soul in the machine, then transplanted it into a . . . *damaged* simulacrum that had been growing for the past five years. The simulacrum itself was already thirty years old by now due to the accelerated growth."

"Damaged? How?"

"It was one of the early experiments Lucien had made. There was tissue damage to the face and body. That's why Lucien used it. He thought it expendable.

"Something went wrong. Over the months that followed it became clear that the copied soul was only partially a success. The simulacrum was still brilliant, a genius, but he was prone to fits of anger, psychotic breaks, a lack of conscience. This was a combination I could not take. A man as brilliant as Sherlock Holmes but without the conscience to stop him from turning that brilliance to evil? That was when I realized the Queen was right. We had to stop the research. We had gone too far."

"But Lucien disagreed?"

"No! He agreed. At least, so I thought. He took the simulacrum of Holmes away, to be destroyed, he said."

"But he didn't destroy it."

"No. I later found out he'd simply locked the simulacrum away in a cell. Lucien thought him far too valuable to destroy. Sebastian, he's had this corrupt copy of Sherlock Holmes under lock and key for *years*. Can you imagine how that must have felt?

"Anyway, that was the last straw. When I found that out I ran, went into hiding. I thought I'd managed to disappear, but Lucien has been using the Holmes copy to do his dirty work. He managed to track me down."

"Why?" asked Tweed. "What does he want you for?"

"Lucien had cancer. He was dying. Had barely months to live. But he wouldn't let go. He was furious when I fled. Because I had imprinted on his soul I was the only one who could save him. I was the only one who could extract his soul and put it into another body."

It all started to make sense now. That was why Barnaby was taken alive.

"So . . . what? He wants you to put his soul into a simulacrum of himself? One he's already grown?"

"No. He tried to grow his own copies, but they all developed the same cancer he was already dying from."

"So what did he want you for?"

Barnaby reached through the hole in the door and gripped Tweed's arm. "I did it for you, Sebastian. They said they would kill you if I didn't do what they said."

Tweed stared into the tired, shadowed eyes of his father. "What? What did you do?"

"Last night they blindfolded me, took me to somewhere. Sebastian, they had their own Lazarus Machine . . ." Barnaby trailed off. "The Prime Minister was there. He was unconscious."

"Barnaby . . ."

"I destroyed the Prime Minister's soul!" shouted Barnaby. "It's gone. And I put Lucien's soul into his body."

Tweed took a step back.

Everything made sense now. That was why they'd seen the Prime Minister at the Clock Tower after they'd witnessed him being kidnapped. It was part of the plan all along. Except it hadn't been the P.M. but rather Lucien now in the Prime Minister's body.

"You're telling me Lucien is now the Prime Minister of Great Britain?"

"Yes! I had to do it, Sebastian! I had no choice!" He choked back a sob. "But there's more. Lucien told me he's perfected the technique to duplicate souls. He says he has big plans for me. That I'm going to help him rule the world." Barnaby pushed his face against the gap. "Sebastian, we have to stop him!"

CHAPTER EIGHTEEN

Tweed turned away from Barnaby and gripped the railing, staring down into the deep shaft. Everything was coming together, things beginning to make a sick, twisted sense. Lucien wanted immortality, but he couldn't use his own simulacra because every time he grew one, it had the same cancer. So why not pick someone who was powerful, someone who had the position he had always wanted? Prime Minister Balfour was still relatively young. He had a long life ahead of him. By switching bodies, Lucien had extended his life by a good forty or fifty years. And after that? Well, who could know where the technology would be by then. Tweed was sure Lucien would keep at it, keep pushing ahead with the experiments.

And he was using the damaged Holmes to do his dirty work, since everything he was doing was off even the Ministry's books. It never had anything to do with Moriarty. He really was dead, just like everyone first thought.

The Babbage engineers! Of course. They had all worked for the Ministry when they were younger. They must have been responsible for building the original Lazarus Machine. Lucien then tracked them down and used them to build his own version of the machine, hidden away somewhere in London. And Holmes had been murdering them to make sure they couldn't talk.

Lucien had been following his own agenda for years now, *decades*. And that was why Barnaby was kept alive. He had been the one to imprint on Lucien's soul. Lucien needed Barnaby to effect the soul transfer. He'd done it now either because the sickness had become too advanced or because it had taken him this long to actually find Barnaby.

As Tweed stared down into the blackness there was a sudden noise. He looked up and saw the elevator swinging around, sliding back up the pole to the top level.

"Stepp?" he whispered. "Is that you?"

"Is what me?"

"The elevator just went back up to the top of the shaft."

"Nothing to do with me. I'm still trying to get the bloody door open."

"Then there's someone else here."

"Tweed," whispered Barnaby furiously. "No one comes down here except for Lucien and Holmes. You have to hide."

"I'm not going to let them take you."

"Don't be an idiot!" snapped Barnaby. "I brought you up to use your head. If you're killed we can't do anything. Hide away, then follow us. There's more chance of you rescuing me on the outside than there is in here."

He had a point. Problem was, there wasn't anywhere *to* hide. He pushed on the cell next to Barnaby's. Locked. The next one as well. And the next. He threw a quick look over his shoulder. The elevator was descending. Tweed could see a flickering blue light shining from inside the cage. That meant it was Sherlock Holmes with one of his lackeys.

Tweed moved faster. Next door. Locked. Next. Locked. The elevator was almost low enough that its occupants would be able to see the floor he was on, see him running along the walkway. He pushed the next door. Locked. The next.

Open.

The door swung slowly inward, revealing a tidy, unused cell. Tweed quickly slid the panel open so he could see out, then darted in and pushed the door nearly closed, leaving a small gap between the door and the frame.

Tweed peered through the gap, watching as the elevator stopped and Sherlock Holmes stepped off. He was accompanied by the man with the strange discs over his eyes.

"Good evening, Barnaby," said Holmes. Tweed could clearly hear his voice echoing around the vast space. "Seems to be a bit of a commotion upstairs. Fires breaking out, unauthorized intrusion into the Ministry systems and such. Lucien—sorry, I really should get used to calling him the P.M. shouldn't I?—thinks we should take the precaution of moving you tonight. Just in case it has something to do with your good self."

"Where? Where are you taking me?"

"This all works rather neatly into my own humble plans, actually," said Holmes, ignoring Barnaby's question. "I was already planning on moving you tonight. But now it's all official. The final part of the plan is ready, Barnaby. Time for you to go to work."

"What plan is this? What do you want me to do, for God's sake?"

Clever old man, thought Tweed. Barnaby was doing this for his benefit, hoping Holmes would say something that would give Tweed a clue. But the simulacrum didn't seem to be falling for it.

"You'll see soon enough," said Holmes.

"I won't. I will refuse to cooperate. You'll have to kill me first."

"I see. I have to say, I'm looking forward to testing you on that. I've found that people's convictions tend to waver a bit once they lose a few fingers. Tends to clear the mind."

Holmes took out a small rectangular card from his inside pocket. He held it against the panel to the side of Barnaby's door, then typed a number into the keypad.

Barnaby's cell door swung open. Holmes grabbed him by the arm and shoved him into the elevator.

But Tweed wasn't really paying attention to that. At the same time that Barnaby's door unlocked, the door to Tweed's cell swung closed and the locks engaged with a very solid-sounding *thunk*. Tweed stared at it in horror then frantically tried to push it open. It wouldn't budge.

Tweed backed up and stared around him at the cell. He was trapped! It must have been some sort of security measure. Before any cell door opens, all the others lock themselves down. Clever. Stopped all the prisoners from escaping at once.

But it meant Tweed was now trapped in a Ministry cell with absolutely no hope of getting out.

∞

"You're *what?*" shouted Stepp.

Octavia tried to peer over her shoulder while simultaneously dodging the Ministry steamcoach that was trying to shove her off the road. The Ministry carriage clipped the side of an automaton, sending it flying into the air to crash up against the wall of building. Octavia saw the æther cage smash open and the soul flicker and die like smoke wafting into the air.

She angrily spun her wheel, trying to knock the steamcoach off the road, but this driver wasn't as easy to get rid of as the first. He jerked his wheel to avoid Octavia's sideswipe.

"What's going on?" she shouted.

"Sherlock Holmes has taken Barnaby and Tweed's got himself locked inside a prison cell!" shouted Stepp.

Octavia's mouth dropped open in shock. How on Earth did all that happen in such a short space of time? "Can you get him out?"

"I can't access the locks. I think they might be on a different Babbage system than the rest of the security programs."

Octavia's mind raced. There was absolutely no way they were going to leave Tweed in there. They had to get him out. But how?

The Ministry cab swerved toward her, but Octavia now considered herself a master at the technique and easily swerved aside. She quickly jerked her wheel left, slamming into the steamcoach and taking the Ministry driver by surprise.

She looked forward. They were approaching a tram line that intersected their street. There were no other carriages in front of them, steam-powered or horse-drawn.

Octavia glanced left and saw one of the Ministry goons actually lean out of the passenger window and level a gun at her. Again with the shooting! Octavia snarled in anger and braked hard. The steam-coach slowed to an almost complete stop, eliciting another shout of anger from Stepp. The Ministry carriage shot ahead. Octavia released the brake, pumped the lever, and pushed the steamcoach forward again. By this time the Ministry carriage was slowing down in response.

"Hold on!" she shouted.

Then Octavia winced, prayed, and smashed right into the back of the steamcoach.

There was the terrific crash and squeal of crumpling metal. The front screen shattered completely, glass flying through the air. Octavia was thrown violently forward. She bounced painfully against the steering wheel, then back against the seat. She heard Stepp cursing her name from the back.

Octavia didn't stop. She pushed the carriage forward, still tight up against the rear of the Ministry's steamcoach. They were locked together, the collision bumpers on their carriages entwined from the crash. Octavia peered ahead. She could see a huge, steam-powered tram approaching the intersection. She pumped the lever some more, getting an extra burst of speed out of the steamcoach. The Ministry driver tried to turn, but he couldn't do anything with Octavia pushing from behind. She simply corrected in the opposite direction.

They were only about twenty feet away from the intersection now. The tram was nearly there. She had to time this perfectly . . .

"What are you doing?" shouted Stepp. "There's a tram coming!"

Octavia watched, gauged, lessened her speed a bit. Too much. A bit more power. The tram's whistle exploded, piercing the night air. A bit more speed. Nearly there . . .

Octavia nudged the front of the Ministry carriage onto the tram lines, stopping Tweed's steamcoach just beyond the lines.

The tram hit the Ministry carriage, wrenching it away from their crash bumper, sending them juddering away to the side with the force of the separation. The Ministry carriage launched into the air, spinning over and over before smashing down onto the tracks. The tram smashed into it again, shoving it along the tram lines, sparks exploding up into the night air.

A terrific screeching wail cut through the street as the tram applied its emergency brakes. More sparks sprayed out from under its metal wheels as it lurched and shuddered to a stop.

Octavia glanced over her shoulder to make sure Stepp was all right. The eleven-year-old girl stared at her with horrified admiration.

"That," she said, "was *insane*!"

Octavia gave her a shaky grin. "It was, rather, wasn't it?" She pumped the lever to see if the steam carriage was still working. It was, but it didn't sound too healthy. "Stepp, I've had a thought. Actually, wait, have you found my mother yet?"

"Not yet, no. I've been rather busy."

"Then start searching. I need to know if she's in there. Please?"

"*Fine.*"

"Thank you. Now, can you still not access the locks?"

"Afraid not."

"Then can you get inside their automata, the ones that are used for security?"

"I think so. Why?"

"I'll tell you in a moment. First we need to find Jenny and Carter."

๑๑

The couple said they would be waiting in the same alley they had used while Tweed and Octavia picked their target outside the Ministry offices. Octavia parked the steamcoach and turned to Stepp. "Still no luck?"

"None." Stepp slammed her hands down on the typing keys. "I really thought I could crack this. I have to say, I'm quite annoyed."

"I'm sure Tweed feels the same."

"Good point. So I take it you have some kind of plan?"

"Pass me those maps." Octavia pointed at the plans and maps Horatio had given them. Stepp gathered them together and passed them over.

"What do you need those for?"

"Never mind that. Now, when you hear the signal, I want you to . . . do whatever it is you do with your Ada and send the automata crazy."

"What do you mean, 'send them crazy'?"

"I mean, *send them crazy*. Make them fight each other—actually, can you do that? Probably not. Make them walk into walls then, make them knock a few Babbages over. Just make sure they're not doing the job they're meant to be doing."

"Why?"

"Because I plan on slipping inside the Ministry and rescuing that idiot Tweed."

"Um, how exactly are you going to do that?"

Octavia grinned. "With flash and style, of course. Just get ready." She opened the door and hopped out onto the road.

"How will I recognize your signal?" asked Stepp.

"Oh, you'll know. In fact, I think you better move this carriage somewhere else. A side street somewhere. Just don't leave it on this road."

Octavia jumped out of the carriage and closed the door. She checked that no one was watching, then took out her Tesla gun and walked to the alley.

"Hoi!" she called.

"Who's there?" came Carter's voice.

"Oh, look. It's the competition," said Jenny, emerging from the shadows with a grin. "How's it going?"

"Rather messy," said Octavia. "I need you to get me inside the Ministry."

"I see. And exactly how would you like us to do that?"

"Can't you use one of those little explosives you've got? Knock a hole in the wall?"

Carter joined them, holding the satchel against his chest. Octavia reached out to take it, but Jenny slapped her hand away.

"No touching. It's dangerous stuff."

"Fine! But will you do it?"

"I have to say," said Carter, "the prospect of you wandering around inside there fills me with a *vast* amount of unease. I mean, I'm talking *huge* amounts here. Jenny?"

Jenny nodded. "I tend to agree, Carter. Octavia, it really does sound as though you're about to do something incredibly crazy. Is that the case? *Are* you about to do something incredibly crazy?"

Octavia thought about it. It *was* crazy, wasn't it? Her plan— if you could call it that—was to basically walk into the Ministry complex and rescue Tweed from the prison he had stupidly got himself locked in.

"Look at me," she said. "Do I look like a crazy person? Your Sebastian Tweed is the loon. *I'm* the sensible one. Now, will you help?"

Jenny leaned forward to study Octavia's face. Then she raised an eyebrow and turned to Carter. "She has that look," she said.

"What look is that, dear?" asked Carter, grinning.

"The one I got when I broke you out of Millhouse Prison. Are you *sure* you two aren't an item?" she said to Octavia.

Octavia flushed and turned away. "Of course not. But we got into this together. We can't just leave him in there."

"Fine," said Jenny. "We'll do it. You go and wait in that alley across the road."

"I want to help."

"Helping you become a terrorist is where I draw the line," said Jenny firmly. "You go wait. We'll take care if it."

Octavia opened her mouth to protest, but by the look on Jenny's face, there would be no point. Instead, she nodded, then turned around and hurried across the empty street, slipping into an alley and watching from the shadows.

Jenny and Carter hurried up the steps in front of the Ministry complex. Surely at this time of night it would be nearly empty. Nobody should get hurt in the blast. She wanted to get inside but she didn't want to start killing people, even if they worked for the Ministry.

Jenny and Carter moved to opposite sides of the building and crouched down. There was a pause while they pushed the explosives up against the wall, then they moved toward the center, stopping on either side of the main doors. Octavia hoped they wouldn't use all of the explosives. She needed two for when she was inside. One for Tweed and one, hopefully, for her mother.

Jenny and Carter huddled together. There was a flare of light, then they moved apart and touched the Lucifer matches to the fuses.

Octavia could hear the loud hisses even from a distance, the fuses spitting sparks onto the ground and acrid smoke rising into the air. Once they had lit all the explosives, Jenny and Carter ran across the street and joined her in the little alley. They each grabbed one of her arms and hauled her straight for the back wall, where they huddled down and waited.

Octavia had never felt *anything* like what happened next, not even back at the docks when Holmes bombed the workhouse. The detonation was a solid kick to her entire body. It stunned her with its strength, the shock wave punching her in the face, vibrating through her chest and out the other side. The orange-white light blinded her, throwing stark, razor-sharp shadows across the walls. The roaring, stentorian explosion rattled the buildings and set her ears ringing in protest. The ground trembled, rumbling beneath her feet.

The next thing she knew Carter was throwing her and Jenny to the ground and she heard the crumping, crashing sound of masonry and bricks colliding, falling apart, skidding across the road.

When the sound died down she peered out from under her arm. Dust cloaked her vision. She inhaled, then coughed as the dust crawled into her lungs.

Tiny stones and fragments of building still pitter-pattered around them. Carter stood up, helping Jenny to her feet. Octavia pushed herself up, then staggered to the mouth of the alley to see the damage.

When she saw what the explosives had done, her mouth dropped open in shock. The whole front of the building was gone, an empty, smoking skeleton. Smoke and flames flicked over blackened, shattered bricks. The three floors stood exposed. She could see into empty offices, could see right along the ground floor hallway into the Ministry itself. Dust and thick, black smoke hung over everything.

It was like a scene from hell.

She gradually became aware that Stepp was speaking to her in her earpiece. "Octavia? Please don't tell me that was the signal, because if it was we're going to be in serious, serious trouble."

Octavia coughed, then fumbled in her pocket for the trigger. She pushed it. "That was the signal," she said hoarsely. "And please don't use my name. Songbird, if you please."

"Fine. Songbird. God, I can't believe you just did that. Interfering with automaton programs now."

"Good. I'll see you later."

"Hopefully."

Octavia turned to Jenny and Carter. They were staring in amazement at the destroyed building in front of them. Jenny turned to Carter and said, "That was a significantly larger explosion than I was expecting."

"You and me both." Carter took one of the small explosive packages out of the satchel and examined it. "They certainly *look* the same."

"Did you ask for our usual?"

"I did. Ethan must have got it wrong."

"Then you'd better have words with him. Actually, no, *I'll* have words with him."

Octavia took the explosive from Carter. "Thank you. And another one?"

Carter just looked at her.

"One to get Tweed out, and a second to get my mother out."

Carter glanced at Jenny. She nodded slightly, and Carter sighed and pulled another explosive out his satchel. He handed it to her, then gave her two fuses.

"Just . . . be careful," said Jenny. "You saw how powerful they are."

"I will," said Octavia. "Stepp's in the steamcoach. You need to go drive her around, otherwise the Ministry will catch her. Tweed and I will see you later."

Octavia sprinted across the street. By this time, those who'd heard the blast were starting to gather outside the building, staring up at the gutted wreckage. Octavia slipped between them, trying to look like just another nosy Londoner.

Octavia clambered over the rubble, making her way up the steps. She put her hands to the bricks, then snatched them back. They were burning hot. But she managed to blacken her hands, and she rubbed it over her clothes and face, making it look as though she was caught up in the explosion.

She stepped over shards of glass. It was everywhere, crunching underfoot. There was movement up ahead. Someone was coming. Octavia stooped over, staggering forward, sobbing.

"Help me! I was just going home! I was nearly caught in the blast!"

The man, a thin, cadaverous fellow in a black suit stared over her shoulder in horror.

"What happened?"

"I don't know! It was just a noise. Everything went black. I . . . I think I'm bleeding!"

"Just stay here." He hurried past her to check the damage to the front of the building. Others were appearing, emerging from offices deeper within the building.

Octavia stepped through the confusion and the panic, realizing as she did so that her disguise to get into the Ministry was going to prove a liability once she was actually inside. The blackened face would most certainly not fit in. So the first thing she had to do was find a bathroom to clean herself up. She had checked the maps—still had them with her, actually—so she knew that after she'd cleaned up she would need to head straight for the elevators that she knew were at the other end of this long corridor.

CHAPTER NINETEEN

O ctavia had another quick look at the map while the elevator was descending. She still had to get across to the other side of the complex and into the elevator that would take her down to the prison level.

She pushed the transmitter button. "You still with me, Stepp?"

"Still here, crazy lady."

"How's it gong up there?"

"The police have arrived. Ministry goons are trying to chase them away. Obviously don't want people sniffing around their secret lair."

Good. More confusion as the Ministry tried to deal with the police meant more time for her. "Are Jenny and Carter with you?"

"Yup. Jenny's driving. Jenny's a *good* driver."

"Excuse me? I'm an excellent driver."

"Sorry, what I meant to say was, Jenny's a *safe* driver."

The elevator slid open and Octavia stepped out into a large, open office area. It was chaos. People were running frantically in every direction, speaking urgently to each other, passing on orders, shouting questions. Automata wandered aimlessly around, bumping into Babbages, walls, and each other. One appeared to be trying to walk up a wall.

No one paid the slightest bit of attention to her as she crossed the space and moved into the next large room. The same thing was happening there. Technicians had the chest panels open on some of the automata, pulling out punchcards, trying to see where the problem lay.

Octavia kept moving until she came to the room with the elevators. She hurried across the floor and slipped inside the first one she came to. She looked at the wall panel filled with numbers.

"Stepp, I'm in the elevator."

"Give me a second. Right. Push 22."

Octavia pushed the button. The elevator shuddered and started to move. Octavia breathed a sigh of relief. She'd been worried it wouldn't work at all, with all the chaos going on.

She'd been on the move for about twenty-five minutes now, making her way through the labyrinthine complex. Despite the confusion, she kept expecting someone to demand her identification or sound the alarm. She felt exhausted. Although, admittedly, it hadn't exactly been a quiet couple of days.

"Hey, Stepp. Any progress on my mother?"

"Still searching through the records."

The elevator doors slid open onto a black, metal corridor. Octavia waited, listening intently. She couldn't hear a thing; it was utterly silent. She found that incredibly unnerving after the chaos upstairs.

She crept forward, moving along the passage until she came to a second corridor that intersected hers. She turned right, then kept walking until she arrived at an open door.

Octavia peered inside. The room beyond was huge, a cavernous space where even her breathing seemed to echo. She stepped hesitantly forward, moving onto a walkway that circled a massive shaft in the ground. She walked quietly forward and leaned over the railing, staring down at the hundreds of prison cells below her. The scale was just . . . enormous.

"Stepp," she whispered. "I'm here. What do I do?"

"You should see a cage of some sort. An elevator. Get in."

About ten paces to her left was the cage Stepp was talking about. It was attached by a metal arm to a pillar that disappeared down into the shaft.

Octavia climbed in and pulled the gate shut. The cage twirled around and dropped, moving smoothly until it came to a stop about ten floors down. There was an open door in front of her. Octavia stepped out and looked inside. It had been in recent use, the bed-clothes scattered on the floor. This must have been where Barnaby was held. Which meant Tweed had to be close. She moved to the right, peering inside the other cells. After looking inside fifteen with no luck, she retraced her steps and checked the cells to the left.

The surge of relief she felt when she glimpsed Tweed pacing back and forth in the cramped confines of the cell was surprising even to her.

But it wasn't as surprising as the look of happiness on Tweed's face when he saw her staring through the viewing hole.

"Songbird!" he exclaimed. "How . . . ?" He rushed forward, trying to peer out the door to either side. "How did you get here? Did you see Barnaby? What's happening? I've got myself locked in," he finished lamely. "A bit silly, really."

"A bit silly?" said Octavia. "Rather stupid, if you ask me."

Tweed quickly straightened up. "Lucky I wasn't asking you then," he said. "Has Stepp figured out these locks yet?"

"No."

"So how do I get out?"

Octavia held up the two packages of explosives. "Bang."

Tweed's eyes widened. "You're joking with me, yes? You'll kill me!"

"It's a risk I'm willing to take," said Octavia. "Seriously, there's no other choice. And I'm hoping the explosion will direct itself outward."

"Hoping?"

"Just give me a minute. Stepp? Any progress on locating my mother?"

"Uh . . . yes and no."

Octavia turned away. "What do you mean?" she asked, feeling dread flowing through her system. She was suddenly unsure if she wanted to know the answer.

"Well, the thing is, she *was* here. You were right. But for some reason she was moved about three weeks ago."

Three weeks ago? Octavia stared into the distance, her eyes filling with tears. Her mother had still been alive three weeks ago. She had been right all along!

"Where was she taken?"

"Not sure. It's all official though. Proper requisitions, proper transfer papers. Doesn't say where she went, though."

Right. Concentrate, Octavia. That can be dealt with later. "Stepp, copy everything down concerning my mother. Her files, the names of the people who signed the transfer papers, *everything*."

"Got it."

Octavia took a deep, shaky breath, then turned and fixed Tweed with a brilliant, happy smile. "She's alive. My mother. They moved her from here three weeks ago. I *told* you, Tweed. I always knew . . ."

Tweed smiled at her. A proper, genuine smile. Not one of his usual half-grins.

"Good work, Songbird. I'm happy for you. Really, I am. Now. About those explosives you want to apply to this door? Are you sure it's a good idea?"

Octavia snapped out of it. "Of course it is. Stop being a baby." She studied the door, then the wall to either side of it. "Actually, I think it would be better to attach them to the wall. Stone is weaker than steel, yes?"

"So I'm told."

"Good. You'd better stand back a bit."

Tweed moved to the rear of the cell, pulling the bed and mattress over onto their sides and crouching down behind them. Octavia attached one package at head height. She was about to put the second one lower down when she hesitated, thinking of the damage that was done to the front of the Ministry building.

She shook her head and put the second package back into her satchel. She stuck a fuse into the soft material of the bomb she'd set and struck a match.

"Ready?"

"Do it."

Octavia lit the fuse, then sprinted along the walkway.

A few seconds later the package detonated. Octavia thought the explosion outside was big, but because this one was in an enclosed space, it *felt* much larger. The roar and clap of the explosion deafened her. Even with her hands over her ears, it was so loud that she staggered back in a daze. She actually felt the concussive wave as it bounced back and forth in the shaft, deep throbbing pulses that traveled right through her body.

Fragments of rock spun through the air into the shaft, tumbling down into the darkness. One massive chunk ripped straight through the safety railings, yanking the whole length out of the walkway and sending it crashing to the prison floor.

When it was over, Octavia straightened up, staring at the smoking hole in horror. What would have happened if she'd used *both* explosives? Tweed would be nothing more than a smear on the walls.

That's if he wasn't already.

Then she heard coughing from inside the cell, and a moment later Tweed clambered unsteadily through the hole, waving the smoke and dust away from his face. There were trickles of blood at his ears and nose. He looked around, then almost walked straight off the edge of the walkway, only catching himself at the last minute and turning to face her.

Octavia hurried over to him.

"THAT WAS LOUD!" he shouted.

Octavia winced. "Keep it down."

"WHAT?"

"I said, *no need to*—" she began, then waved her hands in the air dismissively. "NEVER MIND!"

He grinned and gave her a thumbs-up.

Octavia had a worrying feeling she may have given him a concussion. She really hoped she hadn't. He was bad enough as it was.

❦

There was so much confusion going on around them, it was simplicity itself to slip out of the Ministry. They took the same route Tweed had used to enter, preferring to stay away from the front of the building, and forty minutes after Octavia had blown up his cell they were standing in the alley waiting for Jenny to come pick them up, the prone form of Maximilian still lying where they'd left him, snoring and snorting next to the tracks.

"How are the ears?" asked Octavia.

"Getting better," said Tweed. Still loudly, but at least he wasn't shouting.

"We need to decide what to do next," she said. As they were hurrying through the complex, Tweed had recounted everything Barnaby told him. Frankly, it sounded like something out of an H. G. Wells novel, not something that was happening in the real world. "It's not as if we can go to the police with this. Who's going to believe a story like that?"

"I've been thinking about that," said Tweed. "Whatever plan Holmes and Lucien have, they have to put it into action soon. The state banquet is tomorrow. That means all their pieces have to be in place before then."

Octavia nodded. "True. But then why didn't they have their pieces in place ages ago?"

"I think Lucien wanted to. But they had to wait until they could get Barnaby, remember? I suggest we go to Downing Street and wait for Lucien to make his move. He might lead us to my dad."

"And if he doesn't?"

Tweed hesitated. "I have no idea. We'll cross that bridge when we come to it."

At that moment the steamcoach limped around the corner and dragged itself toward them.

Tweed's eyes widened in horror. "What have you done to her?"

"Ah. Yes. She's been in a few scrapes today. Ministry goons chased us in their own steamcoaches. We . . . may have bumped into a few."

Tweed walked slowly around the carriage, staring mournfully at the dents and scrapes.

"Sorry," said Octavia.

The front door flew open and Jenny jumped out, yanking Tweed into a tight hug. Then she pushed him back and slapped him in the face. After which she pulled him in for another hug.

"Don't you ever do that to me again!" she snapped. "And I'm so glad you're safe," she said in the same tone of voice.

Tweed stared at her with wide eyes and rubbed his cheek. Octavia snorted with laughter. Carter hopped out the back and clapped Tweed on the back.

"So, you saw him? Your old man?"

"Alive and as annoying as ever."

"That's good. I think we should all head home for the night. Lie low till some of this panic has died down, yes? The city is going to be crawling with Ministry goons trying to find out who attacked their home base."

Tweed glanced at Octavia. "Good idea."

Octavia raised an eyebrow slightly, but said nothing. What was he playing at? Why didn't he want them to know they were going to watch Downing Street?

"Come on," said Carter. "Let's get out of here."

Octavia climbed into the front seat next to Tweed. She didn't say anything as he took the carriage out into the night and wended through the backstreets until he arrived at Stepp's house.

He helped the girl carry her equipment inside and stood talking to her at her front door. Octavia watched as he awkwardly patted her on the head.

In reply, Stepp punched him in the stomach. Octavia grinned, watching as Tweed limped back to the carriage.

"What was all that about?"

"Nothing. She just didn't like being patted on the head."

Next, they drove Jenny and Carter back home. The couple hopped out of the coach, but when Tweed and Octavia didn't join them, Jenny leaned over the door. "What are you waiting for?"

"I'm heading home tonight, Jenny. Need familiar surroundings while I think what to do next."

Jenny set her mouth in a firm line. "I don't think so, sonny. There's no way we're splitting up again."

"Jenny—"

"Uh-uh. No way."

Octavia repressed a sigh. She was going to have to do this, wasn't she? It was the only way Jenny was going to let them get away.

Octavia leaned toward Jenny, resting a hand—just! It barely touched the material of his trousers—on Tweed's knee.

She felt Tweed's reflex reaction to jerk away and had no choice but to dig her fingers in. Hard.

"Jenny, Tweed and I . . . we have some stuff we need to talk about."

That wasn't a lie, was it? They *did* have stuff to talk about. She was surprised to realize she felt quite horrid misleading Jenny. She actually liked the woman.

Jenny saw Octavia's hand and grinned, her eyes lighting up. "Oh. Er . . . Fine. I suppose. We'll see you tomorrow. Bright and early, yes?"

Tweed was barely moving. He swallowed nervously and nodded. Jenny banged the steamcoach door with her hand and hopped up the stairs to join Carter, threading her arm through his.

Octavia realized she still had her hand on Tweed's knee and jerked it away as if it were on fire. She stared straight ahead through the shattered window. "We'll never talk of that again. Agreed?"

"Agre—" Tweed started to say, but his voice caught in his throat, coming out in a high, squeaky pitch. He cleared his throat. "Agreed," he said, moving the steamcoach quickly out into the road.

"Now, what's going on?" Octavia asked. "You don't think we could use their help?"

Tweed shook his head firmly. "No. I put them at too much risk tonight, Songbird. I underestimated how this would unfold. You and Stepp nearly got killed. You were shot at, chased through the streets . . ." His fingers turned white as he gripped the steering wheel. "If anything happened to those people, I'd never be able to forgive myself. I'd rather we did this alone."

Octavia was silent for a while. "You didn't force them to do anything. It was their choice. They *wanted* to help you. To help Barnaby."

"And what if Jenny had been killed? Or Carter? You've seen them together. I don't think they could live without each other."

"Of course they could," Octavia scoffed. "But I see your point." Imagining Jenny cradling the body of Carter in her arms—or vice versa—sent chills of horror through Octavia. Maybe Tweed was right. They were endangering too many people. Not to mention Stepp, an eleven-year-old girl.

"So we're going it alone?"

"We are."

Tweed headed toward Whitehall once again. He turned onto Richmond Terrace, a road almost directly opposite Downing Street. He parked the car far along the lane, so they could keep an eye on Number 10 without being seen by anyone passing by.

"Now we wait," said Tweed sleepily. "You take the first shift, I'll take the second."

Octavia opened her mouth to say that she'd had just as difficult an evening as he had, but she saw the glint of his eyes as he watched her through half-closed lids, the ever-so-slight tug at the side of his mouth.

She snapped her mouth shut and faced forward. She wouldn't give him the satisfaction.

∞

About an hour after midnight, Octavia shot up in her seat (where she had her feet up on the empty window frame, shivering in her jacket) and slapped Tweed on the head.

"Wake up!"

"Husah? Wha . . . ?" Tweed struggled upright, swatting invisible insects from the air.

"A steamcoach just pulled up."

Tweed yawned and leaned forward, squinting into the night. "How long was I asleep?"

"About three hours."

"Three . . . ? Why didn't you wake me?" he asked in surprise.

Octavia shrugged. "Wasn't tired. Thought one of us might as well get some rest. Look, he's coming out."

The Prime Minister exited 10 Downing Street and hurried to the carriage. "Look at the way he walks," said Octavia.

"Off balance," said Tweed. "Used to walking with a cane."

Lucien climbed into the carriage, and it chugged off along King Street in a cloud of steam. Tweed pumped the lever and released the brake, pulling out of the side road and onto Parliament Street. Octavia glanced over the divide, keeping an eye on Lucien's carriage. Tweed kept their pace slow, allowing Lucien to get far enough ahead so that when the two roads merged into one they would be far enough behind that they wouldn't be noticed.

The carriage headed east through the sparse traffic, heading along the Strand, then onto Fleet Street, past Newgate Prison and into Smithfield.

Tweed let Lucien take a longer lead now, as they headed through narrower roads, taking back lanes and muddy alleys. There were hardly any carriages around at all now.

"What a disgusting place," Octavia murmured.

"I live around here," said Tweed cheerfully.

Octavia closed her eyes and shook her head slightly, silently swearing at herself. *Well done, girl.* "Sorry."

Octavia wracked her brain for something else to say that wasn't patronizing or insulting, but she knew she'd mess it up, so she just left it.

Lucien's carriage pulled to a stop outside a rundown, two-story house. Most of the windows along the street were dark. In fact, the entire street was dark. No street lamps here. No Tesla power. Here and there she could make out the soft glow of candles in some of the houses, but that was it.

Tweed stopped his steamcoach before turning onto the street. They watched as Lucien climbed out of the coach and hurried into the building. After a few moments a light bloomed in one of the upper windows as a candle was lit. They saw Lucien appear as he pulled a tatty curtain closed.

Tweed climbed into the back of the carriage and fished out one of his spiders. He frowned and looked out the window.

"What's wrong?"

"I'm going to have to take it in. I don't know the layout of the building well enough to send it up using the viewing screen. You get the transceiver warmed up. I'll be right back."

Before Octavia could say anything, Tweed slipped out into the night and closed the door firmly behind him. She saw him sprinting across the road, heading straight for the house.

CHAPTER TWENTY

T weed paused at the front door to the tenement and listened. He couldn't hear anything so he pushed it slowly open and slipped inside, finding himself on a dark landing. There was a door to his right and a set of stained concrete stairs to his left.

The building had an unused, empty feeling to it. That made sense. Lucien wouldn't want anyone else around when he was having secret meetings.

He sprinted up to the next floor. A single, guttering candle had been placed on the floor outside one of the rooms, casting flickering shadows across the walls and ceiling. Judging by its position it was the room Lucien was in.

Tweed moved to the door of the adjacent room, staying close to the wall so he wouldn't creak any of the floorboards.

The door was unlocked. Tweed pushed it open just enough so he could squeeze inside. Dim light filtered into the room from outside the dirty windows. The room was empty, its contents long since scavenged.

Tweed entered the bedroom, leaving clear footprints in the dust that coated everything. He moved to the wall that adjoined Lucien's room. He was hoping to find a hole or something he could slip the spider through.

It turned out he didn't need to. The walls were thin, rotting. He could hear their words almost as if he were in the same room.

"I do wish you'd stop looking at me like that. It's most disconcerting."

"I apologize," said a second voice. An accented voice. "It is just . . . we have talked about this for years, but I still find it hard to believe it is you."

Octavia whispered in Tweed's ear, "That accent is Russian."

Tweed jerked around, then swallowed nervously, trying to force his hammering heart to calm down. "What are you doing here?" he whispered.

"There was no image on the transceiver. I came to see if you needed rescuing again."

Tweed ignored that. But Octavia was right about the voice. It was definitely Russian.

"Do you have it?" asked Lucien.

"Of course."

There was a pause, then Lucien continued, "And it's definitely real? The Ministry has ways of checking for forgeries."

"It is real. We have had *Herr* Klein in custody for years. He was the leader of a German anarchist group that was trying to cause trouble back in Russia. Just make sure your man flees along St. James's Street. The authorities will find Klein lying in the road with a fresh bullet hole in his head . . . a disagreement among comrades."

"Who do you have doing it?" asked Lucien. "He is trustworthy?"

"Of course. The head of my secret police. He has been with me for over a decade. Speaking of which. Your man, he is careful, yes? I am seated next to the Queen. I do not wish to be shot by mistake."

"Don't worry about that," said Lucien. "The shooter is one of the best. A man called Moran. He won't miss."

Octavia and Tweed looked at each other in shock. The Queen? They were talking about shooting Queen Victoria!

"What will you do with the passport?" asked the Russian.

"I will feed it to the authorities. It would look suspicious if it was just found on Klein's body. No one would believe an assassin was carrying his own passport with him while murdering the Queen. Better it turns up a day or so later."

"*Da.*"

There was the sound of hands clapping. "Then we are done!" said Lucien. "By this time tomorrow the Queen will be dead and Germany will be blamed. How does it feel, Nicholas? Knowing that all our planning is finally coming to fruition?"

"I feel relief, Lucien. Relief that I do not have to keep pumping money into your research. You have nearly bankrupted me."

"It will all be worth it. You know that."

Nicholas? Tweed sat back on his haunches. Nicholas II, the Tsar of Russia? The way he was talking about his secret police, about how he was sitting next to the Queen at the banquet . . . It had to be him.

The Tsar of Russia, plotting with Lucien to assassinate Queen Victoria. Tweed had gotten it wrong. So very, very wrong. All along he'd been thinking the *Tsar* was the target, but he wasn't. It was the *Queen*.

Tweed nudged Octavia, gesturing for her to follow him. He carefully moved through the rooms, out into the hall, and down the stairs into the street.

"What are we doing?" asked Octavia.

"Heading back to Meriweather's house. Barnaby said Lucien used the engineers to build their Lazarus Machine, then killed them so they couldn't talk. Meriweather's the only one left alive who knows where the machine is—where *Barnaby* is! We have to find him."

ᴘ ᴏ

Forty minutes later Tweed and Octavia stood in the dark landing of Meriweather's house. Tweed found a candleholder on the entrance hall table—a precaution for when the Tesla Towers stopped working—and put a Lucifer to the wick.

"Bedroom first, I think."

They climbed the stairs and entered Meriweather's bedroom. It was exactly as Octavia had described it: empty of anything that indicated it had ever been used. Nevertheless, they started their search. Tweed opened the bedside cabinet and peered inside. All it contained was a Bible. He riffled the pages, but there was nothing inside. The cabinet on the other side was empty.

He checked under the bed but there was nothing there. Tweed ran a hand over the floor. Not even dust. That made him wonder. Was there a way to track down his housekeeper? Perhaps she knew something.

He dismissed this thought. No time.

"Here. Give me a hand," said Tweed, indicating the mattress.

They both heaved the heavy mattress up, but there was nothing beneath it.

The drawers and cupboard were likewise empty.

"I told you," said Octavia. "It's like no one has ever lived here."

"Let's check the office."

Tweed sat down at the desk in the office, placing the candleholder in the center so he could see what he was doing. He opened each drawer, but all of them were empty. He glanced up at Octavia, who was busy searching the writing desk on the other side of the room.

"Anything?" he asked.

"Nothing. A few used pen nibs. An empty ink pot."

Tweed sighed and got to his feet. Every filing cabinet had been cleared out. The man really had done a thorough job. He turned back to the desk and started pulling the drawers out, placing them in a pile on the floor. Once he'd finished he picked up the candle, got down onto this knees, and peered into the enclosed space where the drawers were housed. Hope flared slightly. There were items there, items that had been pushed out of overfull drawers and fallen down the back. There was some blank paper, a few envelopes, but nothing that could help him. He checked the other side. More of the same, including a full pad of cream-colored writing paper. Of good quality, but no help to him.

He was about to toss it back when something caught his eye. At the top of the pad was a name and a logo. He held it to the candle.

"The Savoy," followed by the address of the hotel. Tweed quickly checked the paper from the left side of the desk. It was older, but it also had the name and address of the Savoy at the top.

Meriweather had obviously been to the hotel a few times in the past and had stolen the stationary. Could this be where he'd gone? To his favorite hotel?

He showed it to Octavia. "It's possible," she said, "and we don't have any other options anyway, do we?"

øq

Octavia looked a bit of a mess. Most of her clothes were black from the smoke at the Ministry, and there were scratches on her cheeks and forehead from broken glass. But Tweed, well, he reckoned he looked pretty good actually. He'd wiped the blood away from his ears and nose, he had his long charcoal jacket on again, and he was feeling like himself once more.

But he didn't look rich. Which meant they couldn't just walk into the Savoy as if they belonged. They needed a plan.

"I just saw you get run over by a steam carriage," said Tweed as they hurried along the Strand.

"No. How does that help us find out if Meriweather's there?"

"You can faint and I'll check their books."

"And you think Meriweather will have used his real name? Not too smart."

"He's not smart, is he? Otherwise he wouldn't be involved in all this."

"He's a Babbage engineer. A programmer. He's *very* smart. How about this? I found you wandering outside the hotel in a daze and the only words you will say are a description of Meriweather. Otherwise you're a dumb mute."

"No one would believe that."

"No, you're right," said Octavia thoughtfully. "The mute thing? Don't think you'd be able to pull it off."

"Actually, I was referring to the dumb part. Why don't we just go with my original idea."

"Which was?"

"To bribe the desk clerk."

"Because we don't have any money. At least, I don't. Do you?"

"Not enough," said Tweed.

By this time they had arrived at the hotel. Wide, well-swept stairs led up to polished glass doors. The inside was brightly lit, tasteful chairs and small tables placed elegantly around the cavernous lobby.

Tweed dashed up the stairs and swept past the sleepy-looking doorman—it was just after five in the morning, after all—striding purposefully to the front desk. He flashed his leather wallet at the startled clerk. "Henry Meriweather. Where is he?"

"W-what? I'm sorry?"

Tweed slammed his hand on the wood. "Don't waste my time or I'll have you down to the Yard quicker than you can say large and lonely cellmate. This woman," he said, indicating Octavia, who was just approaching, "this poor, defenseless woman. Have you no pity?" asked Tweed. "Have you no *shame*?"

"Wha . . . ? I don't understand," the clerk almost wailed. "What's happening?"

"One of your guests, a Mister Henry Meriweather, agreed to a deal whereby Miss . . ." Tweed turned to face Octavia as if searching for her name. He winked. "Miss Jade Aurora would be paid for services rend—"

"Actually, the truth is, he's my father," interrupted Octavia, sweeping forward and elbowing Tweed out of the way. "He's a scoundrel and a cad and he recently ran out on my mother, myself, and my sisters—my *five* sisters, two of whom have whooping cough— to depart these shores with his mistress, a villainous gold digger. I simply want to try to convince him to stay, to face up to his responsibilities. And if . . . if he still wishes to go, why, then I simply hope to say goodbye to my father."

Tweed stared at Octavia, admiring her performance. She even managed to squeeze out a tear! Magnificent.

It would never work, though—

Tweed turned to the clerk to find tears running down his cheeks. He leaned forward and grabbed Octavia's hands. "Oh, Miss. What a sad story. Of course I will help! Just let me know what I can do."

"I merely wish to know his room number, so that I may have my last words with him."

The clerk nodded and sniffed. "And you said his name was?"

"Henry Meriweather. But he won't be using that name for fear of my mother. She does have a terrible temper."

"Can you describe him to me, then?"

Octavia opened her mouth, then she froze. Tweed tried to hide his smile. She was just realizing they had never seen Meriweather before. She didn't know what he looked like.

Tweed let her stew for a few seconds, then stepped in. "Can't you see the woman is distraught! Asking her questions and things of that sort! You know women's brains overheat if they have to think too much! For *shame*. Her father is quite rotund, bald on top, a round face, very small eyes, and a small tuft of ginger hair around his strangely small ears. Now, do you have anyone fitting that description staying here?"

The clerk frowned. "I . . . I think so, yes. That sounds like Mr. Almore."

"What room!" demanded Tweed, slamming his hand down on the desk again.

"Uh . . . room 306."

"Oh, thank you so much," said Octavia, patting the clerk's hand then turning to the elevator. Tweed frowned at the clerk, then pointed to his own eyes, then at the clerk in an "I'm watching you" gesture.

He caught up with Octavia as the elevator arrived. They stepped inside.

"That went well," he said as the doors slid shut.

"Jade Aurora?" said Octavia.

"Quite catchy, I think."

"And am I right in guessing that you were about to call me a prostitute who had entered into a deal with Meriweather?"

Tweed looked shocked. "Perish the thought, Songbird. I would never do that. I respect you too much. As a person. As a *woman*."

Octavia frowned, then squinted at Tweed. "Sebastian Tweed, I do believe you are loosening up a bit. Perhaps that explosion at the prison rattled some sense into that tiny brain of yours."

"Hah. Not likely."

"No," Octavia mused. "Probably not. How did you know what Meriweather looked like?"

"Sound deduction."

Octavia was silent for a while. "A picture of him on the Babbage computer back at the business register?"

"Possibly," said Tweed, with bad grace.

The doors slid open and they hurried along the richly carpeted hallway and stopped before number 306. Tweed glanced at Octavia.

"Ready?"

She nodded. "Ready."

"Then let's finish this up. I really need some sleep."

Tweed banged loudly on the door and leaned down to shout through the keyhole, "Fire! Fire!"

Octavia nudged him. "Not so loud. You'll have everyone up."

Tweed lowered his voice to a barely audible whisper. "Fire. Fire."

"Ha-hah. Very funny," said Octavia, knocking rapidly on the door.

It was eventually opened by a confused and half-asleep Henry Meriweather. Tweed didn't even give him time to register their presence. He shoved the man back, pushing him into the room. Henry stumbled and fell onto his backside. Octavia closed the door behind them and Tweed pointed an accusing finger at the frightened man.

"There is one thing I want to know from you, and one thing only: Where did you build the new Lazarus Machine for Lucien?"

Meriweather's eyes widened. He tried to backpedal away, but Tweed bent down and grabbed him by the pajama top.

"We're not here to harm you. At least, not if you tell me where it is."

"I . . . I don't know what you're talking about!"

"You do realize what they are using it for, don't you?" asked Octavia.

Meriweather glanced over Tweed's shoulder at Octavia.

"They're hatching a plot against the Empire. Against the *Queen*. You don't want to be remembered as a traitor to the Crown, do you, Mr. Meriweather?"

He shook his head.

"Then tell us where it is. We want to stop them. We'll keep you out of it, I assure you."

"You're the only one left," said Tweed. "All your old friends. All your old business partners—dead. Lucien and his goons are picking you off one by one."

"Don't you think I know that? Why do you think I'm hiding here?"

Tweed looked around. "You could have picked a less conspicuous hotel."

"I like my comfort," said Meriweather defensively.

Tweed prodded him in the belly. "I can see that. Now come on. Tell us. Right now we're your only hope. If we stop this you won't be chased anymore. You can return to your old life."

"What can *you* do?" scoffed Meriweather. "You're just children."

"Is that right?" said Tweed softly. "Mr. Meriweather, if we—*mere children*—managed to find you, how long do you think it will be before Lucien does as well?"

Meriweather's face paled. His eyes flicked between Tweed and Octavia. "All right! Fine," he said, pushing himself up from the floor and sitting on the bed. "The machine is below the new Clock Tower."

Tweed and Octavia shared a confused look.

"Below the Clock Tower?" asked Tweed. "Why there?"

"The Lazarus Machine requires a lot of power. I mean, a *lot*. It had to be somewhere no one would notice. It was Lucien who put forward the plans for the new Clock Tower, you see, and Lucien who approved the designs. He's been planning this for years. The power the new clock draws will cover any uses of the machine."

"How do we access it?"

"Years ago, the Ministry—well, Lucien—had a tunnel built beneath the river, leading from Westminster to the opposite side of the Thames. He said it was for security. In case they were ever attacked and needed to evacuate the government. That's how he got it approved."

"That's . . . very long-term thinking," said Octavia.

"Isn't it just?" Meriweather replied. "Lucien owns a shipping company on the opposite bank called Sherrinford Industrial, just before the Charing Cross Bridge. That's where the tunnel comes out."

Tweed glanced at Octavia and raised his eyebrows questioningly.

"Let's go," she said.

CHAPTER TWENTY-ONE

Octavia and Tweed drove across Westminster Bridge in the early morning chill, heading toward the docks and salvage yards along the south side of the Thames. They stared up at the new Clock Tower as they passed, a dark, ominous shadow against the grey sky. The rain started to fall. Not just a drizzle, but a heavy, monotonous downpour that soon had them both soaking wet as the water blew in through the broken windows.

"This is pleasant," said Octavia.

Tweed turned to her and grinned. He wore small goggles to keep the rain from his eyes, but she could still see the manic glint in his gaze.

"Cheer up, Songbird! It's the endgame. We've nearly got him."

Octavia said nothing, instead turning to watch the rain falling into the river. It was all right for him. Despite the obvious danger, there was every chance they were about to rescue his father. But her mother was still missing, and Octavia still had no idea where she was.

Tweed must have realized what she was thinking.

"We've got her records now," he said, "everything they have on her, including who moved her from the prison. We'll find her, Songbird. Don't start getting all emotional on me. You're always telling me to stop living up here." He tapped his head. "But the same goes for you. You have to stop living every moment in here." He tapped his chest. "Use your head for once. She's alive. You *know* that. They're moving her around. That's good. It means there should be a trail. We'll get her back, Songbird. I promise."

Octavia thought about what he'd said. He was right, in a way. She spent all her time chastising him for living in his head, making all his decisions based on reason and logic. But she was the opposite, letting emotions do her thinking for her. Surely there had to be a middle ground.

Tweed steered off the bridge and turned left onto Belvedere Road. The street was pitted, filled with holes from the heavy carriage and steam engines that carried equipment and supplies to the wharves. They passed a number of timber yards, the high-pitched sawing and screaming of woodcutting slicing through Octavia's brain. How could anyone work in those places? It would drive her insane.

After the timber yards was the Government India Store depot, then just a short distance later they came within sight of the Charing Cross footbridge. Tweed slowed and then stopped his steamcoach.

They were silent for a while, staring out the window at the bridge. The metal of the structure glinted dully in the rain.

"Guess we should start walking from here?" said Tweed.

They climbed out. Tweed checked his Tesla gun and Octavia quickly did the same. Her stomach twisted in fear. She looked at Tweed, but he didn't seem frightened at all. Which was insane, surely. They were about to enter an underground tunnel that would lead them directly into the clutches of people who wanted to kill them. He *had* to be scared. He was just good at hiding it.

Octavia couldn't help feeling they were getting caught up in the flow of all this, like pieces of driftwood trapped in the currents, swept along with no way of controlling the outcome. Maybe they should take a step back to think about what they were doing and decide if it was the right course of action.

But one look at Tweed's face made Octavia realize there would be no talking him out of this. He would go in with or without her.

Which meant she *had* to go in as well, to back him up. If something happened to Tweed because she was too frightened to see this through to the end, she'd never forgive herself.

They walked along the embankment until they arrived at Sherrinford Industrial, a decrepit yard fenced off with old, moldering wood.

A locked metal gate barred their way. Octavia peered through the gaps in the fence. A messy yard lay beyond. In one corner was a pile of old, green and brown-stained anchors, covered with dried-out barnacle shells. Iron pilings and girders lay scattered everywhere, rust eating flaking holes in the metal and staining the puddles brown. At the far end of the enclosure, built up against the embankment, was a large warehouse with wide double doors.

The gate was padlocked, but it was a matter of moments for Tweed and Octavia to climb over, landing with a muddy splash on the other side. Octavia looked warily around, but the yard seemed deserted.

There were two deep ruts in the ground. Octavia and Tweed followed them to the warehouse, where they found a smaller door built into the wall. Octavia tried the handle but it was locked. She put her shoulder against the wood and hit up against it. It didn't budge.

"Give me a hand here," she said.

Tweed came to stand next to her, and they both raised their feet and kicked at the door. The lock splintered, the door shifting slightly. They kicked again, and the lock broke apart, the door banging open to reveal the inside of the structure.

A stained concrete floor stretched into the dim shadows. Holes in the roof allowed in the dismal grey light and rain, the steady *drip drip* echoing around the warehouse. Against the left wall lay piles of massive, rusted chains, the links almost as long as Octavia's leg. The center of the floor was clear, while the broken wood from smashed-up crates was stacked up against the right side.

They walked in and looked around. They checked the rear wall facing the river, but it was just a thin barrier riddled with holes, allowing them to look directly onto the rain-churned river.

Octavia and Tweed split up, walking along opposite sides of

the warehouse as they looked for the tunnel Meriweather had told them about. It would have to be big—massive, really—to get all the machinery through. How big was this Lazarus Machine anyway? She had no idea. They really should have asked.

The only logical place for a tunnel of any size was in the floor. Octavia moved to the center of the warehouse, checking the floor for any gaps or cracks. She glanced at Tweed and saw him doing the same thing.

About twenty yards in from the wall she saw a line in the ground. A deep groove that was filled with muddy water and dirt. She poked her finger in and wiggled it about. She followed the course of the groove with her eyes. It went around the floor in a large circle.

"You see this?" she called to Tweed.

Tweed was already moving toward the walls, heading for the pile of old crates. He disappeared behind them.

"Step back," he called a moment later.

Octavia quickly jumped back out of the circle. As she did so there was a loud grinding sound. There was a puff of air, and muddy water jerked into the air. Then the circle dropped into the floor.

Octavia hurried forward. The huge circle of stone dropped just below floor level, then slid along underneath the floor until it disappeared from view.

A gentle ramp led down from the warehouse floor into the tunnel, easily a hundred yards wide.

Tweed appeared at her shoulder and took out his Tesla gun. Octavia reluctantly did the same as she said, "Tweed, I really wonder if this is the right thing to do."

"Of course it is. We can't go to the police. They'll either arrest us or lock us in Bedlam. And we can't just do *nothing*. The Queen's life is in our hands, Octavia. We're the only ones who know what's going on. That means it's our responsibility to see this through."

Octavia sighed. He was right. "Fine. Let's go."

They descended into the tunnel. A continuous strip of small lights had been attached to the wall, not bright enough to illuminate everything, but bright enough that they could see where their feet were going. The lights stretched far ahead, appearing to come together at a point in the far distance.

"Long walk ahead," said Tweed.

He was right. They hurried through the tunnel, but even so it took them about forty minutes before they saw any kind of change in their surroundings. Small rooms now opened up on either side of the tunnel. They checked each one, but they were just for storage: dusty crates of drills and hammers, spades and picks covered with tarpaulin . . .

They kept moving. After another ten minutes, Tweed put his hand in the air.

"What?" whispered Octavia.

Tweed pointed down. The path they had been following through the tunnel was a track gouged out by constant use. But right where they had stopped the track veered into the wall.

Octavia looked up. The wall was brick, just like the rest of the tunnel. Then she started to look to either side, searching for some sort of release mechanism.

"Look around for a hidden switch—a lever or something," said Tweed.

Octavia turned from where she was already running her hands over the wall, giving Tweed her best "Really?" look.

"Sorry," he said, and carried on searching on his side of the tunnel.

They searched along the walls and back along the track, eventually finding the switch behind one of the lights on the wall by the simple method of looking for footprints in the dirt. It was too high for her, so Tweed reached up and pushed the button.

A wide section of the wall swung back into a second tunnel. It was just as wide as the first, but less well lit. Octavia could only see three lights along the crudely carved walls, and one of them wasn't working properly. It flickered erratically on and off.

Octavia and Tweed entered the new passage. It carried on for about a hundred yards and ended at an iron door. This time they didn't have to search for any hidden switches. There was a long lever close to the wall.

Tweed released the break on the lever and pulled it toward him. The round door started to move sideways, sliding into the wall of the tunnel.

Bright light spilled out onto the earthen floor. Octavia fingered the Tesla gun, her index finger curling and uncurling around the trigger. Tweed hurried across to her and they moved to the side of the tunnel, where the door was disappearing into the wall.

They waited, the door trundling noisily only inches from Octavia's ear. The white light chased the shadows away, illuminating the passage almost halfway back to the main tunnel.

The door finally drew level with them, then slid neatly into the wall.

The first thing Octavia noticed were the two members of Sherlock Holmes's gang. The thin man with the metal discs over his eyes and one of the others who wore the long smoke masks. Except the mask was now lying on the ground, revealing an ugly, scarred face that blinked at Octavia and Tweed in utter surprise.

They carried a long box between them. It looked as if they were in the process of loading it onto a cart when the door had started to open.

The four of them stared at each other for a frozen second.

Then chaos erupted.

Tweed fired his gun. The bullet of electricity hit the wooden box the two men carried. They flinched and let go. It hit the ground edge first, the wood splintering and falling apart.

Revealing the ancient, withered body of Lucien.

The body slithered out of the shattered coffin onto the floor. The two men dived for cover behind one of the many boxes piled up in the room. Tweed fired again, running forward to take cover behind one of the larger crates just inside the door.

Octavia quickly followed after, hunkering down next to Tweed. He reached around the box and fired four more bolts of lighting. He tried again, but this time the gun did nothing. He cursed and quickly unfolded the small manual lever, winding it round and round as fast as he could to build up a charge inside the weapon.

Octavia peered around her side of the crate. She sincerely hoped that whatever was inside the crate was heavy—heavy and solid. Preferably made from steel.

"Did they have any weapons?" asked Tweed.

"I didn't see any."

"So . . . should we rush them?"

Octavia looked at him to see if he was joking. He didn't appear to be.

"What?" he asked. "You just said they didn't have any weapons."

"I said I didn't *see* any! That doesn't mean they don't have—"

Octavia saw a shadow moving on the wall directly in front of her. She craned her neck around the crate and saw the man with the scarred face rushing toward them with a heavy metal pole in his hand. Octavia flung her arm out and fired the Tesla gun. Electricity arced out, drawn to the pole. It coruscated along its length, then up along the scarred man's arm, crawling and wrapping around him like a net. The man stumbled to a stop, his limbs jerking uncontrollably. The pole went flying from his hand, spinning through the air and hitting the second man full in the face. The metal discs were ripped from his eyes, the blue light flickering and dying.

The thin man staggered into the wall, making a horrible

mewling sound. Octavia looked on in horror. He didn't have any eyes! Dangling from his sockets was some sort of thick wiring, pulled out of his head when the discs were broken off. His head jerked rapidly from side to side, twitching uncontrollably.

Tweed finished winding the Tesla gun and leaped to his feet. "Right. Let's get this fini—oh."

He dropped the gun to his side. "You killed them all!"

"I did *not*. That," she said, pointing at the man with the wires in his eyes, "wasn't even me. The other one did it. Anyway, they're not dead. I only shot him a little bit."

Tweed walked to the big one lying on the ground and poked him with his foot.

"He *looks* dead."

"Oh, for goodness' sake." Octavia joined Tweed, then reached down and felt for a pulse. She frowned and shifted her fingers slightly.

"Problem?" Tweed asked.

Octavia frowned and straightened up. "He must have had a weak heart," she said.

Tweed hesitated. "No time to feel bad about it now. We're getting close to the end of this, Songbird. I can feel it."

They hurried through the room and found themselves in an old tunnel. The stonework looked old, the arched ceilings dripping with moisture. There was an aqueduct running along the bottom of the tunnel, but it had been covered over with a metal walkway.

"This looks Roman," said Octavia.

"If you say so. Looks like bricks to me."

"Yes, but it's the *type* of bricks. Well over a thousand years old."

"Top marks," Tweed whispered, leaning close. "But I think we should be quiet now. Listen."

Octavia paused. In the distance she could hear a very slight humming sound. Tweed hurried over the metal walkway into another tunnel. Bright globes were attached to the wall, linked together by thick black wires.

The passage led to a mine shaft that dropped down into the ground. It was nowhere near as large as the one back at the prison, though. There were two elevators: one big, reinforced one, probably for machinery, and a second, smaller one for people. Octavia and Tweed peered downward. The hole descended into blackness.

"What do you think?" asked Tweed. "Only way down, but the noise might alert them."

"Not necessarily. If they hear it they'll just think it's those two goons coming back."

"Good point." Tweed nodded up at the ceiling. "See that?"

Octavia followed his gaze. There was a metal pole descending into the shaft. She followed its length up to the ceiling and saw it was mounted by a bulbous metal shape.

"A mini Tesla Tower," said Tweed. "We must be directly under the new clock."

They climbed into the elevator and pulled the door closed. The only control was a single lever. Octavia was closest, so she pulled it back, and the elevator began its jerky descent.

After descending about a hundred yards, Octavia saw a light below them, coming from an opening at the bottom of the shaft. The elevator bumped to a stop and Octavia made to get out, only to be pulled up short by Tweed.

His face was serious, his eyes dark.

"Octavia, whatever happens in there... I just want to say, all jokes aside, I'm glad we met. And . . . and I wish we'd met under different circumstances. You're all right. For a member of the weaker sex, that is," he added, grinning slightly.

Octavia frowned. Why was he talking like that? It was as if he didn't expect to come out alive. She opened her mouth to reply with something witty, but Tweed turned abruptly away and stepped out of the elevator.

He walked to the opening in the wall, his frame silhouetted against the bright light. She could see his untidy hair sticking up, the shape of his greatcoat, and in his left hand, the Tesla gun. Ready for use.

CHAPTER TWENTY-TWO

Tweed felt as if the gun were about to slip out of his hand. He tightened his hold on it, curling his sweating fingers around the grip. He could see the other end of the tunnel from where he stood, a large rectangular opening through which emanated a flickering yellow light.

He checked to make sure Octavia was next to him, then he moved slowly forward until he could see into the room beyond.

The low-ceilinged chamber was dominated by machinery. It took up nearly all the available space, connected to the walls by thick, curved pipes from which condensation dripped, forming oily puddles on the floor. Steam hissed into the air, clawing up toward the ceiling, where thick cables twisted around and through even more pipes.

The machine itself—the infamous Lazarus Machine—was an immense brass and chrome monstrosity, an ugly piece of design covered with dials and switches.

Tweed's eyes were drawn to Barnaby. He was strapped into an upright chair, positioned in the exact center of the machine. A metal helmet, so tight as to seem like part of his skin, had been placed over his head. The helmet and chair were festooned with cables. They draped and coiled along the floor and disappeared into the heart of the Lazarus Machine.

Behind and above Barnaby was a large glass globe. Tubes connected this globe to two glass coffins positioned on either side of Barnaby. The right coffin was empty, but on the left, the remaining goon was busy strapping down an unconscious figure. The goon had taken off his smoke mask. He was the exact twin of the one Octavia killed with her Tesla gun.

"Is he in?"

Sherlock Holmes strode into view. He had been hidden in the shadows, fiddling with some kind of control panel on the wall.

Octavia leaned very closely to Tweed, "That person being strapped into the machine!" she whispered urgently. "It's Prince Edward!"

Tweed narrowed his eyes and tried to see the man in the dim light. She was right! It was Queen Victoria's son. What was Sherlock Holmes doing with *him*?

No matter. They had to put a stop to it. Now.

Tweed leveled his gun, still keeping to the protection of the tunnel. "Put your hands up, Holmes!" he shouted.

Holmes whirled around, darting behind one of the massive pipes. Barnaby stiffened, his eyes searching the shadows. The goon, obviously not one of the clever members of the simulacrum's gang, turned and ran directly at Tweed, letting out a long, guttural howl as he did so.

Tweed fired. Electricity surged out of the Tesla gun and smacked into the man's chest. He stumbled to a stop, smoke drifting up from the wound, then he sagged to his knees and flopped forward onto his face.

Tweed swallowed nervously, staring at the man's body.

"Sebastian, what do you think you're doing?" said Barnaby. "Get out of here. There are others—"

"The others have been dealt with. Everyone left is in this room," said Tweed.

"Then I must congratulate you," said Sherlock Holmes from his hiding place.

"I also know about the Tsar," said Tweed. "I saw him meeting with Lucien. Or should I refer to him as the P.M. now?"

There was a pause. When next Holmes spoke he really did sound impressed. "You surprise me, boy."

"I surprise a lot of people," said Tweed. He crouched down, trying to see past the pipes, hoping for a clear shot. Nothing. "One thing I don't understand," he said, moving to the other side of the tunnel. "What does Prince Edward have to do with the Tsar? How does he fit in?"

"Oh, he doesn't," said Holmes gleefully. "Lucien and Nicholas, they've been plotting for years, you see. Lucien is a loyal subject of Mother Russia. It is Nicholas who has been secretly funding Lucien's research."

"Yes, yes," interrupted Tweed. "They plan on assassinating the Queen and blaming Germany."

"Indeed. And then the Prime Minister will team up with the Russian Tsar and declare war on Germany for this *horrendous* act of war. Over the next few years, Russia will slowly increase her influence over Europe while Britain, seemingly trying to prevent a world-wide war, will in actuality be handing more and more strategic power over to our 'ally,' the Tsar."

"And then?"

"The Tsar has his own lab in Russia. He has been growing copies of himself there for years. Barnaby will be forced to duplicate the Tsar's soul and place these duplicates inside his simulacra. They will then be placed strategically throughout Europe and Britain, where they will be well-placed to eventually take over the British Empire in the name of the Romanovs. With Lucien's help, of course."

Tweed took a moment to digest all this.

"It's a pity it won't happen," said Holmes cheerfully. "All that planning gone to waste."

"Why?" said Tweed. "Why won't it happen?"

"Because I do not wish it to."

Tweed looked around the room. There was no sign of Lucien or Nicholas Romanov. It could be that they were busy with preparations for the banquet, but that was still hours away. If this was part of the plan, surely they would want to oversee it.

"You have your own agenda," said Tweed, as understanding dawned. "You're going to hijack their preparations." Tweed glanced at Prince Edward. "Barnaby imprinted on you back when he was working at the Ministry. You need him to eject Edward's true soul so you can take over his body. No great loss to you. The one you have doesn't seem as though it's working too well. I think the mask is for more than just disguise."

"That is true. I'm finding it harder and harder to breathe of late," said Holmes. "More defects in the process. Please. Continue."

Tweed thought about it. "You're going to kill everyone. The P.M., the Tsar, and the Queen?"

"*And* Parliament—with a rather large bomb detonated by a rather small Tesla-powered remote device."

That threw Tweed. "Parliament? Why?"

"Why not? Once they are all out of the way, Prince Edward will return to the palace with a believable story of escape and bravery. About how it was all a plot by the Ministry to gain more power. With the Queen dead, I will become King. A few new laws to make sure the same thing does not happen again. A few more laws later— reducing the power of the government while increasing the power of the monarchy—and before you know it I will be the most powerful figure in the Empire. A position to match my intellect."

"The people won't stand for it."

"Of course they will! Their own government, trying to kill the royal family? They will *demand* it. My only regret is that I won't be there to see Lucien die. That animal kept me locked up for years. And he thinks he can simply set me loose to do his dirty work? That I would just go along with his orders? He deserves to die.

"You've had your little bit of fun. You know what's going on. That's fine. I feel you've earned that much. But now I must insist you step out of the shadows and put down your gun."

Tweed laughed. "Why on earth would I do that?"

Barnaby let out a scream of pain. He arched back in the chair, his arms straining against the shackles holding him in place. A second later it was over. Barnaby slumped in his chair.

"*That* is why."

Tweed hesitated, then indicated that Octavia should remain where she was. Holmes didn't know she was here. Perhaps they could use that to their advantage. Tweed stepped out of the tunnel and tossed the gun onto the floor.

Sherlock Holmes stepped around a large conduit, moving into view through a cloud of steam.

He didn't have his mask on. The left side of his face was even more horrific when seen up close. His throat was covered in pustules and weeping wounds. His lips were flaking off, the skin covered in open sores. Tweed thought he could even see into his mouth through a gangrenous hole in his cheek. He heard the ragged, painful breathing of the man, and he couldn't help but feel a slight stab of pity.

Holmes moved closer. There was an odd expression on his face. He was frowning, peering at Tweed, studying his features.

Finally, he let out a bark of laughter and glanced at Barnaby.

"It all rather makes sense now. The tenacity. The cleverness. Does he know?"

Tweed hesitated. Know what?

"Does the boy *know*?" pressed Holmes. "Don't make me hurt you again, Barnaby."

Barnaby gritted his teeth. "No."

Holmes laughed and strolled forward until he was only a pace away from Tweed. He stared deep into Tweed's eyes, then shook his head in wonder.

"How can it not know?"

It? "Know what? What are you talking about?"

"Tell him," Holmes insisted.

"No, I—"

"*Tell him!*" Holmes screamed, spittle flying from his mouth.

"I won't!"

Holmes forced himself to calm down. Then he shrugged. "Fine. I will." He smiled at Tweed. "You, my boy, are me. That is, you are a product, a simulacra grown from the tissue of Sherlock Holmes. You and I? We are the same."

It took a moment for what Sherlock Holmes had said to sink in. Tweed shook his head. "Don't be absurd."

"Absurd? Look at me, boy. I am an older version of you. We are identical."

Tweed looked into Holmes's eyes. He studied the shape of the eyebrows, the forehead, the hairline. He reached up and tentatively touched his own nose, the nose that was the same shape as Holmes's. He mentally erased the lines in the man's face, the creases and wrinkles that age and years of pain had etched into his features, seeing—

—seeing his own face looking back at him.

Tweed took a shocked step backward.

It was true.

Holmes nodded. "Yes. You see? Acceptance. We are one and the same, young man. We are kindred."

"He is nothing like you!" snarled Barnaby.

Tweed slowly tore his eyes away from the man in front of him, turning to his father. All he wanted in that moment was for Barnaby to refute it, to have an explanation. But the moment he saw Barnaby's face he knew his hope was in vain.

"Barnaby?"

"I . . . I didn't tell you the whole story, back at the prison," he said. "Remember when I said Lucien took the corrupted copy of Sherlock Holmes away? That he was supposed to destroy him? I knew it wouldn't end there. Lucien was a man obsessed. He would keep experimenting, prodding and prying into the soul of Sherlock Holmes—into *other* souls as well!—until he created something even more horrendous and twisted than . . . than *that*." Barnaby nodded in disgust at Sherlock Holmes. The man smiled sardonically and bowed.

"What did you do?" whispered Tweed.

"The only thing I *could* do. I took the *real* soul of Sherlock Holmes—not a copy, the original soul I had extracted before he died—and I inserted it into one of the undamaged simulacra of Holmes that Lucien had been growing. But this clone was no more than a baby, newly formed. This kind of thing, it had never been done before. The brain of the child was not developed enough to cope with it. The insertion did something to Holmes's memories and experiences. It wiped everything clean, so to speak." Barnaby stared at Tweed, tears falling into his beard. "Then I fled with you and raised you as my own son, trying to keep you hidden, out of sight, away from the Ministry's spies."

Tweed said nothing, just stared at Barnaby in shock as his whole world crumbled around him.

"You *are* Sherlock Holmes, Sebastian. The *real* Sherlock Holmes. You have his soul inside of you."

Tweed shook his head. "It's not possible."

"It is. I've looked after you, tried to guide and teach you. Why do you think I tried to cram so much knowledge into that brain of yours? Why do you think I trained you so hard in logic, in rational thinking? Over the years, I've seen the brilliance that once defined Sherlock Holmes show itself, but always, *always*, it was tempered by *you*, by the person you had become. You are your own person, Sebastian, but something of Holmes still exists inside you."

Tweed tried to back away, but bumped up against the wall. It wasn't possible. Sherlock Holmes? *He* was Sherlock Holmes? He was not born but . . . *grown*?

It couldn't be.

You have no soul to call your own, said a voice in his head.

It was true. He had no soul. He was like a cuckoo, laying its egg in another bird's nest, only to destroy the other eggs as soon as it hatched and claiming the nest for itself. That was what he had done. He had taken Sherlock Holmes's body, taken his soul, and he had laid his own thoughts and memories on top of the original, claiming it all for himself.

He was nothing.

"Sebastian, please . . ." Barnaby pleaded.

Tweed ignored him.

"Come now, boy," said Holmes. "Don't mope. You have the soul of a genius in you. In fact . . ." Holmes stared thoughtfully at Tweed, then shook his head. "No, third time round I think I'd like a different body. Just stand aside so Barnaby can get to work."

Holmes stepped toward him. Tweed, in a daze, heard a high-pitched whining behind him. He blinked. What was that? It was familiar—

Tweed's eyes widened and he dropped to the floor just as a surge of electricity soared over his head and crashed into the æther cage above Barnaby's head. The glass exploded, showering thick, gluttonous fluid over the Lazarus Machine. Octavia stepped out of the shadows and shifted the gun, moving the stream of electricity all over the machine. Sparks exploded. Dials flew off the machinery, pipes burst their rivets, steam exploded into the air.

Octavia released the trigger. A low, guttural howl broke through the air. It was Sherlock Holmes. He was staring at the machine in horror.

"What have you done?" he screamed. *"WHAT HAVE YOU DONE?"*

He whirled on Octavia just as she pointed the gun at him. His eyes widened. He flung his arm up and spun behind a conduit just as she fired again. The bolt of lighting surged around and up the metal pipes, illuminating the room in icy blue before fading away.

A second later Barnaby arched his back, his teeth gritted in pain. Tweed peered into the shadows and saw Holmes running through a door in the rear of the room. Tweed scooped up his Tesla gun and sprinted after him.

"Tweed!" shouted Octavia. "Your father!"

Tweed hesitated. He glanced back at Barnaby, the man's face writhing in pain, then back to Holmes's receding form. "You get him out!" he shouted, sprinting around the machine and through the door.

It led into yet another tunnel. At the opposite end Sherlock Holmes was already pulling the door closed on one of four small elevators. He threw a lever and it started to climb rapidly upward. Tweed ran forward. He leaped into the air, trying to grab the bottom of the elevator, but it was moving too fast. He slammed into the wall and slid downward.

Tweed swore and climbed into another elevator. He yanked the lever, starting his jerky ascent. There were no dials on the wooden structure. The lever acted as a simple brake that started and stopped his movement.

Tweed was about fifteen feet below Holmes. He craned his neck back, making sure the man didn't try to escape. Eventually, Holmes's elevator bumped to a stop and he threw the door open and bolted.

A few seconds later Tweed followed suit.

Everything was a blur as he raced after Holmes. A short, earthen tunnel. Then a crudely dug room, more a hole in the earth than anything. Another earthen passage. There was a grinding noise from up ahead. Tweed burst into a final room to find a thick, reinforced door swinging open. On this side, the door was solid metal, but on the other it was covered with rock and stone.

Sherlock Holmes was nowhere in sight. Tweed hurried through. The wall on this side of the room was made from the same rock and stone that covered the door, so when it was closed it would blend in, hidden from sight.

The room led into a basement of some sort, filled with building supplies. A long set of stairs led up into a vast, square room.

Except it wasn't just a room. Tweed felt a breeze on his face and looked around. A huge, square structure soared up above him, the ceiling lost in the dim darkness.

He was in the new Clock Tower.

Sherlock Holmes was in another elevator, moving upward. This one was a metal cage with safety grills all around it. Tweed looked frantically around and saw another one, this one holding a large toolbox and paint.

Tweed sent the elevator upward. Holmes was already disappearing into the shadows above. As they climbed, Tweed pulled out the gun and checked it. Empty. He wound the lever furiously around, but even so there would only be enough charge left for one shot. He'd have to make it count.

The elevator slid up floor after floor, rising through the different levels of the tower all the way to the top. Tweed dropped into a crouch and leveled his gun as the elevator bumped to a stop.

The four transparent clock faces surrounded him. The rain hammered down outside, the clouds black and threatening. The grey morning light revealed the huge cogs and gears that dominated the space, the machinery that would one day power the clock. Ten bells hung from the roof. They were huge, all hanging in a line, ready to strike the hours for all of London.

No sign of Holmes, though. Tweed stepped slowly from the elevator.

There was a rush of movement to his right and Holmes darted

out from behind the machinery, running straight for one of the clock faces. There was something on the floor there, a small metal box. It looked like the transceiver Tweed had in his steamcoach.

The trigger for the bomb.

Holmes was going to detonate it now, to cause what damage he could.

"Stop!" Tweed shouted.

Holmes froze, then turned around to face Tweed as he stepped forward, the gun leveled in front of him.

"Don't be stupid, boy," said Holmes. "Fight against me, you fight against yourself."

"I'm not the same as you," said Tweed.

Holmes laughed. "How can you even argue? We are *exactly* the same. That's the whole point. Come with me. I'll teach you how to think. I have those memories. I *am* Sherlock Holmes. I'll teach you how to observe, how to reason. How to make use of that mind. I'll make you great."

Tweed said nothing.

"What can Barnaby give you? What *has* he given you? The life of a pauper? A life spent hiding away? Scamming people for money? Do you honestly think that's good enough for the likes of you?"

Holmes moved slightly, heading for the switch. Tweed followed him with the gun.

"Barnaby lied to you," the villain went on. "Your whole life he's kept the truth hidden from you. You deserved to know your origin. You deserved to know where you came from. He didn't respect you enough to tell you. *I* respect you, boy. Just from speaking to you for ten minutes I can see the brilliance in you. The *potential*. I can make you the greatest thinking machine the world has ever seen."

Tweed's hand lowered slightly. He felt . . . lost. Confused. For the first time in his life he didn't know what to think. It was true.

Barnaby *should* have told him. Tweed should have known his true heritage. To keep that from him . . . It wasn't right.

"Use your head," said Holmes. "Don't feel guilty about wanting more. Feelings are for the weak. You have a brain that is better than everyone else's. Use it. Think about it rationally."

Think about it rationally.

His whole life, Tweed had thought about things rationally. Had used his head. Had analyzed everything. Reasoned things through.

Then he met Octavia. What was it she had said? *You can't break everything down into patterns and logic, Sebastian Tweed. Sometimes you just have to have faith and feel life. Experience it.*

"Claim your true name, boy. Sherlock Holmes. That's who you are. With our intellects we could rule the world if we so choose. No one would be able to stop us."

If this had all happened a month ago, before he'd met Octavia, who knew what decision he would have made. But Tweed realized she was right.

"My name," he said grimly, raising the gun, "is Sebastian Tweed."

Holmes stared at him for a moment. Then he snarled and made a dive for the detonator.

Tweed fired. The weak bolt of electricity hit Holmes in the leg. He spun around with a shout of pain, staggered, then carried on moving toward the box. Tweed pulled the trigger again.

Nothing happened. The Tesla gun was empty.

Holmes was only a few feet away from the detonator. Tweed threw the gun down and raced at him. Holmes saw him coming, tried to move faster, but his injured leg slowed him down. Tweed was ten paces away. Holmes lunged forward, his fingers stretching out for the button. Tweed screamed in anger and launched himself into the air, colliding full into Holmes and lifting him off his feet. They flew through the air and crashed into the clock face.

It exploded outward in a thousand glittering fragments, soaring out over the Thames. Holmes and Tweed fell from the Clock Tower. Rain lashed Tweed's face. He spun and tumbled through the air, still holding onto Holmes. He saw the water rushing up toward him. Then the Clock Tower receding above him. Then grey sky, the rain.

Holmes screamed, "Not again!"

There was fear in his voice. Real, genuine, primal fear. And as Tweed heard the words, he felt it too, a sudden panic, the flash of a waterfall, of plummeting, falling, smashing into water like a brick wall. Rocks, blood, darkness . . .

Tweed looked into Holmes's eyes. There was an instant, a brief moment where there was the slightest connection between them. Understanding.

Then Tweed released Holmes, letting go of his jacket, separating from the man.

Tweed smacked into the water. It was freezing, yanking his breath from his body, pulling it from his lungs. Down he went, like a piece of lead dropped from the sky. He opened his eyes, but could see nothing. Which way was up? He moved his arms, trying to swim, but he suddenly felt as if he were swimming downward. His lungs strained. He needed air.

Tweed closed his eyes again and calmed his mind. Then he opened them and blew one single bubble of air out of his mouth. He watched as it bobbed away from him, then he followed it upward.

He exploded through the surface of the Thames with a gasp, sucking in air. He looked around frantically, but there was no sign of Sherlock Holmes anywhere. No body bobbing in the water. No figure swimming away. Just . . . nothing.

There was a shout from up above. He looked up and saw the distant face of Octavia peering down at him. He waved weakly, then spread his arms out and let himself float on his back.

They had done it. They had stopped Sherlock Holmes.

And now they had proof of Lucien's plan. They had the Lazarus Machine. They even had Lucien's body. They could tell the Queen what had been planned. The authorities would have no choice but to believe them now.

He supposed that meant he should start swimming.

EPILOGUE

Four days later Tweed and Octavia waited in a large drawing room, watched over by a frowning man in a black suit, who by the looks of it thought they were going to steal the silver and run off with it at any moment. The man looked vaguely familiar to Tweed.

The sofa was firm and slightly uncomfortable. Tweed shifted his backside and looked up at the huge paintings mounted on the walls, the elegant sideboards covered with flowers.

He frowned down at the floor, then peered into the corners.

"What are you doing?" whispered Octavia fiercely.

"No dust," said Tweed.

"What?"

"There's no dust."

"Of course there's no dust. It's Buckingham Palace!"

"It's not natural."

"Don't be silly. Have you and Barnaby spoken yet?"

"No."

"Don't you think you should?"

"No. Anyway, it's not just me. He hasn't forgiven me for leaving him in the chair while I chased after Holmes." Tweed was silent for a while. "I don't know who I am, Songbird. I don't know how much is me and how much is him leaking through. I can't trust my own thoughts."

"Of course you can. You are who you are. What do I always say?"

Tweed thought about this. "'Tweed, you're an idiot?'"

"What else?"

"'Stop being so annoying?'"

"Yes. And also, don't *analyze* everything. You are who you are, Sebastian Tweed. For better or for worse."

Tweed pushed himself to his feet and went to look out the large window. The parade grounds stretched out below him. Guards dressed in red jackets and helmets were . . . doing whatever it was guards did. *Guarding* things, he supposed. He had been rather surprised to receive the summons this morning. Actually, that was an understatement. He had been *very* surprised. Yes, they had told their story to an endless number of government flunkeys, but he hadn't actually expected a summons from Queen Victoria herself.

He swiveled around and walked the perimeter of the room, coming to a stop before the servant. He squinted at the man, who *definitely* looked familiar. He was in his fifties, bald, oddly small nose, with red marks around the nostrils. Frown lines creased his forehead and eyes, eyes that also seemed slightly inflamed and red. Tweed leaned forward and sniffed.

The man recoiled. "What are you doing?"

"Nothing."

Tweed stepped back, running his eyes over the man's clothes, his shoes, his clasped hands. He locked eyes with the man again.

The door opened.

The servant blinked in apparent relief and turned to attend.

It was the Queen.

She swept into the room, waving the servant away. He left and closed the door behind him. Octavia shot to her feet, and Tweed hurried back to the couch to stand next to her.

Queen Victoria was a lot shorter than Tweed had expected. There was a determined expression on her face, but Tweed didn't think it necessarily had anything to do with them. He thought it was just how she normally looked.

She sat down on the couch opposite them.

"Sit," she commanded.

Tweed and Octavia did as they were told. Octavia fidgeted nervously, clenching and unclenching her hands. It was making Tweed nervous. He elbowed her, but all she did was elbow him back, harder.

"My people have spent a very long time talking to both your-selves and Mr. Barnaby Tweed," said Queen Victoria. "And from all that has been said, I gather I have you two to thank for my life."

Tweed said nothing. Neither did Octavia. It hadn't exactly been a question.

The Queen turned her hard gaze on Tweed. She studied him intently.

"And if Barnaby is to be believed, not only are you a simulacrum of Sherlock Holmes, but you have his soul inside you?" She spoke with disapproval.

"It wasn't my choice, I assure you," said Tweed.

"No. So much of what happens to us isn't," she replied. "And you. Girl." Octavia jerked and tried to straighten up even more. "You were involved? You assisted him?"

"With respect, Your Majesty, I did not assist him. We assisted each other."

The Queen nodded. "Good answer."

Tweed cleared his throat. "Lucien, I mean, the Prime Minister—?"

"Locked away in the Ministry cells, ranting and raving like a man possessed."

Tweed let out a breath of relief. He had still been worried that Lucien would be able to escape.

"He denied it for a while. But then he changed tactics. He admitted it was he, Lucien, but said he did what he did for me, for the Empire. Keeps going on about scientific progress. Odious man."

"And the Tsar?" asked Octavia.

"Ah, well there we had to stifle our pride and leave him be, I'm afraid."

"*Why?*" exploded Octavia. "He plotted to kill you! He was going to try to take over the Empire."

"Oh well, I'm sure it was nothing personal."

"Nothing personal?" said Octavia in amazement.

"It is politics, child. All is fair in love and politics. Or something to that effect. Who is to say I would not have done something similar if I were in his position?"

"I don't think you would have," said Octavia.

Queen Victoria smiled briefly. "Thank you. It is nice to know some still have faith in me. But the thing is, who would believe such a tale? I barely believe it and I've seen the evidence. No, we do not want a war with Russia. It is best he thinks we know nothing of his involvement. He will reveal his hand eventually, I am sure."

Queen Victoria turned her attention to Tweed. "I find myself . . . nonplussed, young man."

"How so, Your Majesty?"

"I know how you were created. In fact, you were created against my express wishes. By your very existence, your are evidence of treason against the Crown."

"And yet?" prompted Tweed.

"Who said anything about 'and yet'?"

Tweed shrugged. "It was implied by your choice of words."

The Queen set her mouth in a thin line. "Hmph. I can definitely see something of the man in you, my boy. *And yet*," she continued, glaring at Tweed, "I find myself rather glad that my word was ignored. Just this once."

Queen Victoria stood up and walked to the window. "I have a proposition for you. For both of you. It is evident I have enemies within my own government. *And* without, but that goes without saying. Now, more than at any other time, I need people I can trust, people I can turn to when I need certain . . . *matters* looked into."

She turned around to face them. "What I suggest is that you work for me. Not the government. Not the Ministry. For me. The

Crown will pay for your training, plus a monthly retainer. And if I have need of your assistance, you will drop everything and come running to me. What do you say?"

"How much of a retainer are we talking here?" asked Tweed.

Octavia jammed her elbow hard into his ribs again. She smiled and said, "We would be honored, Your Majesty."

"Good."

"But if I may . . . ?"

"Yes?"

"I'd like your permission for us to use our newly available resources to search for my mother. She was investigating Holmes and the Tsar. She was kidapped by them."

The Queen nodded. "By all means, child. It is the least I can do."

The Queen started to move toward the door, but Tweed stood up. "Seeing as we're now working for you, I should probably tell you that the servant that was in here just now? He's stealing silver from you. Quite a lot of it."

Queen Victoria paused. She narrowed her eyes at Tweed, then bellowed out, "Jenkins! In here at once!"

The door opened and Jenkins hurried inside. He hesitated when he saw everyone staring at him.

"Yes, Your Majesty?"

"Mr. Tweed? If you would be so good as to expand upon your theory?"

Tweed walked slowly forward.

"What silver polish is used at the palace?" he asked Jenkins.

"Messrs. Rombut and Slim's patented brand. Very expensive," said Jenkins.

"Indeed. So not jewelers rouge?"

"Definitely not," said the Queen. "The stuff is horrible. Scratches the silver."

"Yet it is very obvious to me that Jenkins has been using jewelers rouge over an extended period of time. Using it to polish up
the silverware he steals from the palace before selling it to a dealer in
Whitechapel." Tweed squinted at Jenkins. "In George Street, to be
exact."

Jenkins's eyes narrowed in anger. He looked to the Queen. "Your
Majesty, I must protest. I have never stolen *anything* from the palace!"

"Note the rash on your fingers," said Tweed calmly, "and the discoloration of your teeth. You have been having trouble with an upset
stomach, yes? Don't answer. I know you have. All these symptoms are
side effects of ferrous sulfate, the main ingredient in jewelers rouge.
You have either accidentally ingested some or it has been absorbed
through your skin. And for that to happen, you really must have been
using it for a long time indeed."

Jenkins stared at Tweed in shock.

"And the dealer on George Street?" pressed the Queen.

"There was an accident in George Street last week," said Tweed.
"A cart carrying quicklime to a building site overturned, spilling
the contents into the rain. The quicklime reacted violently with the
rainwater. The slight redness around Jenkins's nose and eyes indicates
healing from these burns. Plus, his shoes, although highly polished,
bear discoloration from the quicklime. I deduce that Jenkins was on
his way to the dealer when the accident happened. He was caught
right in the middle of it. Isn't that right, Jenkins?"

Jenkins stared at Tweed, his mouth hanging open. Then he
turned and bolted from the room.

The Queen watched him go. "Good job, Mr. Tweed. Looks as if
you just might be as clever as you think you are. Excuse me." The
Queen walked to the door. "Stop that man!" she shouted. She waited
a moment. "Good job! Hit him for me, if you will—not *too* hard!
There. Thank you."

The Queen closed the door and turned to Octavia and Tweed. "Remember, you work for me now. If I have need of you, you will attend me at once. Understand?"

"We understand," said Octavia.

Tweed nodded.

"Good," She smiled again, that brief smile that was gone almost before it appeared. "'Sebastian Tweed and Octavia Nightingale, Consulting Detectives to Her Majesty, Queen Victoria.' It has rather a pleasing ring to it, has it not?"

She nodded at them both, then turned and left the room.

"So, how did you do it?" asked Octavia.

They were walking down the steps of Buckingham Palace, heading out into the late afternoon. The autumn sun was breaking through the clouds, limning the buildings around them with golden light.

"What do you mean?"

"Come on. It was a trick, wasn't it?"

"Not at all. I saw the evidence and I deduced the answer. I used *rational thinking*," Tweed said, glancing at Octavia as he emphasized the words.

"I don't believe you."

"Not my problem."

The steamcoach was parked at the bottom of the steps. It hadn't been fixed after the events of the past week. Tweed couldn't afford the repairs. But maybe now, with this monthly retainer, he could send her in to a mechanic. The rather battered carriage was attracting a lot of disapproving stairs from the royal guards.

Tweed and Octavia climbed inside.

"Just tell me how you did it," said Octavia.

"Stop being annoying," said Tweed.

"You think *this* is annoying? Just wait. I'm going to keep going on about it until you tell me the truth. *Then* you'll see what annoying really is."

"Fine! But it wasn't a trick. I thought I recognized Jenkins when we first arrived. I saw the burns on his nose, the discoloration of his shoes. Then I noted the stained teeth and the rash on his hands and deduced he had been using jewelers rouge. I remembered there was a rather shady secondhand dealer on George Street, and that's when I remembered where I'd seen him before. I was on the street when the quicklime spill happened. I saw Jenkins that night, carrying a package. When the accident happened he ran into the dealer's shop. But obviously not quick enough to avoid some ill-effects."

Tweed pumped the handle and released the brake. "Satisfied?"

Tweed started the carriage moving.

Octavia was silent for a while.

"So what you're basically saying is, you *saw* Jenkins take the silver into the dealer's shop."

"*No . . . !* Yes. But I didn't remember that at first. I made the *deduction* first, then remembered that fact later. It doesn't invalidate my cleverness."

"Oh, I'm afraid it does."

"It doesn't!"

"Does."

"Doesn't"

"It *does*!"

"It doesn't! I arrived at my conclusion *before* remembering where I saw him."

"Liar!"

"I am not a liar. You . . . you flap dragon!"

"How dare you! You . . . you rump-headed miscreant!"

"Barnacle."

"Over-used codpiece!"

Tweed paused, then said, "Well, that's just disgusting."

Octavia smiled. "Thank you."

Tweed was silent for a while. Then he asked, "Should we get something to eat?"

"Are you paying?"

"No. I'm poor. You can pay."

"Fine. But I get to pick where we're going."

"Nowhere fancy. I don't think I want to be surrounded by other people like you."

"How dare you . . ."

🙼

And the steamcoach lurches and judders into the traffic, joining the stream of London commuters as they wend their slow way through the claustrophobic city. Tweed and Nightingale's argument trails behind them as they crawl through the streets, causing those who overhear to raise their eyebrows and peer inside the coach, hoping to catch a glimpse of the couple having such a fierce fight.

They raise their eyebrows even more when they see that the occupants of the coach are actually smiling as they argue.

ABOUT THE AUTHOR

Paul Crilley is a Scotsman with absolutely no tolerance for tropical climates and a love of all things cold. So naturally, he and his family now live in South Africa. When he is not sitting in front of the electric fan writing he can be found chasing monkeys out of the kitchen. (Really.)

Paul has also written a middle-grade fantasy series called The Invisible Order, about secret societies, faeries, and Victorian England, and spent a year writing on the computer game Star Wars: The Old Republic. He also writes scripts for comics and television. His website can be found at www.paulcrilley.com, and you can follow him on Twitter @paulcrilley. (Only if you want to, of course. No pressure.)

Paul is currently at work on the sequel to *The Lazarus Machine*.